C 16-

TERMINATION SHOCKS

TERMINATION SHOCKS

Janice Margolis

University of Massachusetts Press

Amherst and Boston

ISBN 978-1-62534-420-5 (paper)

Designed by Sally Nichols
Set in ArnhemFine
Printed and bound by Maple Press, Inc.

Cover design by Kristina Kachele Design, llc
Cover art by Janice Margolis, courtesy of the artist.

Library of Congress Cataloging-in-Publication Data

Names: Margolis, Janice, author.
Title: Termination shocks / Janice Margolis.
Description: Amherst : University of Massachusetts Press, [2019] |
Identifiers: LCCN 2018051825 (print) | LCCN 2018054349 (ebook) |
ISBN 9781613766682 (ebook) | ISBN 9781613766699 (ebook) |
ISBN 9781625344205 (pbk.)
Classification: LCC PS3613.A7425 (ebook) | LCC PS3613.A7425 A6 2019 (print)
| DDC 813/.6—dc23
LC record available at https://lccn.loc.gov/2018051825

British Library Cataloguing-in-Publication Data
A catalog record for this book is available from the British Library.

Pages 4 and 5 feature *Stowage of the British slave ship Brookes under the regulated slave trade act of 1788*, Broadside Port. 282, no. 43, Printed Ephemera Collection, Library of Congress, LC-USZ62-44000.
"Desires" from *The Complete Poems of Cavafy*, translated by Rae Dalven. English translation copyright © 1961, and renewed 1989 by Rae Dalven. Reproduced by permission of Houghton Mifflin Harcourt Publishing Company. All rights reserved.

CONTENTS

ACKNOWLEDGMENTS

Since I couldn't figure out how to choreograph an intelligible thank-you on paper, or submit an elaborate otherworldly doodle—my favorite way to express gratitude—I want to thank the following for their generosity of spirit and providing smooth air along the way: Nzingha Clarke and Mellisa Franklin, fearless global citizens, fellow gelato lovers, and readers extraordinaire who helped shape this collection; John Dugene, enthusiastic reader and generous supporter who shared my desire for a garden and for witnessing the Northern Lights; Thomas Frick, the emissary from Planet Brain, for encouraging all of my creative incarnations; Karen Johnson, structural wizard, gracious reader, steadfast cheerleader, and perpetual generator of fantastic ideas; Sheree Latif, remarkable sister, unswerving supporter, and kind lifeboat; my parents "Y" and "Z" for sharing their DNA and nourishing my curiosity; Sven Birkerts for his pithy thoughts and sharing his boundless well of impressive language on my behalf; Reed Bye for coming along at exactly the right moment with his perceptive insights; the late William Moritz for entering my life like a jolt of lightning; Lisane Lapointe, warrior optimist, who provided a soft landing on cue; the Juniper Prize readers and its judge Sabina Murray for selecting my manuscript; everyone at University of Massachusetts Press who

ACKNOWLEDGMENTS

brought it to life; editor Dawn Potter, who disentangled my grammar and ideas with delicate poise; the editors of *Western Humanities Review* for publishing "21 Days" in December 2017 as part of their Mountain West Writers' Contest; Voyager 2 for braving the termination shock and exploring the ever-expanding universe; history for being so damn compelling; to everyone whose orbits I've been graced to have fallen into; to those who refuse to live at the limits of others' imaginations; and for my being born in the year of the dog, meaning I don't know when to let go of the sock or stop chasing the bone.

TERMINATION SHOCKS

21 DAYS

Day 1

The Ebola ambulance men take Mama's fevered body. They dig out the dirt from underneath her and take that too. Splash. Spray. Everything gone. Can't touch Mama's hand. Can't take Papa's color rope from her wrist. Me naked in the corner. Dwe up in our palm tree gets a good look. His eyes don't lie. He likes all of me.

A white grub with black tusks sprays me. It stinks. It stings. My skin cracks so wide a lion enters. Its fur insulates my lungs. More grubs come. Blanket Grub. Bowl Grub. Spoon Grub. Water Grub.

Bucket Grub nails a bar across the window so I can't crawl out, then ties a blue bucket to the bar. No Dirt Grub comes to fill the hole where Mama fevered. The hole is wider than my arms and big as Papa. It will be a hungry deep ghost. If I fill it with water, it will never be thirsty.

Clothes Grub brings a green-and-gold dress and points a white gun at my forehead. My heart crawls away. It will come back as a coconut, my husk hair woven into President Sirleaf's doormat, my heart beating from the soles of her shoes. Clothes Grub shows me a red-flashing number. 98.4. If only I could get that grade on my algebra test. The

1

grub dances but he's not from Liberia. His feet are dead. He may be from America. Where the slave ships took so many. Where the slave schooner *Feloz* tried to take my mama's mama's mama in 1829.

My eyes want to hide inside the white gun and flash memories onto others' foreheads so they'll know what it means to be someone else.

I am not where I am. I am not this girl. I am concealed. Aboard the slave ship *Feloz*. I am seasick.

I put on the green-and-gold dress. It stitches my breasts together. *It's soft as Mama's favorite hen,* I tell Clothes Grub. Words can't make it through the grub's tiny tusk holes. *Papa gave it to her. He's in the mines. Uncle took Obi and Esther into the jungle. You took my schoolbooks. History won't wait. Grade 9 exams won't wait. Rice won't wait. The rice needs me. Obi and Esther need Mama. They're six. They couldn't decide who would come first, so they came together. History's going to forget Dwe and I are promised. He hasn't given Papa the letter yet. Hasn't brought Papa the rice bowl. The kola nut. The palm oil. The white chicken. Bodies won't wait. What do I do?!*

Clothes Grub writes in the dirt: 21 days.

Day 2

Before yesterday there was a straight path from my heart to Mama's. A straight path from the end of this village to the beginning of another country. There is nothing in that country to tell us we are no longer in this one. On Fridays Mama sold cassava gari over there. On Saturdays fufu here. It took her five minutes to walk from here to there. Everywhere people are drawing lines and circles. Don't walk this way. You are outside. I am in. Our bodies are getting lost.

I draw a circle around the hole where Mama laid and curl up inside. Mama's hole still has paths. Our village hatches beneath me. Uncle's hut pokes my knee. The school separates my toes. Dwe's roof pillows my head. When I roll over, our collarbones fuse into a new village made of teeth. The map of this village eats borders.

Miss Browne likes to open her arms wide when she teaches history. Her arms are wider than Mercator's world. Her fingers like keys when they point at you and call your name. Miss Browne says that when we study a map, we become part of it. Our eyes enter a town but our feet stay.

On Miss Browne's history wall there are yellowy maps with gray tapeworms cutting towns in half. Streets that die in corners. Oceans full of two-headed fish with gigantic red-mouths swallowing ships. This is the same ocean that drowned our history. That still holds part of me. Miss Browne does not have a map of our village on her wall. She says none exists.

My friend Hawa stands at the window in blue rubber gloves and the wooden deangle mask we made in Grade 6. The mask's slit eyeholes are pure night. Her breathing is scared. I tell her:

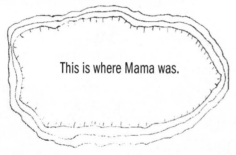

This is where Mama was.

I don't think Hawa wants to look at me, or see how big Mama's hole is. She drops the schoolbooks, notebook, and pencils she's collected into the blue bucket. She keeps the history book. Somebody already left one.

Some people are so scared they've sent their kids to Bush School. My cousin Felicia was dragged there by her hair. Hawa will try to get a message to Papa about Mama, but soldiers are guarding the road in and out of our village. She promises to bring me rice later. Hawa has a pure heart.

Dwe drops a coconut and a stone into the blue bucket on his way to the river to fish. His brothers are watching, so he doesn't husk it for me. I press the coconut to my lips where Dwe touched it. I feel his skin on mine. The stone is sharp on one side and fits my palm perfectly. It burns to think Dwe is at the river without me. The way his arms move the oars in time with my heart.

Day 3

I have been told it is dangerous to dream of cheetahs, so I crawl into Mama's hole with my history book and tell myself, don't dream of cheetahs. On page 379 is a picture of the slave ship *Feloz*. I close my eyes and see the seasick girl in the ship's hold. Waves rock my sleep. My green-and-gold dress becomes a home for endangered bush babies. They leap from hut to hut spreading our dreams.

In Dwe's dream, his words wrap my body. "Corrugated zinc roof." "Wild honey." They're like new skin that dances. A bush baby carries my word-wrapped body to the edge of the world. When I look over the side, I can see back in time to the day the *Feloz* set sail.

226 below deck each has 13 inches

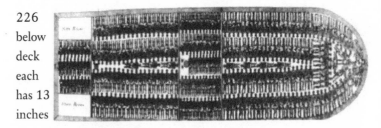

The seasick girl is shackled to two others in the ship's prow. They sit in a row, knees bent, between the others' legs.

Day 4

I draw a map of our village out of rice in Mama's hole. I draw the path to school and from the end of the village to the other country. The guards don't stop the rice. It could go all the way to America. The guards don't know I've written my name on a grain of rice that crossed the border. I'll join a gang of rice that will swell into an army that feeds the seasick girl aboard the *Feloz*.

A baby palm rat drops through a crack in the palm-leaf roof. It is the size of a small mouse. It falls into Mama's hole, right in the middle of my village. If it's not dead, maybe it will stay.

The rat's tail sweeps away Miss Browne's rice classroom and half the school. I think of Hawa and Dwe tumbling out of their desks. Of Miss Browne's maps colonizing new territory. Africa smothering America. Europe covered in penguin poop. The baby rat scurries out of my village and across the border. If it hurries it may rewind time and catch the *Feloz* before it sails.

The seasick girl's knees are younger than the knees she sits between, but older than the shoulders she sits behind. The ship's hold is 3 feet, 3 inches in height. Its prow is 18' x 16'.

The prow is the part of the ship
that draws the path across the ocean.
It is a breast and a torpedo.
It is furthest away from the hatch's
promiscuous dark acts.
It will touch America first.
Making them slaves longer.

The palm rat eats the grain of rice I've written my name on, then runs in circles looking for a way out. It never dizzies or tires. It is like a slave.

Day 5

Mama,

A baby palm rat fell from the sky. It looks at me the way I looked at you. It sleeps flat on its stomach in the hole the ambulance men dug out from under you. It likes rice more than freedom. It ate the last hut remaining in the rice village I drew. I want to teach history like Miss Browne. I am teaching the baby rat about the *Feloz*. About your mama's mama's mama. I don't know her name, so I call her the "seasick girl."

Hawa brings me food and water. Dwe brings coconuts. Everyone's afraid of me except the palm rat. Dwe comes to the blue bucket when he thinks I'm asleep, but I know how he sounds when he breathes. Sometimes Hawa sings near the well. If I don't sing back, she shouts my name. Sometimes old Abraham sits across from the window and tells me what's happening. "The big blue chicken walks in circles. There are five people at the well. Miss Browne has on an orange dress." He doesn't want me to forget language.

I sit inside your hole and pretend I'm aboard the *Feloz*, the seasick girl in front of me. My bent knees are the borders of her world. I've braided a map of our village in her hair.

I've learned how to dance with just my knees. Discovered a beat with my feet I've never felt before. I taught the seasick girl the beat, and how to braid a village on the head of the girl in front of her. Her feet and fingers taught that girl how to do it. Together we've mapped our country's coastline so no slave ships can make landfall. We unbuilt the coastal forts and braided them into palm trees. Our feet have reversed the tide. Our mapped braids have erased borders.

Day 6

In my history book the plantation map says 1 inch = 1 foot. An arrow points at an 8-inch shack. "Slave Quarters" it says across the missing door. The master must have lashed it gone. I quarter the slave quarters with lines. My pencil point severs a fiddler slave and infant. Half the fiddler's music and a slave baby's foot are set free. Two other children huddle, faces so sunk they've lost their noses. I draw wings on their arms and an arrow pointing east toward me in their hands.

They need to learn how to play "Oh, Mama." Their hands ready to clap Liberian when the ships return. Under. Over. Back. Across. Together. Faster. Faster. Over. Under. Slap. Slap. Together. Back. Across. They watch from the shack as I teach them. *Oh, Mama, Mama! Oh, Papa, the war! I met my boyfriend in the candy store. He bought me ice cream. He bought me cake. He brought me home with a bellyache. Mama, mama, I'm so sick. Call the doctor quick quick quick. Doctor, doctor. Will I die? Count to five and you'll be alive.*

1	2	3	4	5

Hawa and Dwe don't come today. The baby palm rat whines for rice. It nibbles my finger as I tell it about the hungry seasick girl squeezed into the city below the waves. To show it how many men and women the *Feloz* took on at the coast, I write the numbers in Mama's hole and add them. 336 males + 226 females = 562. I write 17 to show how many days the *Feloz* was out at sea, 55 for how many were thrown overboard.

My finger fills Mama's hole with wavy waves, but when I look from the other side they are birds in flight. I join the numbers in Mama's hole and try to forget how hungry I am.

Day 7

It must be Sunday. The blue bucket overflows with rice and coconuts. My stomach is grateful.

Outside is full of Dwe's laugh. Through the barred opening, I sometimes see an elbow or foot chase past, and my shoulders soften. I stand there forever, watching the dust from their game drift close. If the wind blows toward me, I breathe deep and let Dwe's speed fill my lungs. It feels bright green. I want to battle with stones. I want to play "Who Is in the Garden?" with him. We've been playing since we were five. In ten years he's never caught me.

Miss Browne brings me two clean dresses and her map of medieval Europe with the red-mouthed monsters. This is to remind me how wrong people can be. When I tell her those streets were full of plague, she clicks her tongue and waves her blue rubber-gloved hands at me. She may be casting a spell or letting me know I'm a fool. It doesn't matter. It's so good to see her wider-than-the-world arms scatter time that I beg her to stay and tell me more about the *Feloz*.

Instead, she tells me how animals groom each other in the most vulnerable positions. How humans groom each other with language. Miss Browne grooms me for hours, bringing messages from classmates too afraid to come.

I stretch the map across Mama's hole. Side by side the slave-quarter shack is half the size of Germany. The palm rat pokes around France, though Belgium is shaped exactly like a palm nut. There is a ghost ship on the Atlantic with twenty transparent sails and a gray hull. It's bigger than ten countries but can only sail in circles since it's trapped inside a square.

My foot has as many blue roads as Spain has gray ones. The vein from my big toe to my ankle is as straight as the trade winds. A grain of rice that sets sail from my anklebone easily lands in the Caribbean. I launch ten more rice ships before my foot cramps and my rescue flotilla stalls in the windless horse latitudes of the Sargasso Sea.

Beneath the map are the wavy waves, the birds in flight, and the *Feloz's* 562. I sit among them shivering. This floating coffin feels off course, my body hot and cold at once. The palm rat nuzzles my neck, chews my hair. I can see the hole it slipped through in the thatch above. It's easy to get lost among the braided fronds. A map of trees that could be anywhere, or somewhere that hasn't been mapped. It could be streets of circles. Circles chained. It could be somewhere that isn't somewhere. Somewhere that isn't a pitched roof. Anywhere that has a central beam. It could be the bottom of a boat. The keel of a capsized slave ship tangled in the Sargasso Sea. This could be what the red-mouthed monsters see. Beam and pitch and slope. Bodies braided in weed. Shackles done noising. Done rubbing. Undersea wind blowing. They could be balloons. They could be sirens luring slavers.

Where is the *Feloz* on the earth's belly? I should turn its deck on history.

Day 8

On her way to school, Miss Browne leaves me scissors, a box of postcards she's collected from everywhere, and a red yarn baby with seed eyes. The palm rat grabs its hand and runs off. Poor Yarn Baby. Some of the postcards say strange things that no one would ever say to Miss Browne. Some are addressed to people with funny names. There are more trains and statues than can possibly exist. One postcard has a picture of a man on stilts and is addressed to London. It says: *This is a race, Myron. That's all it is. A race. I don't know how else to put it. A race. I wish it wasn't, but*

Another has a glass pyramid floating on water. Above it is a three-quarter moon. Either the glowing pyramid lights the moon, or the moon makes the pyramid glow. The pyramid's face is hundreds of diamonds braided together from triangles. There is no way to know if 1 inch = 1 foot, or 1 inch = all of medieval Europe. It could be a map of an Egyptian glassmaker's shop, except on the flip side it says: Le Musée du Louvre. There is a smudged fingerprint on back. The postcard may or may not have made it to Mary in Tulsa, OK 74112. I hope not. If I were Mary and received this beautiful pyramid lighting the moon, I would want nothing written at all. I would not want: *I think you know I love you. Do you?*

I cut out the man on stilts and the glowing pyramid, and stand them in Mama's hole. The man on stilts is taller than the pyramid, but not tall enough to walk over it, so I cut out a railroad track, lean it against the pyramid for him to climb, and set a train on the pyramid's roof so he can get across town. There are so many fountains to lay side by side they spout an ocean. I free the trapped ship sailing in circles inside the square. Free the noseless slave children, the fiddler slave with half his music, the infant slave with half a foot. They board the ship and sail for the pyramid. If only I could cut out myself and walk on stilts. See Dwe the way a coconut does.

The yarn baby is no more. Red wool twists through the hut, intersecting at tangled figure eights. The palm rat sleeps in a knotted cul-de-sac having worn itself out. While it rests, I will map it a village different from the one we live in.

Day 9

The map of this hut is 1 foot = 1 foot. My thumb knuckle = 1 slave-quarter inch. The baby palm rat = 3 thumb knuckles without its tail. When I close my left eye, the tip of my thumb can swallow the full moon. When I close my right eye and open my left, my thumb can erase Dwe and the palm tree. No matter which eye I close, Mama's hole swallows my whole arm.

There are dimensions inside my body. Someone is lighting a fire. Throwing red-hot sun into my stomach. It's possible I ate the glowing glass pyramid and I'm full of chattering diamonds whispering nonsense. *Love is a broken line of ideas. It used to be the inside of a person never caught fire.* I might be covered in bush babies. I might be a hut in the other country. There is seashore between my eyes, seashore and ghosts sitting on coconuts hatching sounds. A diamond taps against my teeth, *so eh . . . I might have to, eh . . . ride a cheetah to Monrovia.* The baby palm rat is lost in the village I built. I never gave it a name. It's Baby Palm Rat, or Palm Rat, or It. I think I'm crying. Or falling toward something red and wet. I hear *Eh, about that, so, I think it's time to look down and see whether you're falling.* I may look down. May see Baby Palm Rat riding a cheetah. May see the glowing glass pyramid enter me. I'm dizzy with diamonds and full of miniatures. Baby ships. Baby huts. Villages too small to map. The world shows its flesh. Big blue pockets around its hips. Gravity gone. *Love might be a cheetah,* a diamond taunts, and I scream, scaring Miss Browne at the window, asking if I need another notebook.

Day 10

Everything crackles inside me. I could be made of lightning. A dying bird beats against my brain, swoops between my ears, pecking songs Mama sang me. It makes the notes bleed between my legs, and I cut the gold-and-green dress into beautiful rags to catch the falling sounds.

A trail of ants un-build the rice ships I stranded in the Sargasso Sea and return them to the Atlantic. I set the ghost ship with the twenty transparent sails among them. The trade winds will send it in search of slavers.

On one of Miss Browne's postcards a woman flowers from an enormous pink-and-white cake. Her waist is very small and her teeth very large. Her arms are flung in the air, her legs and hips buried in frosting. In one hand, a big balloon says: Happy Birthday! I hold it up to Miss Browne and tell her I'll be 16 in 80 days.

She says there is a book about a man flying a balloon around the world in 80 days. She draws a picture of that balloon, folds it into an airplane, and flies it through the window. I tell Miss Browne that on the man's 75th day afloat, he might have soared over my ghost ship as it converged on the *Feloz.* If I can describe what he saw, she'll give me credit for the test I missed.

I close my eyes and search for page 379 in my history book. Huge black kettles steam on the *Feloz*'s bow. Five slavers swivel an enormous cannon mounted on a circle of iron and aim at the ghost ship.

The seasick girl hears two whooshes overhead. The overseer's whip cracks. The hatches slam closed. Darkness chokes off her air. There was a time before today she thought she'd live forever.

Day 11

When the fever breaks the jungle clock will unborn Charles Taylor.
The boys he kidnapped will forget they killed.
The girls he stole will dance again.
Earth's blue pockets will save the seasick girl.
Foreheads will sing.
Diamonds will become drummers.
Skin will become fabric.
Bush babies will teach history.
Cheetahs will be motorcycles.
Words will outweigh meteors.
Mama will return.

Day 12

If I move, I'll catch fire. Baby Palm Rat won't come near me. It's scared I'll singe its fur. The back of me squeezes the front of me. My space inside is gone. A bush baby must have braided the *Feloz*'s anchor in my hair. My head is the cannonball fired over its bow. The whoosh heard by the seasick girl, hot metal gouging raw air.

My head is an egg stuck inside a hen. There are voices inside me. This is how the people who live in Miss Browne's medieval map must sound. Crazy. And mean. I beg Baby Palm Rat to bring me some water, but it shreds what's left of Yarn Baby. It eats so much yarn it'll poop its own yarn baby tomorrow, a yarn baby big enough to smother Germany.

The voices shout, *WAKE UP! EAT!*

A steady rain flows over me. Miss Browne stands on a chair outside the window in her blue rubber gloves. A palm frond stretches from her to me. Dwe pours jug after jug of water down the frond until a river runs from my arms and floods what's left of the village I built in Mama's hole.

The seasick girl cries out, *Viva*.

Baby Palm Rat comes to drink at Lake Mama. Its tongue is yarn-baby red. I submerge my fingers in the water. The fire leaks from me into Lake Mama's big blue pocket. Dwe's face swims at the window. His teeth are happy to see me.

Day 13

Baby Palm Rat has taught itself how to do back flips. Watching it is better than music. The notes flow slower between my legs at sunset. Hawa walks past and sings: *You and me and me and you together are strong. You and me and me and you together are one.*

Miss Browne stops at the window and calls Hawa a beautiful songbird. Her voice is so loud it can break open words. Her hands are full of Grade 9 exams. The national test is in 9 days. She begs me to eat some rice. I beg her to tell me more about the *Feloz*. She reads from Reverend Walsh's account of the *Feloz*'s interception by the British Navy. His words bloom in her mouth.

As soon as the poor creatures saw us looking down at them, their dark visages brightened up. They perceived something of sympathy and kindness in our looks, which they had not been accustomed to, and immediately began to shout and clap their hands. One or two had picked up a few Portuguese words, and cried out "Viva! Viva!" They knew we were come to liberate them.

The seasick girl was branded under the breast with a red-hot iron. The air on deck cools her raw skin. Her tongue tastes water again.

Day 14

Mama floats through the window and lays her cool hand on my forehead. She sings Baby Palm Rat and me to sleep. When we wake, a new red yarn baby lies on the shore of Lake Mama.

Hawa visits in her slit-eyed deangle mask. It's like listening to an ancestor. When she laughs, the deangle mask shakes its head no. The rain makes it look as if the mask is crying. Everyone is studying for Grade 9 exams. Hawa tells me soldiers patrol the jungle and roads. The other country five minutes from here is full of Ebola. Our chief says no one can come. No one can go.

She wants to know the yarn baby's and palm rat's names. Yarn Baby and Baby Palm Rat, I tell her. I am a terrible mother.

Day 15

Deep inside the history book left in the blue bucket, someone wrote a confession in the margin. They must have drunk palm wine laced with gunpowder. It starts above a photo of Desmond Tutu and Nelson Mandela, the one where they hold hands in the air. The confession curves around their heads and snakes down the page.

> *felicia*
> *come last*
> *friday from*
> *bush school*
> *straight to*
> *chocolate city*
> *belly full of*

dumboy we
soak our
tongue with
palm wine
i satisfy
her fish
she stop
five days
i write the
letter
collect
the dowry
give her
kola nuts
and
plenty
a white
chicken
she try to
steal my
gold it
make me
so mad
it just
happen
knife too
sharp
palm wine
too thick
i make
mistake
for true-o

Day 16

Someone comes to me in the night. It must be Felicia's ghost. I write Obi's and Esther's names in the dirt where they slept to hold part of them here. Miss Browne always says that we are living history. That what befalls falls. I throw her postcards around the hut until the floor is a sea of rectangles. I hop from train station to train station, cruise ship to cruise ship. I stomp on a place called Piccadilly. Walk on tiptoe from Jakarta to Rome. What was left of the village I built for Baby Palm Rat evaporates with Lake Mama.

Spread across the hut, the postcards map this world. I tear out the confession and lay it on the Sistine Chapel. If I circle it enough, the name of Felicia's killer will enter my feet through God's finger. On the postcards, there are lots of statues with breasts but no heads, or heads but no arms. Maybe Charles Taylor and General Butt Naked made their boy army worship pictures like these before giving them machetes.

Felicia and I were near the old cassava patch when General Butt Naked came through with his boys. She buried me under leaves, then hid up a tree. I peed myself as Butt Naked dragged off Dwe's cousins. Miss Browne said, never forget that day. Everyone else said, forget.

I can feel Felicia's killer up in Dwe's coconut palm. How many nights has he waited for me to read his confession? Each circle I make around God's finger, I see his hunched shadow between the fronds. Whoever it is, has on a wooden Dan bird mask. He wants me to know he's crossed the boundary between the human and spirit realm.

I crouch in the moonlight licking imaginary knots from my fur. There are plenty of boundaries to cross, plenty of spirits to quarter inside me. Let him think I am not who I am. That I am the seasick girl come back as a lion.

Mama,

Crawl through his dreams and shake him loose.

Day 17

Mama leans into me and releases her memory. My spirit is now part cheetah, part thorn. Felicia's killer thinks I don't know he climbed down before dawn. He thinks the boundary between realms makes him invisible and quiet, but he is louder than the *Feloz*'s cannon.

Baby Palm Rat and I wait for night near the Sistine Chapel. Yarn Baby perches in the window where I put her to keep watch. Her red body turns purple, then black at sunset. She is like a red antelope covered in mud. Baby Palm Rat won't leave my side. I still can't tell if it is a he or a she, so I think of it as both. We share each other's sleep. Last night I walked upside down on the ceiling and Baby Palm Rat sang Mama's favorite song. Felicia's killer will have to confront what we've become. Feral. Unknown.

Yarn Baby trembles in the wind. Felicia's killer is back. He is a masked snake, slithering up the tree. His body bends at strange angles. His bones are getting softer. Soon his flesh will have no choice but to fall away. Is he counting days? Waiting to see if the sun will touch me again?

Day 18

Mama,

When the ambulance men took you, your hair beads left a wavy trail in the dirt. Three snakes splitting your path. I thought that meant you'd come home. Now I know you are gone and already returned to me. You are Yarn Baby and Baby Palm Rat. The seasick girl and the braided village. Cheetahs and bush babies. Sharp and still. The machete that never needs to cut.

Rain punctures the night to feed the ground. The killer's bones are giving way. Things slide out from under him. Slick feet and hands can't keep hold long. Soon he will lose history.

Day 19

Miss Browne shouts my name over and over until I crawl to her. She points a white gun at my forehead. A soldier at the border to the other country points the gun at everyone before he'll talk to them she says. He let Miss Browne borrow it for ten minutes. The red number flashes 100. *If this were my Grade 9 exam, I'd have a perfect score.* Miss Browne laughs and tells me she doesn't want me to have a perfect score, but she's happy it's a lower score than yesterday.

Something is wrong. Miss Browne has never pointed the white gun at my forehead before today.

Mama once told me people try to reach something inside other people that they can't. Is Miss Browne reaching? Is that why I'm shaking in there? Shadows slip around me. Mama's hair beads scatter between my ears. I hold up the history book confession to the window. Miss Browne won't shut up. I want her to read the confession, but she reels off numbers: 104.6. 103.9. 103.1. 102.7. 101.8. 102.4. That's how many times she's pointed the white gun at my forehead.

Baby Palm Rat stands between my feet, screeching. Baby is mad at Miss Browne. I am mad at Miss Browne. She says I slept for two days. That I wouldn't wake up. That I scared her. Her blue rubber fingers fly in the air and drop the white gun.

I describe Felicia's killer in the palm tree. His sticky climbing feet. His Dan bird mask. His dissolving bones. I'm scared the cheetahs are eating Felicia gone. She saved me from General Butt Naked. I want to find her while she still has a face.

Miss Browne stabs a blue finger at the confession. She is trying to reach my rage, Mama. I think she wants to steal the seasick girl from where I've hidden her. But she's held too deep. Miss Browne will never find her. Between the seasick girl and her there is an ocean. Miss Browne always says history is the long neck of time. My neck is too long to climb.

Miss Browne folds her blue arms. Says she recognizes the writing and I should too. She sounds angry. Baby Palm Rat cowers between my toes. It doesn't understand what's happening. Neither do I. My insides feel full of unraveling braids. Villages long gone. There are dark circles circling darker circles the way buyers circle slaves. The way stars circle nowhere they can see. I beg Miss Browne to find Felicia before her face is gone.

I'm falling toward something red and wet. I'm so hungry my stomach could be thunder. A bush baby has lost my dreams. I cry out *Mama* and feel ice drip inside me. Something is thawing. Another thing burning. Miss Browne says she forgives me. She holds her blue thumb and forefinger together so there's no air between them and explains that one finger is life, the other death. A drop of water couldn't squeeze through.

Miss Browne knows people so near death they imagined friends a continent away sitting beside them while they fevered. She tells me that I didn't want to get lost to history forever, so I brought history here. I needed an anchor to stay. Without it, I would've died. She is proud of my imagination. Proud of the confession I wrote. She thinks my pencil was dipped in palm wine and gunpowder.

Dwe runs past, playing "Who Is in the Garden?" His red T-shirt leaves streaks in the air. He is like sunrise and sunset all at once.

I dress Yarn Baby in the history book confession until she looks like an Egyptian mummy. Baby Palm Rat doesn't recognize her. Today I see two small sacks drop between his back legs. It's time to cut the *Feloz* out of the history book and snip its prow. *Viva,* I cry, as the seasick girl is set free for the last time.

Day 20

On the back of empty postcards I write one sentence each: My first history.

21 DAYS

This is growing up.
When my oar goes in our river, I want it to ripple continents.
Next time I battle with stones, I'll know how to forgive.
When my skin dances, it will be time to change.
Obi and Esther are my passage to somewhere.
Papa may never know who I really am.
I could be something other than me.
Map everything I don't know.
Play "Who Is the Garden?"
Let myself be caught.

Day 21

Dwe pulls out the nails in the bar across the window. Hawa takes off her deangle mask and shows me her new tattoo, a songbird with braids. Miss Browne brings Felicia home from Bush School. They put a clean dress in the blue bucket and aim the white gun at my forehead one last time. It's not a perfect score. Miss Browne reminds me tomorrow is Grade 9 exams. Now it's time to get 100.

Yarn Baby and Baby Palm Rat watch me fill Mama's hole with my postcard history. We picnic on the shore of dry Lake Mama. With the leftover rice I christen them Yewande Bakko and Boe Peter Retta. Then I teach them how to count to 21.

I AM TOM WAITS!

At first I went on as normal. If someone misguidedly said, "Hey, there, Sydney," I'd laugh. Later, when I couldn't purge the name from my being, I'd gag "Syd ney," the two syllables dead saliva, utterly meaningless, a joke.

On days when I'd lost all hope, or found myself near the swan boat embarkation point at Echo Park Lake, it was obvious the lounging hipsters knew precisely who I was but chose to play the coma girl/boy game they'd perfected on stage at Spaceland when Beck was still a boring beer from Bremen and not a musical wunderkind, if I'm not mistaken.

There was a time after *Rain Dogs* peaked at #188 on *Billboard*'s Top 200, when I was convinced that my acne scars allowed people to pretend they didn't recognize me.

Once, I walked from Echo Park Lake to Griffith Observatory via the hidden Angelus Avenue stairs to gauge how the stalwart bands of Korean hikers on Mt. Hollywood would respond to me. Confusion and fear was not what I expected from people who bang their backs against tree trunks in the Berlin Forest at the base of the hill.

To be fair, my record label never compiled accurate demographics about my sales, so it's possible there wasn't a booming Korean market for my work.

In frustration, I sometimes scribbled I AM TOM WAITS! on my palms with a magic marker stolen from the laundromat in the mini-mall where a podiatrist erected a gigantic neon green foot capped by a screaming orange bunion. I'd flash my palms at passersby, often children licking corncobs dipped in heavy mayonnaise, a disgusting habit that seemed borderline pornographic. The mayonnaise-licking children claimed they'd never heard of me, though their grasp of English was doubtful.

By that, I don't mean to belittle the little ones' intelligence. Once you realize California's written driver's test is offered in seventy-two languages, it's just common sense to assume the worst.

In the beginning, when suicidal feelings swamped me, I'd go to open mic night at the Tiki-Ti or Troubadour. Surely someone in the audience would realize I was me, I'd thought. I'm still mystified no one ever did, even when I sang "Clap Hands." The jerks just clapped their hands.

Incidentally, while I was strolling near the malodorous La Brea Tar Pits, mesmerized by another violent purple sunset courtesy of Mt. Pinatubo's cataclysmic eruption earlier in the year, a white vapor trail streaked overhead in chaotic loops before exploding into billowy gray smoke reminiscent of a mammatocumulus cluster, often referred to as boob clouds by amateurs. Those of us who knew a missile launch gone wrong when we saw one, shared an aha moment—what billion-dollar satellite did Vandenberg Air Force Base lose this time?

I don't remember my reasons for walking the length of Sunset Boulevard in a sandwich board, but when I arrived at Gladstone's on PCH the smell of fried fish and crusted guano made me seasick. Since then, I've avoided the ocean and feared seagulls, whose inland flight range is equivalent to a medium-range ballistic missile. Seagulls have been known to lift off from Gladstone's dumpster and land at Denver's aquarium. En route they pass over Salt Lake City, where some stop to poop on the Miracle-of-the-Gulls monument erected on Temple Square to honor their ancestors who saved the fledgling community's first harvest from a plague of Mormon crickets.

Speaking of Mormons, shortly after the episode at Gladstone's, the trembling began. Trembling beyond trembling that made my voice warble and fingers bungle C-chords. Music was likely rebelling against being trapped in someone mistaken as an imposter. Audiences got progressively ruder. I'd be singing "Way Down in the Hole" or "Christmas Card from a Hooker in Minneapolis" when people would shout, *Sit the fuck down, Bobby McGee!* I had no idea what that meant, or what they wanted from me, except to sit down, of course.

Here is one unmistakable fact: Mainlining was not glamorous. Heroin addiction was shit on shit toast. Heroin withdrawal was death on death toast.

A few weeks after crashing the UFO Expo West at the Airport Hyatt, I began to notice I could no longer rhyme. Previously, writing a song was as easy as solving quadratic equations. At the Expo, I attended a packed lecture by the eloquent ethnobotanist, Terence McKenna, whose writings on alien intelligence acting through psychedelic mushrooms were beyond mystical.

Actually, I'm not sure what "beyond mystical" means, or if anything can be beyond mystical.

On another psychedelic note, the pad I used to crash at had a Jimi Hendrix poster tacked on the wall. Hendrix was wearing his "Purple Haze" jumpsuit, a two-piece affair that defied the term jumpsuit, and was red, not purple.

The original "Purple Haze" chorus was "Purple Haze, Jesus Saves," which may explain why I devoted three years to creating a rock opera concept album—*The Passion of Black Jesus*—that my label refused to release. The album's title cut was a sonic tour-de-force of cabaret-R&B-gospel that lasted a mind-bending eleven minutes.

My opinion has always been first thought, best thought. Allen Ginsberg had the same opinion, though it's difficult to say which of us had it first.

It's possible Allen Ginsberg wrote a poem titled "The Passion of Black Jesus," though it's equally possible I just wish he had. I'm fairly certain Ginsberg's poem would've ended the Vietnam War.

Come to think of it, the character of Hendrix as Black Jesus, an AWOL helicopter pilot preaching peace and love on Skid Row, was conceived on my sandwich-board walk.

The opera unfolds during Apollo 11's moonwalk mission. Rounding out the cast was: Thief—an apostle; Glory—a devout chorister with dementia; Cate (aka Great Ass)—Glory's daughter; Francis Xavier (aka Doc)—Glory's VA Hospital orderly son; Ricky Diver—a drug dealer; and Michael Collins—the loneliest man in the universe, circling the moon solo in the Command Module. I've never understood my label's hostile reaction to the material.

The day I discovered my favorite falafel joint Eat A Pita was owned by the original Catwoman, Julie Newmar, I composed "I Don't Want to Grow Up" on a napkin over baba ganoush and pickled radishes. The line *Makes me wish I could be a dog* was for a stray beagle I hung with that afternoon.

On my way to Little Ethiopia, I got lost in Little Armenia, and wound up in Little Tokyo. It's almost impossible to do this, but there you have it. The foot blisters from that escapade were excruciating. I can now see where I grossly miscalculated. It wasn't the first time I mistook north for south and east for west. There was the horrible day when I mistook the Parthenon for the Pantheon. Imagine being in Athens when you think you're in Rome. I don't know who we have to thank that the Apollo 11 astronauts didn't suffer from similar directional impairment.

Having said that, I don't hold myself completely responsible for the Parthenon/Pantheon debacle. It seems ancient cartographers and epicists had a sarcastic streak. Why else would Mt. Ida be mapped in Crete and Turkey? And, why would the Mt. Ida in Crete (a Greek island) not be the Mt. Ida the Greek god Zeus kidnapped Ganymede from to take to Mt. Olympus (a Greek mountain)? And, to make matters worse, why would Zeus pop all the way over to Turkey's Mt. Ida to abduct the lad, when Zeus could've abducted any pretty boy from his own neighborhood to rape and pour wine? The whole thing strikes me as a mind fuck. And people wonder why so many Shakespeare characters are location- and identity-challenged.

The only time I rode in a helicopter was when I was ten. After that I no longer wanted to be a pilot or astronaut. Every flying aspiration I'd had flew out the helicopter's open side door that afternoon, scattering my dreamains over the Wisconsin Dells.

I doubt dreamains was the term I'd thought at ten, not knowing about cremation, or that cremains were the end result of that process. Nevertheless, dreamains seems exceptionally apt shorthand for the annihilation of childhood desire, while cremains could be a non-dairy creamer.

I used to ask people on the street if they'd ever felt a brontosaurus running inside them. At the time, I was preoccupied by the possibility that the human body could represent the land time forgot. Call it the long chain of knowing or being, though conceivably there's a vast difference between knowing and being, as there is between a brontosaurus and a giraffe, except perhaps as seen from a distance on the savannah when they might be indistinguishable from one another.

Another question I used to ask people was whether they thought concrete's teleological purpose was to showcase colorful gang graffiti. Those who responded "yes" were generally covered in tattoos, which may in fact represent the skin's ultimate teleological purpose.

According to John Lear, the son of Lear jet inventor Bill Lear, gravity is instantaneous. I've no idea what that means, but it sounds true enough. I've never dropped anything and had to wait for it to fall.

Sometimes, when confronted with uncontrollable gravity, as happened when I fell out a third-story window, I'm reminded of John Lear's lecture at the UFO Expo West. Apparently, alien spaceships use gravity generators to pull the fabric of space toward them. Then, when the aliens turn the generator off, their spaceship coalesces with the space they've pulled toward them (hundreds of millions of light years away), and moves there at much faster than the speed of light. Who knew the universe could be traversed in the time it takes the Wilshire bus to get from downtown to Santa Monica during rush hour?

Many Junes ago, I became obsessed with the film *Teahouse of the August Moon*. Presumably, I'd been heavily influenced by the lotus blossoms on Echo Park Lake and the illusion of ventilation kimonos offered. Picture my shock when Marlon Brando, the shrewd Japanese villager to Glenn Ford's misfit American captain, was awarded the "Golden Turkey Award" for "Most Ludicrous Racial Impersonation." I'm ashamed to admit I saw Brando's name in the credits, but thought he was impersonating Eddie Albert. I've no idea who I thought Eddie Albert was impersonating.

Speaking of déjà vu, Black Jesus' first aria was like regression therapy minus hypnosis. Imagine Skid Row, Sunday, July 20, 1969. The eagle has landed in the Sea of Tranquility. Michael Collins orbits the dark side of the moon. Black Jesus preaches to his stinky, penitent flock. Frances Xavier (Doc) searches among them for his demented mother, Glory. Black Jesus feels the spirit take hold. He must bless someone. Anyone. Who is this plaintive man in orderly's scrubs repeatedly shouting "Glory"? Why not grab his head and sing . . .

> *Go slow, brother, go steady.*
> *Your steps will bring on the water.*
>
> *I've surfed the muddy Mekong on a water buffalo,*
> *Celebrated Thanksgiving in the killing hills of Dak To,*
> *Seen My Lai's ditches flow with women and children,*
> *So listen up. Listen good.*
>
> *There is never a good time to make a run for it.*
> *Never a bad time to pray.*
> *Two men are on the moon,*
> *Three are in a foxhole,*
> *Four are in a rice paddy.*
> *Only one has his head between my hands,*

His brain pounding out orders.
Disobey them all, brother.

I once tried eating lunch naked but found out ants are real assholes. Even more so than flies. In fact, I'm pretty sure the insect world is five, no six times more assholic than Norman Mailer.

About the time that I began *The Passion of Black Jesus,* I quit meditating. I'm fairly certain that the causal link between losing my mantra and finding my soul resulted in others' disorientation.

Speaking of Norman Mailer, he and I had a brief correspondence in the '70s. For some reason, a fan letter I'd written gave him the impression I was a tall dirty blonde. I didn't disabuse him of his mistake, and allowed a non-existent part of my body to be described in a particularly lascivious exchange he later insisted was meant for Gloria Steinem. As requested, I destroyed the letter, which, as a lover of history, I deeply regret.

Incidentally, am I the only one who notices that incessant ringing?

I originally recorded Saint Vibiana's cathedral bells to accompany Glory's "Long Love" aria, but some tones rub lyrics the wrong way. Virgin martyrs aren't always the best begetters of harmony . . .

Holy moly, Mr. Armstrong's on the moon.
What does the Lord think of his creation?
Use to be the sky above the birds was all his,
Use to be no one but the Lord could see the whole earth,
Use to be the inside of a person was sacred.

Mr. Armstrong's on the moon seeing us spin,
Seeing day and night at once,
Seeing all them yellow children burning in the villages.

Stay and watch the moon set, Doc.
We'll kiss Mr. Armstrong goodnight,
And when the sun rises tomorrow,
Me and Black Jesus will walk to the ocean for all those burnt yellow
     babies,

Walk straight into the water and dive under the waves,
Oysters waiting on the long love.

By "lover of history" in relation to my Mailer letter, I did not mean to imply that I love all history equally, and that some history should not, if it were possible, be destroyed. I'm a bit uncertain about that double negative, same as I was about the potential of a brontosaurus and giraffe being confused with one another when seen on the savannah from a distance.

Isn't it strange how the same thoughts circle around and around. It's why the best choruses embody refrains that stick in the heart, while the best refrains engender choruses that stick in the brain. I've never forgotten my first music teacher cum heroin dealer's advice: *Remember, Tom, all choruses are refrains, but not all refrains are choruses.*

Now that I've said that, I'm not entirely sure if that was my music teacher's advice or William Burroughs's.

William Burroughs was a thin old man with bad teeth and the kind of paranoia people would die for. He saw doppelgängers everywhere and often said over buttermilk pancakes: *Tom, from a great distance I see a cool remote naborhood blue windy day in April sun cold on your exterminator there climbing the grey wooden outside stairs.* It made perfect sense to me at the time, like throwing the *I Ching* on New Year's Eve, though, in retrospect, I had to admit to being thoroughly confused.

It wasn't until I was at the Central Library years later and found Burroughs's *Exterminator!* on the shelf that I realized he wasn't imparting wisdom but quoting from page 4.

Speaking of doppelgängers, there was a panhandler outside the Music Center in October who could've been Hendrix's twin. He pretended that he'd never heard of me even though he was singing "Heartattack and Vine." It felt like the Echo Park Lake hipsters all over again. Very dispiriting. Nevertheless, that wasn't a good reason to kill him.

Perhaps I should've mentioned that the morning of my panhandler oops, I got a blinding headache at discovering there is another Mt. Ida, in Colorado of all places. So it came as a deafening blow to also learn a celebrity subdivision in Laurel Canyon was named Mt. Olympus.

By deafening, I don't mean to suggest I'd lost my hearing. If I had, I wouldn't have heard Hendrix's doppelgänger sing "Heartattack and Vine," and presumably not killed him, headache or not.

Speaking of murder, there isn't a murderer better suited to a horror opera than the fifteenth-century child-sodomist-serial-killer Gilles de Rais, who had princess frocks and page's doublets sewn for his hundreds of victims before assaulting, decapitating, dismembering, and cremating them in his castle fireplace. Compared to Gilles de Rais, Mack the Knife could've headlined *A Charlie Brown Christmas*.

"Jupiter is a bitch-ass planet" was one of those repetitive thoughts that frequently circled around at that time.

Eager to see celebrity Mt. Olympus for myself, I trudged up the Sispheanly steep sidewalk past Electra, Oceanus, and Zeus Drives. There was nothing at the top but a loud posse of small dogs hurling themselves at a picture window. Apparently I made a right turn at some point because I was found unconscious at the intersection of Achilles and Hercules. A mythologically obtuse paramedic with a woeful sense of humor officially reported that I demanded he return my shield.

"God Bless Rust-Oleum" was another thought on frequent replay. It sweeps through whenever I reminisce about Black Jesus' apostle, Thief, an addict and graffiti aficionado. His "Lights, Camera, War" tag on the 3rd Street overpass was pure genius.

While scoring some heroin (his "chicken fix"), Thief witnesses Glory's foxy daughter Cate rip into Black Jesus for laying his "filthy crackpot hands" on her brother's head. I laid an awesome hiss track of paint exiting a spray can behind his "Day of Days" aria that closed Act 1.

> Ricky Diver, my man,
> Why do chicks with great asses always got sharp tongues?
> Why are they such a carnival of trouble?
> OK . . . I see you wanna get on with my chicken fix.
>
> God bless Ricky Diver's needle.
> God bless the veins in my arms and between my toes.
> Take your pick, my man, and God bless.

This is the day of days, my man.
Just look how blue that vein is,
Blue as Miles, blue as God's eyes.
You good with that needle, Ricky D.
God will surely reward you in this life and the next.
See you on the moon, my man.

A person with a vagina once suggested that Ricky Diver was a rip off of Fitzgerald's Dick Diver from *Tender Is the Night*. Clearly, the vagina never read the novel and never heard my *Passion*. Only an illiterate imbecile could think Ricky D and Dick D had anything in common, except a penis.

"Ignorant imbecile" was not meant as an insult toward my dear vagina-possessing friend Nicole, who like many women of a certain age and gender, find themselves out of their depth and confused.

Physical violence was central to *The Passion*, though I suppose that goes without saying since everyone knows "Passion," when used this way, is a euphemism for an unjust painfully horrific death.

In fact, euphemisms are such a tender way to communicate I'm not sure why anyone bothers with the truth.

After my deadly encounter with Hendrix's doppelgänger, I decided to take some time off. I spent a year in Uruguay, though for six of those months I thought I was in Paraguay. Since Spanish is spoken in both countries it can be complex. Something I learned from that episode is time travels faster when I don't know where I am.

Speaking of dislocation, for longer than I'd care to admit, I thought harum-scarum was an abandoned ghost town near Addis Ababa.

This may not be pertinent, but around the time of the L.A. riots, I discovered a gold tooth at the back of my mouth and have no idea how it got there. I discovered it after eating Ma Yi Shang Shi but before I knew Ma Yi Shang Shi meant "ants creeping on trees."

Ordering Chinese food always makes me feel as if I'm speaking baby.

Whenever the temperature hits 92.7, I've had the distinct sensation that my head might fall off. In fact, shortly after my homicidal oops, I became convinced that whatever was sitting on top of my neck was much lighter and more ethereal than my actual head.

I'm also convinced that Michael Collins survived his time orbiting alone in the Command Module by letting his body parts float about, which is why his rhapsodic arias ripple God-like through my *Passion*. After Doc confronts Thief about stealing Glory's jelly donut, Thief howls his recitative—*I know what you think. You think I want to spread my shit on your shit until your shit got no place, until none of our shit got no place*—while Collins soars above it all, singing . . .

> *This familiar ship,*
> *We circle and watch and wait.*
> *I am not lonely. I am.*
>
> *Not since Adam, they say,*
> *Not since Adam before his rib.*
> *Such loneliness, they say.*
>
> *Blue-and-white star, circling fire,*
> *I've lost you forty-four times.*
>
> *Near Greenland's icecap,*
> *You are shedding oceans.*
> *Whorls rip across your equator dragging sound waves.*
> *Houston, I have my eye on you.*

Shortly after I returned from Paraguay, the headaches had abated, but distance became fluid. It was wild to set out for the Greek tragedy *Electra Glide in Blue* at the Regent on La Brea and, ten steps later, wind up at the Egyptian on Hollywood.

It took years before *Electra Glide in Blue* screened again and I realized it wasn't a Greek tragedy. And that the title wasn't a coy reference to the dress Electra wore while plotting her father Agamemnon's murder, but a blue motorcycle favored by Robert Blake, an Arizona cop. In the end, everyone was killed in either case, and Arizona's bleak khaki scrub wasn't such a far cry from ancient Greece, so I suppose I got my money's worth.

Among Los Feliz Boulevard's majestic pines, a good Samaritan handed me coffee, two donuts, and, strangely, a handful of tampons. My hair was quite long at the time in the Paraguayan style, which may have accounted for their confusion. Still, I was miffed and burst into the second verse from "Singapore," thinking that would set them straight about who I was. They had an allergic reaction to the rhyme *Cross your heart and hope to die, When you hear the children cry.* Likely, they were the person who called the police.

Imagine my surprise when I later needed one of those tampons.

There was a chance I might have ridden horses while in Paraguay, which presumably cured my headaches. If in fact I did ride horses in Paraguay, they may have also irretrievably jumbled my insides. Nothing else makes sense. Speculation beyond Paraguayan horses seemed fruitless.

I no longer remember where I lived during the L.A. riots, or why anyone would care. Around that time it enraged me that people still called chamber music chamber music when it was played in a 3,000-seat hall. The same held true when people stopped drawing in drawing rooms.

After Griffith Park became untenable to live in because of the puma stalking me, I resided at Forest Lawn necropolis for six months, near the Wee Kirk o' the Heather Chapel. While there I did my best to avoid Babyland, a horrible heart-shaped hillside with epitaphs like "Lil Booger" and "If only . . ." Twice I stopped by the Great Mausoleum to view the 30-by-15-foot stained-glass replica of Da Vinci's *The Last Supper.* Subsequently, I experienced schizophrenia. Both times.

That adventure was a perfect example of how we can never know what lies dormant within us. As was my unprecedented need for a tampon.

Speaking of black and death, apparently the squirrels on Mt. Ida in Colorado of all places have bubonic plague.

It didn't take long for me to learn that suspended animation was an important state to be able to conjure at a moment's notice. On occasion, time needs to catch up with where you are and the only way to let that happen is to not let it move forward or back.

Another critical state to be able to enter at a moment's notice is California.

On the other hand, it may be more important to be able to exit rather than enter anything.

My headaches returned with the total solar eclipse. Everything became greenish-yellow, like living inside a liver. In fact, my liver experienced deep malevolence, an emotion I'd previously thought off limits to organs.

While in Paraguay I developed a problem. On the road to Montevideo, which may in fact be in Uruguay according to a map I saw in the Central Library while inserting that stray tampon, a river presented itself. I've no idea what prompted me to remove my clothes, but when I did, I discovered my penis was missing.

The experience was similar to jumping off a surfboard near the L.A. County Jail and thinking: Who needs the ocean?

During my Paraguayan sojourn I never quite felt like myself, so who knows if I was even there. I certainly would've preferred to have been in the Galapagos than Paraguay, given the choice.

Despite my distaste for polyester, and Hendrix's purple jumpsuit not being purple or a jumpsuit per se, when it came to costuming Black Jesus for *The Passion*, I chose a purple polyester jumpsuit. After a few days on Skid Row, he stinks a boil and refuses to bless the pigeons, but nonetheless corrals Cate with his compassionate "Argonaut" aria . . .

> *Hey, sister, calm yourself.*
> *The first job of life is to listen.*
> *The young can't know what the universe will bring,*
> *But when it brings it, you answer.*
>
> *Enter that attitude of no disturbance*
> *Where your Argonaut dwells.*
> *Practice stripping away what stops you from a quiet mind.*
>
> *When your bird gives you a view of earth,*
> *Contrary to the rules of nature,*

Don't lift your nose and retreat.
Don't arrest your descent.
It's called level flight attitude for a reason.

So level your flight attitude, sister.
Respect what you see before you,
Give yourself over to what you don't know and what scares you.
C'mon, sister . . . Step up and I will listen.

Let's face it, since Paraguay my body was in an ongoing state of diminishment and leakage, and couldn't meet my anger. I had no idea it was possible to become a smudge.

I wrote a long philosophical letter explaining my dilemma to the great composer/arranger Nelson Riddle, who apparently had already died.

Incidentally, Riddle's middle name was Smock.

For as long as I can remember I've felt deeply geographical. As if made up of seven continents still in a state of Pangaea, a supercontinent awaiting dispersal and repositioning.

Being 60 percent water, we likely merge and go adrift all of the time, I wrote to Riddle, who for obvious reasons never responded.

Speaking of Pangaea, the opera *The Emperor of Atlantis or The Disobedience of Death,* had a similar dispersal and repositioning as myself. Written by two inmates at the Theresienstadt concentration camp, the score survived its makers and entered the metaphysical realm before its premiere. The opera's Dutch conductor consulted a spiritualist to contact the gassed-at-Auschwitz inmates for instructions regarding the instrumentation of Death's aria near the opera's end. As my first music teacher cum heroin dealer explained it, the dead composers asked for flute and trumpet to be added, and strings to replace harpsichord.

Trumpet is the most honest instrument. It never smiles when it doesn't mean it, cries when it does, is mean as hell when deserved. While Thief basks in the afterglow of his "chicken fix," his oily motor mouth, backed by a pulsing ghostly trumpet, sets death in motion in his "Great Ass" aria . . .

> Great Ass is one carnival of trouble, my man.
> Someone needs to fry her jelly donut,
> Unbend her angles until grace fills her belly
> And frosts her mind.
>
> Bingo, baby, ain't that what you always say, Ricky D?
> That you can get back any day,
> That you can Bingo time.
> Go Bingo Carnival of Trouble with a chicken fix,
> Prime her caboose, doodad her universe,
> Give Great Ass the ride of her life,
> And get back this day.

Yeah, get back this day. And while you're at it, whoever I'm talking to, doodad my childhood.

I've had a fear of the Hollywood Bowl since I showed up to play on the wrong night and stumbled into a *Sound of Music* sing-along. Being surrounded by men in nuns' wear crooning "Climb Every Mountain" was harrowing. Curiously, I seemed to be the only one who was outraged that Julie Andrews's hairdresser used a bowl to cut her hair.

After I abandoned Forest Lawn's necropolis, I embarked for Lake Hollywood but ended up in Long Beach. This was an even more traumatic directional disaster than my Little Ethiopia, Little Armenia, Little Tokyo triangle. For weeks after, my heels developed frightening claw-like growths and I became convinced I'd traversed the human-animal divide.

With that in mind, I bedded down with the peacocks at the L.A. Zoo for a week. Of course that meant I had to sleep in a tree. It came as quite a surprise as I thought peacocks were too fat and clumsy to fly.

The same puma that stalked me in Griffith Park eventually showed up at the zoo. Thankfully the raucous peacocks protected me, while the poor koala got its face eaten.

I may have forgotten to mention that soon after the trembling started, slurring set in. It was hard enough to go unrecognized, but to be accused of perpetual dipsomania was infuriating.

William Burroughs was a dipso and a murderer, but he didn't take much flak for it. And here I was a murderer, but no dipso, forced to sleep with peacocks.

On the other hand, the peacocks were absolutely lovely hosts.

Then again, after the ongoing Paraguayan strangeness, I might've been wrong about killing anyone.

It wouldn't be the first time since collaborating with William Burroughs that I made erroneous assumptions about events, later to discover they were markedly different than I'd thought.

The lyric "I'm at the end of my rope" rhymes with a lot, but not with "frog" or "lily pad."

My headaches returned with the total solar eclipse, though I may have already said that. However, if I didn't, my headaches returned with the total solar eclipse.

As it turns out Ricky D's needle was laced with fairy tales. Terror and wonder in one. Consequently, the police roll in while Thief crawls through the pandemonium, a symphonic overdose spilling from his throat . . .

> *Black Jesus say the mechanics of intelligence*
> *Reside in my thump ditty thump.*
>
> *Ricky D's needle knows how to plant a seedling*
> *In life's thump ditty thump.*
>
> *Great Ass goin on the ride of her life,*
> *Silver ponies gonna stampede her veins,*
> *Mustang her tongue, Harley her venom.*
>
> *I'm gonna skinny-dip in her city of rainbows,*
> *Gonna peel back her skin,*
> *Dissect her thigh gap,*
> *Insert my camera.*

> *I'm coming in for a close-up,*
> *We're about to go airborne,*
> *Rust-Oleum on the wind.*

Deep disgruntlement seized hold of me after that. I never was able to get to the root of the issue beyond the sense that the end of a song is much like its beginning.

For longer than was healthy, I worried that the reason people shouted *Sit the fuck down, Bobby McGee!* at me was because that might be my nickname. Then I realized it was mass psychosis.

If you don't believe in mass psychosis, just ask the average Joe or Jane if they think Apollo 11 ever landed on the moon. Or, for that matter, where harum-scarum is?

Since Paraguay, my memory has ceased to be my most reliable asset. My penis, which had previously held the post, obviously lost that spot when it went missing at the river.

The Passion of Black Jesus did not have a happy ending. By that I mean everyone died. The only characters who survived the police assault on Skid Row were outside earth's atmosphere. Michael Collins's final aria hovers like gossamer over the bullets and teargas . . .

> *A quarter of a million miles mapped,*
> *The vacuum of space,*
> *The truth of the matter,*
> *New world take my picture.*

I've decided to return to Paraguay by way of Wisconsin's Dells and Mt. Ida in Colorado of all places. Surely I'll discover what I lost, or haven't yet been able to locate. I plan to ride horses again since they were so helpful with my headaches last time around.

Since I've never learned Spanish, if a Guayan misguidedly says, "Sydney," it's likely I'll think they burped. As for Bobby McGee, I doubt he even exists.

Allen Ginsberg once howled, *Follow your inner moonlight; don't hide the madness.* I prefer Black Jesus' wisdom. *My home is beneath my hands, your home is beneath yours. There is nothing truer in the universe.*

I've said goodbye to the swan boats, the lounging hipsters, the Tiki-Ti. All that's left is to pull some fabric of space toward me to generate momentum and a song. I've dug out Black Jesus' purple jumpsuit for the trip. Distortions of perceptual reality are on my agenda.

LITTLE PRISONERS

Prologue

Farah let the soldier guide her through the labyrinthine Ras el-Tin neighborhood, though he didn't know Alexandria. Voices splintered through shutters flung open to collect the sea air; a weave of Arabic, Greek, Turkish. Polyglot fringe on the pearl of the Mediterranean's coastal tarboosh. That curious hat worn by waiters, dervishes, and diplomats.

Her fingers stroked the grit caked on the soldier's uniform. He smelled of desert and oil, coated and creased with sand and the things he'd seen. There was an unfamiliar scent too. Something American.

Gloom smothered the cobblestones. The sky was a speckled ribbon between the pitched roofs. They could have been threading their way through an unmapped valley. Farah still hadn't told him it was her thirtieth birthday. Was that why she accepted his invitation to the Athenios Café? To mark a milestone her family ignored? Or was there something more that compelled her to linger in the bookstore to translate his question to the miserable bookseller? Was it the book he was searching for? How odd to translate Antar and Abla's love story to a stranger over tea. His haunted blue eyes pleading . . . go on go on . . . his finger turning the page each time she hesitated.

Neither had spoken since leaving the café. His easy silence, the pressure of his arm around hers, revived her childhood walks with her father. She could taste shisha smoke. Hear the blind fortuneteller deliver fate. Felt the urge to move faster, not be left behind with her mother and sisters.

Farah wanted to wander in circles with this man until dawn, when they'd arrive in the dazzling pale sun of the harbor. With him she'd walk straight into the sea. Let the waves make love to them, drowning her restlessness and buoying the weight of the lovers' story she'd left unfinished just at its point of doom. She ached to tell him how it ended. Ached to read him the final passage. Anything to keep him near a bit longer. Her desperation terrified her. How long had she craved a man without knowing it? What else lurked within? Is this why she fled Cairo for Alexandria?

Ras-al-Tin's air was vehement. Its summer grip a lover refusing to let go long past the point of pleasure. Putrid leaching garbage slicked the cobblestones with ooze and guts.

Farah marveled at the soldier's confidence. Did he really think he could find his way to her apartment through this maze because he was American? She couldn't have found her way. Not in a blackout, not without help. Was there something about his uniform? Did it possess superpowers? Her students had showed her the comic book propaganda. America soldiers busting their seams. Becoming planes. Bombs. Bullets to Hitler's brain. She wanted to try on this American's uniform. See how it changed her.

Farah noted every sensation, every smell and sound, cataloging the moment. She was tempted to break their silence, to tell him her senses were compiling a list she'd label: Aaron. American. May 1943. She would've liked an American song to accompany the list. One of the tunes that wafted through the large windows with balconies overlooking the Corniche, or that leaked from the expensive hotels where the foreigner mischief-makers mingled. She wanted to know what notes, what key, what rhythm aroused him, so she could bend herself into that chord.

Was she G-minor or -major? A quarter or whole note? What part of her body would it take to sustain the perfect vibration so they remained untouched by war. She was lost among chords when a pack of wild dogs descended on them from a side alley. Aaron yanked her into a doorway and folded himself around her. She had never been subsumed—simultaneously singular and plural. Then his limbs unwound and he was back on the street, squinting in the direction the pack came from. Something was there. A soft buzz. An atmospheric moan. A grooved record going round that morphed into a low drone.

His arm shot out to grab her hand. The superhero's "BAM" exploded its bubble. Air raid sirens screamed as the droning erupted into a roar quaking the city. Alexandria's sky ignited with anti-aircraft lights and tracer bullets. Explosions convulsed the ancient ground, choking the air with millennia of blood and dust. Guts churned. Throats spasmed. Blown-out windows hurled glass knives that cut like fire. Farah and Aaron were swept into the wave of panicked people running madly toward the Anfushi Tombs.

People plunged down the crumbling limestone staircase carved out of the hillside. Children's hands slipped free from parents'. Lovers got separated in the pitch-black necropolis. Bombs concussed the harbor. People screamed that the hillside would collapse. A direct hit would breach the seawall and they'd all drown. The Anfushi Tombs inflamed the suffocating sense that this night would be the end of the world. And why not? When the implausible revealed itself daily, gods and prophets must be on the move.

Farah's back pressed against Aaron's chest. Dress and insignia discovering their common fiber. Farah was so familiar with the tombs, her blind ode about the room began in a whisper, until those nearest grew quiet, and calm spread through the vault. This was her favorite time in history, when Egyptian deities came face to face with Greek gods, the decorative blend an architectural feast of assimilation. She didn't know who had once occupied the sarcophagus at the room's center, but for the terrified children she spun a mythic tale of a hunted creature saved by this tomb from extinction.

Aaron's hands rested gently on her shoulders. The feeling of peace that suffused her came as a shock. They were hands that must have built walls to enclose time. Hands that crafted space where things became electric. Hands perfectly designed for those blood years. Adept at creating hidden chambers to unfold within.

From the bookstore to the café to the silent walk, Farah wasn't sure what would happen once they arrived at her apartment, though she'd mapped lines on her body fitting to the era. Red for fortification. Blue for tributary. Dotted for access point. Above her waist was the shabby Siegfried line, robust as a paper fence. Below her waist, the impenetrable Maginot, useless against a low country incursion. And then there was the North African desert's Mareth—French built, German occupied, English and American overrun.

Her boundaries could not withstand a charge of kittens. No matter. Before the all clear sounded, her desire to defend her map had been expunged by Aaron's touch.

Aaron stood naked in Farah's empty bathtub, his skin streaked ochre in the candlelight. Grime swirled at his feet. He had no chocolate bar. No cigarettes. No silk hose. Nothing to offer but himself.

Farah handed him a second pitcher of warm water, unable to tear her eyes away. His body was complex and beautiful, scars vivid and delicate telling an entire life she'd never know. When her fingers felt nothing but the tub's smooth porcelain, she plugged the drain and heated more water so he could soak away what remained of the desert.

Farah sat on the edge of the tub and finished Antar and Abla's love story from memory. Aaron had heard the beginning of the Bedouin romance a year earlier in a chieftain's tent while his five-member unit waited out Rommel's offensive against Tobruk. From there, they'd tagged behind the Desert Fox on his long march from Libya to Tunisia, examining all things metal—looking for signs of weakness in Germany's war machine.

They traversed an entire desert, scarabs scurrying over the sand in flowing djellabahs. Aaron rubbed hundreds of ball bearings, analyzed tank treads, cut buttons from corpses' uniforms, and buried his best friend in that monstrous waste that dehydrates flesh into jerky. They were an elite group of junk men, professional scavengers by trade, set loose in the scrapheap of war. Strategies were designed based on their interpretations. That mission lasted a year and ended in a race to the sea. German and Italian soldiers had hoped for their own little Dunkirk, but Hitler and Mussolini left them stranded on the beach, so they sat in the surf and surrendered.

Farah reached the end of the romance and recited Antar's words after his marriage to Abla was consummated: "My heart is at rest: it is recovered from its intoxication."

Aaron placed Farah's hand on his chest so she could feel the state of his heart's unrest. It was that moment in an opera, the middle of the long second act that delineates drama from tragedy. Aaron knelt before her, eager to hear Farah tell him once more how Antar described Abla's smile.

"When she smiles, between her teeth is a moisture of wine, of rain, and of honey."

He held her face between his hands. No brass-button nose. No ball-bearing eyes. Only golden oiled lips, fine-tuned and slippery. So slippery his words slid straight into her mouth. "Imagine a world where wine, rain, and honey are the ingredients of a kiss."

There was no day or night. A bed, just enough food, water. Farah and Aaron didn't leave her apartment for seven days. When the sun rose on the eighth, they stood in the dazzling flare of the harbor and walked straight into the Mediterranean. Every curling wave, every breath of wind startled and tasted different. Farah had never felt she owned any-thing, let alone time. She knew her body as something, but never this limitless, wet, and wanting.

No sleek-finned eggs dropped from silver fuselages. No tarboosh-topped waiters stormed their stomachs. They had not been found. It was the day that never ended. The one she had dreamed about. Even an American tune drifted out from the Hotel Cecil as they crossed the Corniche and Aaron stopped to ask the manager what it was. Farah's catalog was complete: Aaron. American. May 1943. "You'd Be So Nice to Come Home To."

Part 1

A crackly burst from a nearby minaret sent the museum's interim director off to pray, and left Alexandra briefly alone in his outer office with the photographs of Ebla. Three prints so large they destabilized her with their disquiet—the long-abandoned city caught in a roiling sandstorm; a shadowy staircase vanishing into a gloomy abyss; a lone jackal perched on a collapsed wall, guarding the ruined acropolis. This was where the clay tablets she'd come to help decipher had been unearthed. It was lonelier than she'd envisioned, desolate as discovering a single baby's shoe.

From the moment Alexandra Pierce introduced herself to Dr. Harun Lakhosh, he gave the impression he would have preferred a different intern. His eyes repeatedly drifted to her application file, as if looking for some justification to send her home. He intimated that he'd had nothing to do with the selection process as his predecessor's unexpected death had caused an upheaval in his duties. It was also possible that his behavior merely reflected a socially graceless bureaucrat. For someone so young he was remarkably stuffy, initially refusing to call Alexandra by her nickname because "Alice" was on her passport. But he eventually acquiesced, unlike her new landlord, Eldridge Whitby, the sixty-year-old British proprietor of the Collinwood Arms.

Their silent walk to the museum archive was interrupted when a man darted out of a room. He seemed a few years older than Alexandra's twenty-four, and had a mustache that overwhelmed his better features. He spoke in rapid Arabic to the director, never acknowledging her existence, an unpleasantly familiar experience from Alexandra's undergrad days, peaking in a senior seminar, when her reinterpretation of an Akkadian mythological narrative from a spatial perspective ended up much like the Akkadian language itself—first subjugated, then trivialized, and finally obliterated in a hail of silence.

Her initial thought was, it must be my dress, it barely covers my knees, which made her feel better. Dresses can be changed, knees concealed. But as the men's conversation proceeded, she decided her dress couldn't be the culprit. If it were, the mustached man would've had to cross Damascus blindfolded. Alexandra had seen hundreds of cosmopolitan women dressed similarly on the street in the past week. Exposed lower legs and sandals seemed another sign of the government's modernization campaign. As were the young people lined up outside cinemas screening contemporary eastern-bloc films. And then there was the fact that one of Damascus's oldest traditions had vanished. Alexandra discovered it the day she'd arrived at the Al-Nawfara Café and her tarboosh-topped waiter divulged that the hakawati's performance had abruptly been stopped by the regime the month before on night 158.

Alexandra focused her attention away from the two men and onto the hallway's mud-brick wall. Fragments of it were deeply grooved, other segments charred nearly black. She didn't notice the mustached man had ducked back into his office until the director spoke.

"The French colonials used fire to suppress rebellion. In this case, unsuccessfully." He rapped on the wall. "Fire only made this stronger." He motioned for her to follow him.

"How long have you lived in Syria, Dr. Lakhosh?"

"Seven years. Why?"

"My advisor at Berkeley was from Egypt. You have a similar accent."

"You have a good ear. I was born there. My mother was Egyptian."

"Not your father?"

"No."

Other westerners had seen the Ebla tablets—Italian archeologists discovered the site a decade earlier and had been overseeing its excavation since—but Alexandra suspected she might be among the first Americans to glimpse the Bronze Age records. Square and rectangular clay tablets were arrayed on a dozen tables in the chilly archive. Hundreds more filled shelves along the walls. Its vastness unnerved her. Her shadow fell across a tablet with script that resembled the stick figure her father drew on the scaffold when he taught her to play hangman. Excavation was the first long word he beat her with. She was six, and though she often saw the figure sprout limbs, fingers, and a face, until then she never knew he had glasses or a button-down tunic.

She slipped on a pair of gloves and ran her index finger over a tablet. "Can you make it out?"

The director may have been genuinely curious, but the question sounded like a challenge. Alexandra bent over the cuneiform script. "I'm afraid someone didn't pay their taxes to the king."

She smiled, hoping to soften the mood, but her teeth were the same as every other young American the director had met at conferences or excavation sites, perfectly straight white rows not unlike the marble slabs marking British graves at the military cemetery near his boyhood home. The cemetery was always immaculate and watered, while his neighborhood remained filthy and parched. Alexandra's smile rekindled his fury, and so he changed the subject. "Do you find your accommodations acceptable?"

"Yes, thank you." She followed the director into the hallway. "Dr. Lakhosh . . . That man . . . in the office back there . . . was he upset by—"

"Sayeed can be intense. Do not pay too much attention to his moods."

A balding man in a rumpled lab coat too tight around the middle ran up. His bushy gray eyebrows resembled two arches painted on a terracotta vase. "Please forgive my lateness." His lilting accented English sounded more sung than said.

"Alexandra, this is Dr. Arman. He will be overseeing your work."

Dr. Arman thrust out his hand to shake hers. "So, it's Alexandra . . . not Alice?"

"Yes, I prefer it."

"I will leave you in Dr. Arman's capable hands. Call on me should you need anything."

Before Dr. Lakhosh could slip by, Dr. Arman stopped him. "Harun . . . Has the ministry given their permission for us to visit Ebla?"

"Not yet, Mikha'il."

The director walked off before Alexandra could thank him. As he headed back down the long hall she was struck by his odd gait, more heron than human.

Dr. Arman sinuously gestured with his arm in the direction of his office the way ballet dancers do. Alexandra was instantly drawn to his congenial energy. He was so different from the other men she'd encountered since arriving in Damascus.

"Alexandra . . . If you don't mind putting up with my mistakes, I would be grateful to speak English as much as possible."

"Since I really should be working on my Arabic, how about mornings we speak English, afternoons, Arabic?"

"Capital idea."

Alexandra laughed.

"Is that the wrong phrase?"

"No. It's just very British. No American would ever say that."

"Then we must work on my idioms."

Dr. Arman's chaotic office defied description. How he managed to publish so many seminal articles surrounded by such mayhem astonished her. He gracefully slid his portly body between the 6-foot-tall stacks of newspapers, periodicals, and books, and sat behind his desk.

With nowhere else to sit or move, Alexandra stood rigid between two precarious towers.

"I was impressed by your application. That you can read Akkadian and ancient Hebrew is irrelevant to some of the Italians on the expedition who think Eblaite is more heavily rooted in ancient Sumerian, but I believe it is an asset. Also, to be honest, you were the only postgraduate student who did not write something about the romance of the desert. People have no idea how silly that sounds to someone who lives in it."

"I've only been in the desert once. Camping near Death Valley. Nothing about it was romantic. It was terrifying."

Dr. Arman searched through the files on his desk. "Your necklace . . . Good idea. Better for people to think you are Christian."

Alexandra held up the gold chain. "This is a key, not a cross."

"Oh, so it is. Forgive me. It is very delicate. I had assumed you were taking precautions."

"I'm only half-Jewish, and completely disinterested in religion."

"Half-Christian, half-Jewish . . . If anyone asks, do not mention it."

"You really think that's necessary?"

"1973 was a humiliation. Wounds do not heal in two years." He located the file and handed it to her. "That should bring you up to date on what has been deciphered so far. After you settle in, we will drive up to Tell Mardikh so you can see Ebla for yourself."

"That would be wonderful."

Somewhere amidst the mess on one of the shelves, a clock chimed noon. Dr. Arman sighed and, as per their agreement, switched to Arabic.

●

Alexandra held an ancient tablet midair, her distress mounting by the minute. What at first seemed like a fascinating legal record of a 4,000-year-old rape case now enraged her. A seventeen-year-old virgin had been brutally assaulted, and the assailant, though found guilty, was punished with a small fine because the girl couldn't prove she had cried out for help. "Who was there to hear her?" Alexandra shouted at the thick walls, her outburst registering with no one.

The Ebla tablets possessed an aesthetic allure that Alexandra had described to Dr. Arman as excavational sorcery, a phrase he added to his little black book of everything. Their shape and texture fascinated her; it was their content she chafed at. If decoding ancient intent had been her original desire, that world seemed as misogynistic and greedy as the one she lived in.

Dr. Arman entered to see the tablet gripped between her palms. "Anything interesting?"

Alexandra carefully set it down. "Interesting, but also horrible. A law case with an unjust verdict for the victim. Similar to the witch trials in England."

"I will have to hear more about that, but I came to tell you the good news. We've received the necessary papers for you to travel to Ebla."

"That's great! When?"

"Tomorrow morning. Dr. Lakhosh and I will accompany you. You will be picked up at nine." Halfway to the door, he took out his copy of Cairo's Daily, *El Ahram,* and laid it on a table. "I almost forgot."

"Thank you, but I'm not sure it's actually helping."

"On the contrary, in the past three weeks your Arabic is much improved."

"I still have no idea what half the words mean. I searched for Fatah-land on a map and it doesn't exist. I must have made a mistake."

"No mistake. You were searching for a phantom dream. Like Neverland."

"Really?"

"I'll explain tomorrow. Enough work today. The museum is about to close."

The Collinwood Arms was among the last rooming houses for westerners in a swiftly changing neighborhood. Huddled at the quiet end of a noisy street, worn colonial villas gave way to Soviet-style apartment blocks, necessity feeding the city's exponential growth. Two cypress trees, balding and brown in the middle, flanked the Collinwood's front entrance. A grillwork gate opened onto the villa's chipped tiled courtyard. It had been more than Alexandra expected—graceful curves and ceiling fans—but she had hoped the museum would place her among Arabic speakers.

At the corner of Al-Ma'moun Street, Alexandra could already hear Mrs. August rattling on. The cypresses shielded the patio from the street, and, as Alexandra came through the gate, she found Rafi, a Lebanese businessman who owned a factory, held captive, briefcase still in hand.

Mrs. August, in her customary slouch on the sagging rattan chair, swirled the ice in her 6 p.m. gin. "Alice, darling, stay and chat a bit."

Rafi peered over his glasses, imploring Alexandra to stay, but she kept moving up the four well-grooved steps. "I'd love to, but I must pack. I'm off to Ebla in the morning."

"Eb-what?" Mrs. August squawked as the door closed behind Alexandra.

Eldridge called to her from his desk in the common room. "Alice . . ." He held a manila envelope out to her, not lifting his eyes from a crossword puzzle. "What is a nine-letter word for building?"

"Structure."

Eldridge mouthed each letter as he consigned it to its space with his special crossword pencil, confirming another boarder's description of Eldridge's prewar life as a finicky chaplain. She retrieved the envelope and frowned at seeing it was from a legal firm.

Upstairs, Alexandra's small room held the bare minimum. Six strides to the writing table. Three to the bed. Five to the gouged Art Deco vanity with the crooked mirror. She opened the left-hand drawer and dropped the manila envelope beside the letter her mother had grudgingly handed over at the San Francisco airport. Alexandra had glanced at its postmark—May 16, 1975, three weeks earlier—then tucked it inside the Bedouin romance her advisor had given her as a going-away gift.

Alexandra hadn't heard from her father in seventeen years. Not one birthday card, not one postcard. She didn't open the letter until her flight was over the bottomless black Atlantic.

The note was brief, her father's scrawl unmistakable after all their hangman games. Alexandra chewed on her last remaining fingernail, eyes skimming the words "a trust," "a good sum," "legal papers to sign will follow." His last paragraph struck a different note.

> I forfeited my right to butt into your life years ago, but I've been thinking a lot lately. Trying to make sense of things. Tracking time before you were born. Recording history for myself. Don't blame your mother for what happened. I deserved everything. During the war, I left pieces of myself behind: one in Libya, the other in Egypt. It took until now for me to realize two pieces gone is more than a man can bear.

Alexandra flipped over the page, nothing more—a cryptic admission of wrong, a weightless apology. Her eyes drifted from that page to the Bedouin romance open on her lap.

TEN famous horsemen of the tribe of Abs went forth from the land of Shurebah on a plundering expedition.

The word "plundering" had scattered her mind with its onomato-poeia-like gracelessness, a collision of consonants and vowels wedded to destruction. It was a word steeped in another time, out of her reach. One that distilled a future calibrated to disintegrate. It had upset her to see the word. A reminder that what had attracted her to dead languages and excavating ancient intent was still a mystery to her. Maybe she wasn't the right person to be touching Bronze Age documents. Clay had been known to leave an imprint, and because it was used to join and construct, it also cracked and fell. She didn't like that it could be majestic and dull. Pompous and bleak. It was too much like people.

Through Alexandra's open bedroom window came the usual buzz from an unseen neighbor's radio tuned to a high-powered station out of Israel. In the last few weeks, Bowie's "Young Americans" had etched its way into her bones.

"Alice . . . ," Eldridge called through the door. "Are you decent?"

"Yes. Come in."

Eldridge stepped in, stroking Monty, his canary. "Mrs. August has planned a little outing for this evening. Cocktails at seven, then supper in the souk. She won't take no for an answer."

Outside, a bird called. Monty tilted his head toward the open window. Alexandra commiserated with the bird's sense of being trapped. "Maybe you should get Monty a friend."

Eldridge puckered his lips and cooed in a baby voice to the canary on his way out . . . "Do you want a friend, Monty? No, I didn't think so. Nasty birds. So messy."

Alexandra, Mrs. August, Eldridge, Rafi, and the Fouquets, a retired French couple, navigated the crowded Al-Hamidiyeh souk. Nicole Fouquet stopped at a spice stall and in French asked an old woman where the nice man who usually manned the stall was. As Nicole inexpertly haggled over the price of fenugreek, Alexandra soaked in the souk's raucous improvisation. Above, a luminous sickle moon hung perfectly over the Bab Sharqi, the ancient Roman arch known as the Gate of the Sun. "Alice!" Nicole called. "Please tell this woman I am not some naive tourist. I need this for my diabetes and am willing to pay a fair price."

Alexandra rolled her eyes. Although she'd repeatedly corrected everyone at the Collinwood, they still called her Alice because Eldridge did. He insisted civilization would unravel if everyone thought they could change their first name. Alexandra suspected Eldridge was punishing her for doing what he wished he'd done, and the others deferred out of fear that he'd raise their rent.

Mrs. August flashed an impatient smile. She'd lived a much better life in Damascus when her late husband was part of the British legation. That he'd been a sod and a lousy gambler for the past decade is what landed her at the Collinwood Arms four years ago. Though she felt the Collinwood's residents weren't quite up to her station, after twenty years in the Middle East it was unthinkable to return to England. Her yearly income would require taking a bedsit in an immigrant neighborhood full of dirty children, and for Mrs. August, there was a vast difference between living among westerners in the Third World and living among Third Worlders in the West. She called to Nicole, "Meet us at the restaurant when you're through."

Alexandra approached the spice table and spoke in Arabic with the old woman, who was happy to oblige her. She handed Nicole the tin of fenugreek as they walked on.

"Thank you, Alice. It's so frustrating that some of them treat me like this because I'm French. When are they going to get over it? France gave them independence thirty years ago. You know, that is what's wrong with these people. Why they'll never progress. They're insecure."

Alexandra and Nicole surveyed the packed glorified shawarma stand until they spotted the others at the back. Rafi rose to pull out their chairs, nearly impossible given the closeness of the tables. Nicole's husband, Jean-Paul, an ex-diplomat whose government pension permitted him to live a lazy, dissipated life in Syria but not France, justified his sloth in accented English: "Women don't want that anymore. No chairs. No doors. They don't respect a man who does that."

Rafi wiped his perspiring brow. "What they do or do not want is unimportant. I was brought up a certain way and that is the way I am."

A young American man at the next table shifted his chair to make room for Alexandra. If it weren't for the directions they were facing, they could have been sitting together.

A waiter appeared with a bottle of arak, a bowl of ice, and a carafe of water. He set two glasses in front of each person and slipped away as silently as he'd come.

Alexandra picked up the glasses. "Why do they always give us two?"

Jean-Paul took a glass from her. "If you weren't such a teetotaler, Alice, you'd know why." He filled the glass with arak, then water, then ice. The colorless liquor turned a milky white. "Now watch." He took his glass and reversed the order: ice then water. A thin skin formed on the surface. He dipped his finger in the glass and pulled it off. "The same thing will happen if you mix a second drink in the same glass, even if you do it in the correct order. A clean glass must be used every time." He clinked his glass to hers and knocked back the drink.

Another waiter emerged carrying platters heaped with steaming piles of chicken, eggplant, and beef in garlic sauce, along with a pot of hot water for Nicole. She retrieved the tea ball she kept in her purse and filled it with fenugreek. By then Jean-Paul had appropriated her extra glass and was already on his third arak. She rested her hand on his arm as he lifted it to his lips. "On our way here, Alice was telling me that all of Roman Syria, every ruin but the temple to Jupiter and the gate of the Sun, is just 5 meters below our feet. Isn't that incredible?"

Jean-Paul gave a noncommittal shrug, then held the platter of chicken for Eldridge, who picked out the choicest pieces before passing the platter on to Rafi. "When Monty and I were in the battle of Alam el Halfa . . ."

Rafi froze, the chicken aloft. "You and Field Marshal Montgomery were friends?"

"Heavens, no. Though I do feel if given the opportunity to make his acquaintance, a friendship would have most certainly followed."

Jean-Paul snickered. "Without doubt."

Mrs. August detested sarcasm and turned to Eldridge with forced curiosity. "Was that an important battle?"

"Important, Madam . . . It was critical, momentous even, the turning point of the whole desert campaign. The Jerries lost twenty-two tanks. Rommel was forced to withdraw from his offensive. The Afrika Korps never recovered from the hell we gave them that August."

The American man at the next table cleared his throat. "Excuse me, sir, but many historians have criticized Montgomery's cautiousness in that battle. If he hadn't allowed the Afrika Korps to escape, the second battle of El Alamein never would've had to have been fought."

"You, sir, were not there, and neither were your armchair American historians! And I dare say had you or they been, you wouldn't have survived a night's barrage!"

"I'm sure you're right," the man conceded, sharing a look with Alexandra.

"You can bet on it, young man!"

"There, there . . ." Mrs. August pleaded. "I invited everyone out since Alice is leaving for somewhere tomorrow, though why anyone would step foot outside Damascus is beyond me."

"Where are you going?" Rafi asked.

"Tell Mardikh. South of Aleppo."

Nicole mixed herself a glass of arak. "That's in the middle of nowhere, Alice."

"Yes. It's so exciting. People always discover the best things when they're nowhere."

The 1965 Volga didn't purr. It bore down. As if the only way forward was for the tires to eat pavement. On An'Nasr Street Sayeed hit the gas. The Volga backfired, then lurched forward at an uneasy clip. Alexandra felt self-conscious about her Arabic and stayed mute.

Traffic slowed in front of a movie theater. The film's poster caught Alexandra's eye. The title was in Russian, but the image was thoroughly American—a blond, blue-eyed boy fished beside a steamboat.

"The title in English is *Hopelessly Lost.*"

Alexandra wheeled around. Sayeed had spoken just to see the look on her face. She didn't disappoint. As suspected, she had assumed his English was tenuous.

"That poster looks hopelessly American."

"It should. It is based on an American character, Huckleberry Finn."

"What . . . ? Have you seen it?"

"Three times."

"Is it that good?"

"No, but I see everything."

"Three times?"

Sayeed nodded tersely and turned his attention back to the road. Alexandra wanted to probe further, but it was clear Sayeed was done.

At the intersection of Al-Walid, traffic stopped. Drivers stood on car hoods to rubberneck. Sayeed got out to speak to some men. When he returned, Alexandra waited for him to explain the gridlock, but he shared nothing. It was the same treatment she'd received in the museum hallway on her first day. Alexandra still couldn't tell if his silence toward her was confrontational.

A fruit vendor abandoned his cart to hawk fresh-picked figs among the immobile cars. Alexandra waved him over and bought a half-dozen. The ripe swollen flesh seemed the closest thing in nature to a woman's breast, the moist tips still oozing milky white from where they'd clung to the tree. She offered one to Sayeed and ate one herself, conscious about chewing quietly.

Traffic inched forward toward a square, where a bronze-sculpted soldier with sword and tarboosh sat astride a bronze horse. To its right, a flesh soldier with a machine gun impatiently waved cars through. On the sidewalk behind him, two bodies lay half covered by a tarp.

Alexandra stuck her head out the window. Where were the wrecked cars? The metal tangle that greeted such scenes? Her eyes drifted: Soldier. Pool of blood. Bodies. Soldier. Pool of blood. Bodies. The soldier raised his gun at her.

"Look away," Sayeed hissed. "Do not appear to notice anything unusual."

Alexandra did as he advised, though in the side mirror she noticed the soldier was focusing on the back of the car. "I think he's memorizing the license plate."

"He is."

Again, Alexandra waited for an explanation that didn't come. What terrible thing had she done to so anger the soldier? Sayeed's silence deepened her anxiety, provoking her to disrupt the stillness. She launched into an impromptu history lesson about Damascus being the oldest continuously inhabited city in the world. Birthplace of Apolodor the Damascene, the brilliant architect behind Trajan's column and the great bridge over the Danube. Her hands began to get away from her, pointing at whatever caught her eye. Intricate mosaic work. Arched recesses. Decaying facades. She became fingers and wrists. Elbows and forearms. A sprung coil.

Sayeed took in her history dance. Her exuberance like watching a fire burn. When she realized how ridiculous she looked, she slumped against the seat and apologized for getting carried away. After that she said nothing until Sayeed asked where in America she had come from.

If she'd thought he'd get the joke, she would have said, "Fidgety Bluffs, Oregon, by way of Hopping Toad, Indiana," to lighten the mood, but instead rambled about being dragged from Indiana to Oregon at age seven. There was nothing to gild. No history worth embellishing. She ended by muttering, "I haven't spoken to my father in seventeen years."

Sayeed's foot came off the gas pedal. He spoke to his father nearly every day. Alexandra didn't know why she had admitted it. When anyone asked, she always said he was dead.

She kept her face to the window, and as the car coasted past a beautiful home with a colonnade entrance, Sayeed confided, "That is my favorite house in Damascus."

Alexandra appreciated the distraction. "Have you ever been inside?"

"No. But I have imagined every room. The best is the screening room."

Alexandra swiveled, pleased to see he was smiling. She had never seen him smile and was struck by how it softened his chiseled features.

"I know you came to Syria to do scholarly work, but you could also be a tour guide."

"When this internship is over, maybe I'll stay. Forget the PhD and show tourists around."

"If you do, do not just show them old things. Show them how things are changing, or at least how we hope they will change."

"What do you want to change?"

Sayeed seemed about to reveal something when he spotted Drs. Lakhosh and Arman sitting on their suitcases in front of the modern apartment building where they both lived. His features stiffened as he pulled over to the curb and mumbled, "Many things."

The Volga swerved sharply. Alexandra's eyes popped open to see an animal dart into the scrub. Sayeed reached across her and pointed east. "Ebla."

A barren fifty-foot mound rose out of the desolate Syrian plain. No wonder it had lain undiscovered for millennia. Sayeed turned off the highway and stopped the Volga near two guards resting in the shade of a concrete building beside a sign: IT IS FORBIDDEN TO ENTER THE EXCA-VATION AREA. One sentry wore a white shora on his head and a flowing black dishdasha, the other a black shora and a white dishdasha.

The guards warmly greeted Drs. Arman and Lakhosh, but raised their hands for Alexandra to stop. Dr. Arman showed the guards the Ministry of Culture papers granting Alexandra permission to be there, but the papers weren't the issue. A woman couldn't possibly stay in the encampment all night with three men unrelated to her.

"Tell them I'm no different from the female archaeological students who work with Dr. Matthiae and the Italians," Alexandra fumed.

The guards conferred before refining their excuse. Alexandra wasn't different. The situation was. When the Italians were on site, the guards' task was to protect the perimeter. What happened inside the encampment wasn't their responsibility. But with no excavation going on, their job was to protect all of Ebla, which included Alexandra's honor.

"Oh, for God's sake," Alexandra huffed, walking back to the Volga, where Sayeed unloaded the suitcases. "I can't believe we came all this way and they may not let me in."

"Do not worry. You will get in. This is not about your honor."

Alexandra gestured toward the two guards. "Then why . . . ?"

"These people have nothing. They live in the village that borders the excavation. In a minute Dr. Arman will give them fifty lira for their trouble."

"That's less than a dollar."

"I am afraid that is all your honor is worth."

Dr. Arman strode toward them, bouncing on the balls of his feet. "Mission . . ." He hesitated, searching for the correct expression.

"Accomplished," Alexandra provided.

Dr. Arman repeated the phrase as he and the director headed off with their suitcases. Alexandra reached for hers, but Sayeed kept it. "Do not make things more difficult."

Alexandra followed the others around a crumbling wall, unprepared for her first sight of Ebla. The dull mound she saw from the highway hid the scope of what lay behind it. Ebla was immense, with a lower and upper town connected by impressive stone staircases and red mud-brick walls concealing dark chambers. She walked along the edge of a wall, gaping at its unburied wonders, nearly losing sight of the men headed steadily away from her. Alexandra hurried to the far side of the upper town, where Dr. Lakhosh waved to her from an encampment of white tents arranged in a circle around a fire pit.

Sayeed exited a tent as she arrived. "Your suitcase is in there."

"It's so huge. The only tent I've ever been in barely slept two."

"Yes, they are spacious. Plenty of cots to chose from." Dr. Lakhosh pointed to a small shack at the edge of the encampment. "But regrettably, that is the lavatory."

Dr. Arman joined them. "Ready for your tour, Alexandra?"

"Let me just grab my pad to make some sketches." Alexandra ducked inside her tent and returned with a notebook. Dr. Lakhosh was already disappearing down a steep stairway into an underground room. "Isn't he coming with us?"

Dr. Arman chuckled. "He is going to muse on the basin of the bearded men. That is how Ebla was discovered. A farmer plowing his field hit it."

Dr. Arman flitted off, and again Alexandra was struck by how light he was on his feet. "As you can see," he began with a sweeping gesture, "the city plan is regular, not haphazard, a monumental undertaking, very sophisticated. The Acropolis is at the center, or very nearly so. The fortification walls from north to south are somewhat longer than east to west. So far, four entrance gates have been unearthed. One faces the desert, another Damascus, a third towards Aleppo, and the fourth in the direction of the Euphrates."

Dr. Arman headed west into the sun. "See those ramparts? They show that Ebla existed in at least two periods. Structures of the Middle Bronze period lay right over the Early Bronze. And over there," Dr. Arman said pointing toward the Damascus gate, "you can see the remains of one of the old fortresses. The rampart on top was built so guards could pass through it."

He took a deep breath and surveyed the horizon. "Imagine coming across that plain. At first, you see only a hill. The hill turns into forts, fortresses, magnificent structures rising several tens of meters above the ground. Then out of the mud-red brick suddenly white plaster and limestone ramparts, glinting in the sun. In ancient Arabic, Ebla is 'white rock.' It would have been an imposing sight for Ebla's enemies."

He spun on his heels and darted into the heart of the lower town adjacent to the Acropolis. "Dr. Matthiae has written extensively on the many temples on the site. All are in the classical Syrian style with a single cella of the langraum type. But this is my favorite. Ishtar's temple."

Alexandra strolled along the temple's perimeter, making a quick sketch before joining Dr. Arman in the ruins of the building next door. It was on a lower level than the temple, and, remarkably, grass sprouted among the various excavated features. He rested on a green patch against the western wall in the shade.

Alexandra knelt beside him. "Why is Ishtar's temple your favorite?"

Dr. Arman smiled. "Because Ishtar represents everything taboo. She waged sex the way men wage war, with domination and cruelty. Every god and goddess has their cult. Some worship the sun, others rain, but Ishtar made prostitution sacred."

"She was also the goddess of fertility, not just sex and war."

"Another reason to sing her praises. There is a lovely view from the other side. You should see it while the sun is at this angle."

Alexandra circled the room, hugging the shaded wall. Jagged shadows spread across the ruins as the sun slowly dipped behind the nearby hills. She found a good spot to sketch Dr. Arman as he dozed and didn't sense Sayeed until his shadow fell across her pad.

"Dr. Arman's head is quite oblong, is it not?"

"Shhh . . . He can hear you."

"He is asleep. This is his favorite place to nap. Close to his fickle goddess."

Alexandra glanced up to see if Sayeed was joking. He wasn't. Around his neck hung an expensive camera with a telephoto lens.

"Did he tell you Ishtar's holy city, Erech, was known as the town of the sacred courtesans?"

"No."

"He likes to tell women that to see how they react."

Dr. Lakhosh called Sayeed. Alexandra watched him deftly hoist himself out of the ruin with unexpected grace, the way a pommel-horse gymnast would. She was impressed.

Alexandra scrutinized her drawing. Sayeed was right. Dr. Arman's head was remarkably oblong, and her drawing failed to reflect that. She began a new sketch, carefully gauging the proportion of his head to his other features.

"I hope you are making my head more oblong this time."

Alexandra stuttered an apology.

"Just so you know, Sayeed is only half right. I do tell women about the town of the sacred courtesans, but not to see how they react. I do it to let them know there was a time in the Middle East when society was more open."

"I can't figure Sayeed out."

"That is the way he likes it."

"What exactly does he do at the museum?"

"Helps Dr. Lakhosh with his research and makes a photographic record of all the museum's holdings and exhibitions."

"So he took those amazing photos in Dr. Lakhosh's office."

"Yes. They are amazing. Not pretty pictures, but raw, full of energy."

"Is Sayeed also an expert on water basins?"

"Heavens, no. That is Dr. Lakhosh's bailiwick. Harun joined the Italian expedition years ago to head up research on the basin of the bearded men. That is what brought him to Syria, and then to the museum. The basin has become his mistress." Dr. Arman stood up and dusted himself off. "May I have a look at my portrait?"

"I'm not very good. Please don't hold it against me."

Dr. Arman glanced over her shoulder at the sketch. "You are wrong. That is quite a good likeness. Come. I have a few more things to show you before supper."

Alexandra trailed after Dr. Arman, braving dusk's chill until he led her back to the tents, where clay pots simmered on a grate above the fire.

"Where are Dr. Lakhosh and Sayeed?"

"Praying."

"Ah, you're an atheist like me."

"No. I am a Copt."

"So you're a practicing Christian."

"Yes. Though I do not believe in Santa Claus."

Dr. Arman excused himself to get a pullover, leaving Alexandra alone by the fire. The sky still glowed violet blue, but dozens of stars already glimmered. She'd never tell Dr. Arman, but at this moment, and in this place, the desert did seem romantic.

Dr. Lakhosh and Sayeed stepped out of two different tents, one right after the other, and joined her. The wind shifted and the wood smoke forced Alexandra back. She was shocked by how cold it was just a few feet from the fire, and noticed the others had put on sweaters. She sat on a rock near Dr. Lakhosh, hoping he'd block the wind. Sayeed crouched in the dirt, lifted the lid from a clay pot, and stirred their supper with a battered tin spoon.

"It smells delicious. Did you make it?"

"No. An old widow in the village nearby prepares meals for us."

Dr. Arman called from a tent, "Alexandra would you like to borrow a jumper?"

Dr. Lakhosh was incredulous. "You did not bring anything warm?"

"I know it sounds idiotic, but I didn't think it could get this cold."

"Yes, Mikha'il, bring her a jumper."

The sweater flopped to below her knees. "I'll try not to set myself on fire."

Sayeed headed to his tent and returned with a colorful coat, similar to a short winter robe a Bedouin might wear. It was big in the shoulders, but otherwise not a bad fit. Alexandra thanked him as he served up a chickpea barley stew in a savory chunky sauce. After dinner, when Drs. Arman and Lakhosh pulled out their pipes, Alexandra ducked into her tent to retrieve a pack of Marlboros. She offered Sayeed one and lit her own. "Now all we need are marshmallows."

The men exchanged confused glances.

"Hmm . . . Never had to describe a marshmallow before. Basically, it's a pillow-like cube of sugar that people roast in campfires. The outside caramelizes and then it melts in your mouth."

Dr. Arman sighed. "Sounds delicious."

Harun patted his shoulder. "Poor Mikha'il. All this talk of sugar and we have no dessert."

Alexandra was charmed by Dr. Arman's youthful pout.

"It was how I was brought up, dessert after supper. A meal just isn't complete without it."

Sayeed retrieved a folded handkerchief and held it out to Dr. Arman.

"What's this?" Dr. Arman peeled back the edges and swooned at the sight of four plump figs. "Sayeed . . . You are a savior."

Sayeed gestured with his Marlboro at Alexandra. "She is your savior. She bought them earlier today."

Dr. Arman passed the handkerchief around, but Alexandra refused hers. "It'll be much more fun watching you enjoy two of them."

He held a fig up to the moonlight. "A remarkable fruit. D. H. Lawrence wrote a lengthy poem extolling its virtues as a fruit of female secrecy."

"I thought Lawrence only wrote novels. I'd love to hear one of his poems."

"I'll give you a short excerpt." He smiled mischievously and cleared his throat.

That's how the fig dies, showing her crimson through the purple slit
. . . .
Like a prostitute, the bursten fig, making a show of her secret.

"A very salacious poem, no?" Dr. Arman said, biting into the fig.

"Very salacious," Harun agreed. "Not exactly a poem for mixed company, Mikha'il." Harun tapped his pipe against a rock. "Alexandra . . . What else do you do around fires in America?"

"Tell scary stories, play games."

A high-pitched howl pierced the night. Alexandra sprang to her feet. "What was that?!"

"Desert jackals. Something has been killed," Dr. Lakhosh explained, seconds before a dozen more chilling howls answered the first.

Alexandra covered her ears. "It sounds as if a baby is being eaten alive."

Sayeed flicked his finished cigarette into the fire. "That is how jackals call their family together to feed. This place is full of them. They mate for life. Not like Americans."

Dr. Lakhosh said goodnight, explaining he'd barely slept three hours before dawn prayers.

Dr. Arman leaned toward the pack of Marlboros. "May I?"

"Of course."

Dr. Arman lit the cigarette and inhaled, his tongue flirting with the smoke as it swirled out of his mouth. He pulled out his small black notebook. Added *Marlboro* to the bottom of a list.

"You know . . . American men keep little black books like that with women's names."

"Men who need notebooks to keep track of women do not deserve them."

"May I see your list?" Alexandra reached for the notebook. There were the usual suspects, *Winston, Kool, Camel,* and then Alexandra chuckled. "Virginia Slims?"

"I am eager to try everything." Dr. Arman stretched his back. "I need a walk before bed."

Alexandra watched Sayeed absently stir the dying fire. She fixated on the embers consuming the last log. When they reached a certain spot she'd retreat to her tent, feeling she had stayed long enough not to appear rude.

"What kind of games did you play around the fire?"

"All sorts of games, but the one I really liked was Truth or Dare."

"Dare? What is that?"

"Um . . . a dare is a test . . . or a challenge. Like . . . I dare you to go look at those jackals."

"How does the game work?"

"We'll play a round and I'll show you. First, you have to make a choice. Do you want to answer a question truthfully or perform a dare?"

"But I do not know what it will be."

"That's the point."

Sayeed threw the stick into the embers and leveled his gaze at her. "Truth."

"I should've warned you. This game isn't about being nice."

64

"Go ahead."

"What is it about me that makes you dislike me so much?"

Sayeed flinched, but kept his eyes on hers. He didn't speak for a long time, so long Alexandra was about to suggest they forget it when his voice startled her. "I do not dislike you in particular, but people like you in general. You come to this part of the world thinking you have the answers to everything. Many of us believe in the same things you do, freedom to speak, religion, the freedom to marry who you love. It will happen if it is done in the right way, which is not your way. If you people in the West do not stop meddling, you will set things back thousands of years." He kicked sand over the fire. "You said it was not about being nice."

"Yes, I did. Well . . . Goodnight." She started to walk away.

"Truth or dare?" he called after her. "It is my turn, right?"

Alexandra hesitated then folded her arms across her chest. "Truth."

"Why have you not spoken to your father for so long?"

Alexandra heaved a sigh. "I'm sorry . . . I'm freezing. I have to go to bed."

⸬

They scrambled across the ruined ramparts. Kicked over baking stones. Their overlong shadows made them seem fantastical. Some of their boots were scuffed and frayed, others so shiny Ebla's dust barely clung. They deliberately disturbed any small animal or insect in their path. The setting moon was a broken tooth on the western hills. The rising sun plowed into their backs.

They preferred to shout. Together, their shouting melded into unintelligible menace. This was how the clean-shaven officer in charge trained them. None had been the smartest in their class. Many had cheated to get this far. Their lidded eyes saw only what they were told to. They smiled when they hit people with their guns or their hands. They also smiled when they shot them. This, too, was how the clean-shaven officer in charge had trained them.

Their shouts buzzed louder. Sayeed was first out of his tent and took the first blow from a startled private. He also took the second when Dr. Lakhosh emerged from the adjacent tent, and Sayeed stepped between him and the private's gun. That was the thud Dr. Arman and Alexandra heard when they ran out of their tents, metal meeting flesh.

"We have permission to be here," Dr. Lakhosh rebuked the clean-shaven officer.

"Permission" was one of those words that riled the man. With a look, his men scattered into the four tents and returned puppy-like with what they'd found. The officer inspected papers and travel permits, dropping what didn't interest him in the dirt. He gazed from Sayeed's papers to his face a half-dozen times, piecing together where he might have seen him before. Alexandra's instamatic camera received special attention, as did a small blue plastic case.

He pointed the camera at Alexandra. "Is that Bedouin coat part of your disguise?"

Alexandra assumed she'd misunderstood. "I'm sorry . . . What?"

The officer took her picture. "Take it off."

Alexandra handed over the coat. A soldier riffled through the pockets."

"Whose coat is this?" the officer demanded.

Sayeed tried to stand, but was pushed back down. "It is mine."

The officer aimed the instamatic in his direction. "Smile." He took Sayeed's picture, then pocketed the camera. Alexandra watched in horror as he examined the outside of the plastic case then opened it. Her diaphragm popped out and landed at his feet. "What is this?"

Alexandra stuttered, "Women use it to prevent . . ." She suddenly couldn't remember the Arabic word for pregnancy. "It is like . . ." She stopped, not knowing the Arabic word for condom. She turned to Dr. Arman and whispered in English, "How do you say condom in Arabic?"

"What did she say?" the officer snapped. Dr. Arman translated into

Arabic. The soldiers snickered, while the officer glared at Alexandra, "I am no fool. This is not a condom."

"It is for women."

The officer kicked at the diaphragm with his boot. It jiggled on its round rubber surface. "So you are a prostitute." He dropped the blue plastic box in the sand beside the diaphragm. "After I examine the photographs, your camera may be returned to you." He handed the confiscated papers and permits to Dr. Lakhosh. "Your permission to be here is revoked." The officer ordered his men back to their vehicles. He chucked Sayeed under the chin like a naughty child as he passed.

Once the officer was out of sight, Sayeed rose. "I should have explained what happened yesterday in the square. I had hoped nothing would come of it."

"I am sure nothing will," Dr. Lakhosh assured him.

The men glanced sheepishly at Alexandra, embarrassed for her, and at themselves for not defending her. She picked up the diaphragm and case, and tried to make light of the incredibly awkward situation. "Well, now I know the Arabic word for condom, so it's not a total loss."

Dr. Arman laughed. Alexandra avoided Sayeed's gaze as she walked toward the latrine. Dr. Lakhosh handed Sayeed his papers. "I am grateful they did not confiscate your camera."

"It was not in my tent. I was experimenting with a long exposure and left it at the site."

When Alexandra returned Dr. Arman was alone, building a fire in the cooking pit. "So now you have had a real taste of Syria."

"All I did was look at the soldier directing traffic."

"No one in Syria looks. Looking is a crime."

"I'm just a post-graduate student. What are they so afraid of?"

"Things here are always on the verge of disintegration. There are so many nationalities and religions. Turks, Armenians, Christians, Sephardic and Ashkenazi Jews, Sunni and Shia Muslims, plus three sects unique to Syria, the Samaritans, Alawis, and Druze, the list goes on."

"America has more nationalities and religions than that."

"Yes, but Syria has no common purpose. Someone once called it 'a country without a nation.' An artificial country carved out of artificial lines."

"I guess this means we'll have to go back to Damascus today."

"We are too close to Aleppo for you not to see it. We will drive there after having tea."

Alexandra insisted she'd seen the enormous stone bridge of Aleppo's citadel in a book of fairy tales. Spine broken, pages stained, edges curled and charred. It smelled of smoke and mold, and some words fell straight off the page, which made the tale seem truer. The viaduct ramp and intertwined snakes carved above the doorway were so familiar, and yet none of the men knew the tale or book she remembered. Drs. Arman and Lakhosh left Alexandra and Sayeed to puzzle it out as they walked on, arguing over whether Emperor Julian sacrificed a white or black bull to Zeus there.

Sayeed led Alexandra down a zigzag of corridors designed to disorient attackers. It was like being trapped in an Indiana corn maze on a moonless night. Alexandra could imagine the confusion of marauders, thundering out of that last dark passage into the blistering midday sun and being set upon by their foes. She followed Sayeed across a square as he expanded on its history. "There are two mosques inside the walls that were once Byzantine churches. During the Crusades, the king of Jerusalem was imprisoned here."

"How do you know so much about this place?"

"I spent every summer here until my grandfather died."

"I wish I'd grown up around such history and beauty."

"It is nice to share it with someone who appreciates it."

The old part of the city gave Alexandra a good sense of Aleppo's former grandeur, but now ruins sat collapsed among meticulously conserved buildings, the government having run out of money or the will to finish the job.

Deep in conversation, Drs. Arman and Lakhosh strolled past a mosque without a glance upward at its multiple domes. Alexandra walked backwards, absorbing every detail as Sayeed explained how the original minaret had fallen in an earthquake hundreds of years ago.

Alexandra felt a strange affinity for the city, more at home here than she'd been anywhere else she'd lived. "Sayeed . . . Do you believe in past lives?"

"I am not sure. Though my mother believes that my father was once the great thirteenth-century love poet Afīf al-Dīn al-Tilimsānī."

A man, his head wrapped in a black and white keffiye, shuffled past wearing one shoe. Sayeed fumbled in his pocket for money, but the ashamed man skulked off. "Palestinian refugee. Probably from Lebanon," Sayeed whispered. "It is unusual for them to be this far north."

"What's going on there? I can't figure it out."

"The problem is Lebanon's National Pact. An agreement giving Christians a dominant role in the government despite Lebanon's Muslim majority. It was designed as a temporary measure more than thirty years ago. Now there is so much bad blood that every insult or attack by one political or religious group provokes retaliation by the other. Added to that is the Palestinian refugees from Israel. Everyone wants something different and no side respects civilians."

"It sounds intractable."

Sayeed nodded, then joined Drs. Arman and Lakhosh, waiting near the entrance to the souk. Alexandra followed the men through a tiled doorway out of the sun. Unlike the Damascus souk, Aleppo's wasn't jammed with tourists but with shoppers in traditional dress. It was as if she had stepped back a hundred years.

Harun breathed deeply, taking in the aromas, good and bad, commingling under the vaulted ceiling over the labyrinth of walkways. A donkey weighed down with carpets brayed behind them so he gently pulled Alexandra to the side. "Donkeys have the right of way here."

"This place is unbelievable."

"It is one of the largest souks in the world. Do not wander off or we may lose you forever."

"What would you like to see first?" Sayeed asked. "There are areas that specialize in gold, textiles, meats, spices, nuts."

"She must see Khan al-Gumruk," Dr. Arman insisted, leading the way toward the heart of the souk that had been restored during the reign of the great Ottoman sultans. Rich details infused even the humblest of shops. Still, nothing prepared Alexandra for the sublime beauty of the grand portal of Khan al-Gumruk.

Sunlight streamed through two stained-glass windows beneath a high-domed ceiling. A delicate hexagonal motif surrounded the dome as if encasing it in a honeycomb. Between the windows, Arabic script rose and fell on waves of light framed by vaulted horseshoe-shaped archways, suffusing the entire portal in amber light that gilded the stone in an iridescent gold.

"For centuries Aleppo was the main trading route between Mesopotamia and Europe," Dr. Arman boasted. "Caravans of the pious and not so pious ended and started here."

Sayeed stayed close as she searched among the thousands of beautiful kilims, speaking softly about the history of the customs house and Aleppo's commercial decline after the French ceded the nearby port city of Alexandretta to the Turks. "You are blessed. Named for not one but two great Mediterranean cities."

"Alexandra's not my real name. It's my nickname."

Sayeed was confused.

"It's a name someone gives you . . . a pet name. Sometimes because you remind them of something or someone, and sometimes for no reason at all."

"And what is yours for?"

"I don't know. Ever since I could remember my father called me Alexandra."

"Your father . . . ?"

"Yes."

70

"So you prefer to use a name given to you by a man you haven't spoken to for seventeen years over your real name. I find that odd."

On a tour of Aleppo's Al-Jdeida quarter, Dr. Arman urged Alexandra inside the Church of the Forty Martyrs to show her the stone-block wall of engraved crosses designed like a patchwork quilt. Each block varied in size, some dominated by a single ornate cross abutting a dozen of simpler pattern. Others, massive and immoderate, gave the wall a sensual beauty that belied the church's name. It assaulted and defeated the senses, yet somehow the decorative excess achieved harmony. It was impossible not to feel its strange sad call.

Dr. Arman placed his outstretched hand on a rough-hewn cross beside Alexandra. "I hate this wall, but I also respect it. It is so . . . what is the American saying . . . sock it to me."

Alexandra laughed as Dr. Arman led her back outside toward Sayeed and Harun, waiting near a memorial commemorating the Armenian genocide. "When I am in Aleppo and see that wall, I feel like Shakespeare's Othello. I must confront the foreigner in myself, Copt living among Muslims, perpetually being something different, other. You see . . . I am hopelessly doomed. Never to marry, never to have a son."

Dr. Lakhosh shook his head. "You are not like Othello, Mikha'il. You are not black. Not a Muslim convert to Christianity. Not tragic enough to think no white woman could ever love you."

Dr. Arman shrugged. "That is how I feel, Harun."

"I've never read *Othello*," Alexandra confessed as they headed back to the car.

"In the play, Othello murders a Muslim for simply hitting a Christian," Sayeed explained.

"It's just a play."

"Yes. But Shakespeare set it here in Aleppo. That must mean something."

"Or maybe Shakespeare laid out a map, closed his eyes, and pointed."

Dr. Arman shook his head. "No. Sayeed is right. Aleppo is the setting for the last lines Othello speaks in the play. 'I took by th' throat the circumcised dog, And smote him thus.' On the word 'thus' Othello stabs himself." He climbed in the backseat beside Dr. Lakhosh, continuing his analysis. "Aleppo is a crossroads, neither east nor west, always teetering between barbarity and civilization. Aleppo is Othello, and Othello, Aleppo, man and city, full of pride and pomp, yet utterly lacking self-confidence."

Sayeed shifted the Volga into gear. The car rattled off, negotiating the twisting streets. Around a tight corner feathers fluttered. A little girl darted in front of the car to grab her hen. Sayeed slammed on the brakes. Alexandra screamed and threw her arms straight in front of her. Her palms thudded against the dashboard and the shockwave rippled up into her shoulders.

The child dashed off down an alley. Sayeed cursed under his breath then turned to make sure everyone was all right, alarmed to see tears streaming down Alexandra's cheeks.

"Are you hurt?"

Alexandra shook her head and wiped her nose.

Dr. Lakhosh leaned forward. "You were frightened, yes?"

Alexandra nodded then feeling embarrassed, glanced out the window. Two old men sipping dark tea peered from a doorway and wagged their tobacco-stained fingers at her.

"Could we please go," she choked out in a half-whisper, mystified by what had just happened. Something about the wall, the child, the looping streets had rattled her.

In ten minutes they were out of the city and back in the desert. Alexandra gazed at the shimmering haze, heat trembling prism-like above the sand, as if an invisible force had trapped a million water droplets to create a lost caravan of ghosts.

Part 2

3 July 1975

My dearest Harun,

This will not be like my previous letters. Today I will tell you new things. You can be grateful for what I say, or curse me for making you reconsider everything.

But first, because you asked, the new doctor is optimistic about my recovery. He is young and vigorous so perhaps his energy clouds his judgment. He studied in America, in a state called Maryland. He promised to show me where it is on a map, and then in the next breath told me in America they simply cut off a woman's breast when it is like mine. The medicine he gives me makes me feel as if I am floating down the Nile. Sometimes I drift among the white-sailed feluccas, ignoring what there is to see on shore with so much to look at in the water.

As promised, I will finally speak of your father. He was not as I told you from England. I feared you would want to go to school where he came from, but I could not have you as far away as America. You may want to continue hating the British. They have much to be ashamed of. So you see, I did not lie about everything. Your father is not buried in the British cemetery near here as you insisted, and the gravestones will be cleaned and the grass watered, no matter how much you wish them to fall into neglect and disrepair. The truth, which some people cling to even when it no longer lets them breathe should not be sought if it will do more harm than good. You should consider this.

When I was ten, my father took me with him to the fortuneteller so my mother could prepare hammem the way she preferred it, poking out the birds' eyes and grilling them with lemon and mint. Since I could not bear the idea that the birds would enter the afterlife blind, I would mercilessly torment my mother.

I sat outside the blind man's stall and overheard that the child inside my mother was a girl. I was the third, now there would be a fourth, and my father, whom I loved more than Allah, wept.

For two months I lay awake, unable to shake the sound of my father's tears. I knew I must change the fortuneteller's truth. When my sisters and I were sick because we had eaten dirt or rancid olives, my mother made us drink a horrible brown liquid she kept on the top shelf. It looked exactly like qahwa, and sometimes she would heat it up, brewing a bit of coffee grounds in the little pot over the fire, adding extra cardamom and sugar to fool us. But an hour later our stomachs exploded, each of us unable to stop vomiting, and so together we prayed to die.

My oldest sister giggled whenever our mother prepared gargir. The nickname for gargir was rocket because it sexually invigorated men. I did not understand those words, so my sister drew pictures in the sand outside our kitchen until I knew where the child growing inside our mother came from. When I saw Mother prepare gargir one afternoon, I knew I must get rid of the girl that was there, so father could finally have a boy.

It was not hard to trick Mother into drinking the horrible brown liquid, and it accomplished my purpose. A child enters a parent's heart in many ways, but can be purged from it by just one. It is terrible to admit this, but it was a relief when Father died eight years later. I wish you could have met him though, because in time I think he would have forgiven me, and embraced you as the boy he so desperately needed, and I as the daughter he once loved.

Given my history, it was not difficult to leave Cairo to make my way on my own. The war made that possible, along with having no male relatives to stop me. Being twenty-nine, I was just one more teacher of unmarriageable age among a dozen in Alexandria.

It is now July 4th. In the spirit of the day your father's country gained independence, I will tell another truth. The pocket watch I gave you on your eighteenth birthday did not belong to your Egyptian grandfather, but your father's grandfather. Your father left it with me, though I cannot be sure if it was purposeful or simply forgotten since he did not leave the key. I know the watch meant a great deal to him. Perhaps it was his way of saying he loved me deeply.

LITTLE PRISONERS

I never tried to contact him to let him know that together we had created this beautiful child. Now I can see that I was being terribly selfish. Having lost my father's and mother's love, I had so much to give I did not want to share you with anyone. It was wrong. And though I cannot say what your father would have done had he known, I believe he would have left America and come back to us. When we were together we were whole, past grievances all forgotten. That is love, Harun, history erased, time irrelevant. Now, now, forever now, all that matters. I will tell you more, but please think over what I have said before I open Pandora's box.

Last night I dreamed about the god Serapis, whom I revered as a child. I would like to think this is a good omen for my recovery; that Serapis, god of fertility and healing, and not deity of the underworld, is watching over me. I hope this does not offend your piety, to have your old mother dreaming of an ancient god. We look for solace where we can, and I believe you will forgive this transgression to Mohammed in me. In the dream I was Isis and you Horus, Madonna and child, me shielding you from the sun with my magnificent gilded wings. That is ridiculous, is it not . . . me protecting you, Horus, the god of the sky from the sun?

Your father had read about Alexandria's Great Library before coming to Egypt, so it is fitting we met because of a book. He was not an educated man as you are, but very intelligent in the way that learning sometimes undoes. I have never been treated with such tenderness by anyone, and I hope you do not find this a blasphemy, but tenderness when combined with love makes religious faith seem like nothing but an adornment with which we dress our dull lives.

I have never regretted what happened, and not only because it created you. For thirty-two years the memory of just a week with him has lit something inside me that no faith can enhance or extinguish. Love is more powerful than God. Some day I pray you understand this, because until you do, part of you will never live. And a life unlived is the worst way to honor Allah.

Your mother

Harun rolled up his prayer rug. In the kitchen—bereft of color or a residue of flavor—he sliced two apricots into six equal sections, then mindlessly chewed, reaping no pleasure. The events at Ebla had unnerved him, but his decision not to go to the Interior Ministry and alert them to what they surely already knew rattled him even more. Some things are to be avoided like death. Was this one of those things . . . ? Or by not acknowledging the situation, had he inflamed its existence?

He was still chewing at the sink. The apricot flesh began to taste untrustworthy. Sometimes this happened, but it hadn't for a long time. He spat it out, a bit of orange to brighten the bland. His sense of perfection grew wobbly. The not knowing if not going burrowed deeper. He had begun to think in circles. Thought entanglement ensued. Word bedlam would follow. This, too, hadn't happened for a long time.

He tried another section. This flesh joined the other in the sink, a spit painting on the canvas-white surface. Soon he would find himself frozen in the doorway. One word cascading into another. It was a process. Water boiled. Gas leaked. Harun vacillated. Privately. Vacillation in public was untranslatable to his sinew. Even if he had wanted to waver, his muscles would never permit it. Everything of import transpired in privacy, even word bedlam occurred within the echoing confines of his skull. The word "privacy" entered it a minute ago, when, briefcase in hand, he'd stopped in the doorway. *Privacy privy toilet loo shithouse pubis oboe . . .* It had begun.

He avoided the main road choked with cars and walked the side streets to the museum. After seven years, he still felt like a stranger in the city. Ahead, the same three businessmen he saw whenever he walked this way fell into their familiar banter. Harun crossed the street to avoid having their words form a stream with his, though it meant braving the already unbearable sun and pungent smell of excrement. For months, squatters had congregated in the vacant lots tucked between buildings. With the current mayhem in Lebanon, Harun couldn't be sure if they were Christian, Muslim, or Palestinian refugees. After Beirut had exploded in the spring, an alarm often rang in his head: Return to Egypt before all of Syria is mired in shit. It rang now. *Shit bog sink . . .*

At Borsaid Street, a military vehicle hurtled through the intersection nearly causing an accident. Harun clenched his teeth. *Oboe shithouse.* He hoped Damascus would stay out of the Lebanese crisis, but sensed Syrian nationalists were eager to exacerbate the situation for their own gain. Every week an inflammatory article appeared in the newspaper inciting readers to embrace the glory that was once Greater Syria. Harun detested one writer in particular, who referred to Lebanon as an amputated limb in desperate need of reattachment.

A young couple zipped by on a scooter. The girl sat sideways, one arm hugging the boy's waist, the other her schoolbooks. Harun felt a brief pang for Sana before his sense of propriety overrode what little desire he'd let emerge. Appetites were reserved for apricots.

His favorite café was still uncrowded. Was there time to stop? Out of habit, he stroked the watch in his trouser pocket before glancing at the one on his wrist. His fingernail shadowed the small black minute lines, counting . . . *two three seven impossible* . . . The staff would beat him to work. Head bowed and mumbling a prayer, he hurried past the Umayyad mosque, where European tourists with pale hair and sharp features huddled around Saladin's mausoleum.

His office door was already open and a new photo hung on the outside wall—a thin blade of light cast a tantalizing stripe down the staircase leading to the basin of the bearded men. The long exposure that had saved Sayeed's camera from the officer at Ebla. An air-letter envelope from Egypt lay on his desk. He slapped it against his chair. He had repeatedly asked his mother to use normal stationery with separate mailers, to no avail. The flimsy paper that doubled as an envelope was so tedious to open.

He read the letter twice. The second time clutching his great-grandfather's pocket watch, awed by its, and now, his history. Over the years he had grown to like the idea that the watch couldn't be opened;

that its face was off limits because he lacked the key. But what if the watch was like a locket and held a piece of his family's history?

Harun considered the gravity of his mother's words. He admired her for writing what she did, but why reveal it now? And then there was the trail of unrepentant blasphemy she'd committed throughout her life. How could he forgive her?

At midday prayers he pondered this. Surely this was a test of his faith, more than a test of his love. If his mother must experience punishment to confront her sins, that was Allah's decision. It was not a son's place to offer love or forgiveness as redemption. That would be piling one more blasphemy on the others, he himself sinking to the debased level his mother had already fallen.

▧

13 July 1975

My son,

You are being dishonest with me or yourself. Repentance does not lead to salvation. Truth does. If I were a man, the "sins" of which you speak would not be sins. I do not seek Allah's mercy. Only hope for your understanding. In the end, people must answer to themselves.

I do not want to waste what time I have left quarreling with you over definitions of shame. I want to share what I have kept hidden. Yes, I do have one photograph of your father taken with soldiers in his unit. The U.S. Army might have other pictures in its archives. You may be able to use your position to get some. After all, your father was somewhat of an archaeologist himself during the war, not of anything ancient, but of man's mechanized folly.

As I understood it, he was a reader of metals. Not like a fortune-teller, but a doctor who looked for signs of illness and breakdown after a battle. He belonged to a small unit that tracked German tanks and artillery. He excelled at his profession and was also a collector of keys. He had two with him when we met. Your watch key, and another that belonged to a neighbor girl when he was young. A key used with shoe wheels children wore for fun. When he taught her how to move backwards on her shoe wheels, they had their first kiss. They talked about being together forever, as children do. Despite your father's rough exterior, his heart was tender. I think this is why he loved keys so much. They opened things and brought light into dark places.

I met him in a bookstore. Your father had just come from a mission in the desert. His face seemed to carry the whole of the battle in it, rocklike, unforgiving. His boots were dusty, his fingernails dirty. The innocence I later saw in his eyes entirely absent at that moment.

Unlike most Americans, he wasn't frustrated when the shop owner did not understand English. I translated his request, and in gratitude he took me to Alexandria's best café. The staff ignored his soiled uniform because of his American dollars, and over tea I began to fall in love.

Your father asked me to read to him the book he had bought. Not once did he take his eyes off me. His gaze was extraordinarily powerful.

The city was under blackout when he walked me home. Then the Luftwaffe attacked. The way your father protected me let me know I'd be safe. He did not force himself on me, or try to seduce me with things women wanted but could only get from soldiers. You need to know that.

The book that led your father to the shop was about Antar and Abla. He had heard part of the story in the desert and wanted to know how it ended. That this book brought us together is especially relevant when you understand how similar our situation was to Antar and Abla's.

When I began this letter I did not yet know if I would tell you this, but now I see I must. You are a grown man. It is time for you to shed unhealthy idealistic notions of perfection. I do not know how else to say this except boldly. Your father was a Jew. His name was Aaron. That is why yours is Harun.

Your mother

This was the second time Harun had been summoned to the interior minister's office since Ebla to hear the same message. Radical elements sought to destabilize Syria. Sayeed and Alexandra took a marked interest in the incident on the street. The film in Alexandra's camera showed places of "sensitivity" to the Syrian government. Harun knew better than to ask to see the photos.

His mother's letter had left a nauseous apricot pile-up in his throat. Behind his ribs a dull ache throbbed between the muscles. He feared it was *sagin zoghayar,* the little prisoner, wanting to be set free. Harun hadn't felt the pressure or heard the unruly British hooligan that accompanied it erupt in a decade. The thought entanglement the word bedlam had intensified, yes, but the little prisoner, no no no no no. Had his mother's revelations unleashed the little shit?

The little prisoner wasn't a recognizable what, or thing, or a who in any sense Harun could define. It wasn't mythological or hieroglyphic in appearance, and didn't correspond to any gods he knew from Egyptian fables. It was best described as a sensation of a specific shape and size, more elliptical than square, ironically, about the size of an apricot pit. The sensation first surfaced when he was eight years old. His mother had taken him to the museum to see the great statue of Serapis, but he fixated instead on a mummified crocodile resting on a wooden bier. The yellowed label near the crocodile's dirty purplish belly read, "Symbol of the cult of Sobek, son of Set, god of turmoil and thunder. Sobek rose from the dark water to create the universe, but allied himself with the forces of chaos."

Harun memorized the words and asked what "chaos" meant? His mother's description was petrifying. He filled a blue notebook describing the pressure behind his rib cage as chaos trying to claw its way out. So he named it the little prisoner. It was different from his other anxieties and fears. The little prisoner lacked any sense of morality, encouraged Harun to do horrible things, think horrible thoughts. The little prisoner was—how exactly to say this to not be too offensive—a motherfucking pig.

An aide slipped in, ending the meeting. Harun fled the ministry at a run, disregarding the heat and odd looks from passersby. Across Martyrs' Square word bedlam took hold *martyr satyr sex* . . . Across Al-Thawra Street *seraph cherub sprite* . . . Across. Across. Across.

Sayeed intercepted him the moment he entered the museum, but Harun waved him away and took shelter behind his office's locked door. His mother's second letter joined her first in his desk's bottom drawer. He sprinkled both with disinfectant. How many diseased hands had they passed through at the hospital before reaching the post? *Disgusting!*

For the first time since the age of ten, he ignored the muezzin's midday call to prayer. Praying was something he had always looked forward to—what subdivided the day into its proper segments—but after his mother's revelation it felt blasphemous to kneel and recite the salat. He curled up on the floor under the ceiling fan, drifting from one fitful dream to another. It was a relief when Dr. Arman knocked and demanded to know if he was all right.

Harun straightened his wrinkled trousers before opening the door. Dr. Arman blew past, sending a stack of papers to the floor. Harun watched them flutter . . . *sirocco föhn meltemi* . . . a word bedlam waterfall of ominous winds.

"What did the minister say that upset you?"

"Who said I was upset? I am not upset."

Dr. Arman made a face and lowered his large frame onto the small chair across from Harun's desk. He rested his interlaced fingers on his belly. "We are alone. Tell me what he said?" Dr. Arman tapped his thumbs together and waited.

"Really, Mikha'il . . . This is absurd."

"Harun . . . If I were to lock myself in my office for three hours, no one would ask why. But it makes the staff nervous when you behave so erratically."

Harun noticed a gouge in his pristine antique desk and licked his finger to rub it out.

"Is it a woman?"

Harun looked up, aghast.

"Very well. Perhaps you should talk to your imam." Dr. Arman hoisted himself out of the small chair with a groan. "I detest this silly chair. It is neither dignified nor quaint."

"Yes, Mikha'il, you have made your hatred of my chair quite clear on several occasions."

"The director, even the interim director of a museum, requires a proper chair. This one makes no statement. Except to say I am . . . oh, what is that American word . . . oh, yes . . . I am sissy."

Harun smiled. "So you think I am sissy?"

"No. I think your chair is sissy."

"And what would you think if I said, 'I am a Jew'?"

Dr. Arman laughed. "Now who is being absurd?"

⁛

31 July 1975

Dearest Harun,

I have not heard from you. I hope you were not too hurt by what I wrote. I am not sure how to read your silence. Sometimes people wish to know more but are afraid to ask. Sometimes they have buried their heads in the sand. I will go on writing until you firmly tell me to stop.

I do not know exactly when I realized your father was a Jew. It may have been something he said. I cannot remember. All I know was I did not care. Not at the moment, not ever.

After I left Cairo, my only passion was for solitude. One can make a religion of it if they are not careful. My life consisted of teaching and reading. I imagined that would be the extent of it until I died. At one time, I had planned to write a book for my students about the Ptolemaic dynasty, my favorite era of history, the blending of Hellenic and Egyptian cultures irresistible. Perhaps that is why your father's religion never concerned me. Alexandria in the time of Ptolemy was not unlike the New York of your father's America. I believe they still call it a melting pot.

I know what you are thinking. Your mother, the history teacher, fell so in love she forgot history. You are mistaken. I understand how this melting breeds economic and social strife. Historical Alexandria also had its ruthless mob, notorious for dispensing sudden justice. It once murdered an official of the Roman embassy after he accidentally ran over a cat with his chariot. If you still enjoy collecting strange facts like you did as a boy, you can add this detail to one of your small blue notebooks.

Your father's eyes were a startling bluish green. The color of the Mediterranean. Working in the desert sun must have been torture. When you were born, I had hoped you would inherit his eyes so I would be reminded of him, but I am pleased it did not happen. Eyes like that would have set you apart.

Before I met your father I had not the slightest notion of who I was beyond daughter, sister, teacher. Meeting your father might have merely given me a new set of names in which to see myself—woman, lover, mother—but it did not. It forced me to break from my old self and, cell by cell, rediscover what it was to be human.

I remember the moment of epiphany, when I knew emotion was no longer my enemy but my redeemer. Your father had left with his unit on a barge bound for Palestine. I did not see him off, but joined a friend at the beach near where the fishermen built shacks for their boats and nets. I am sure you remember the place. Along the sea wall, not far from where the ancient lighthouse once stood. You and I spent two happy summers there after the shacks became cottages. You thought the cottage a palace, even though we had to jump up and down to get the lights to work.

Something had propelled me to this beach and not to the dock with your father. It was Saturday. People were enjoying the sun. Among them, two men around the age you are now. They talked in circles about a woman they had met the night before, each certain he was the one she was interested in. One man insisted, "The war is going to change women for the better." His friend disagreed. "Women are already masters of the home, kitchen, and bedroom. The war will only make them masters of the universe."

It had never occurred to me that I was master of anything. Fear has a way of eating away courage. I leaned against the sea wall, and as I considered the men's words I suddenly knew why I had not gone with your father to the dock. I could not bear the feeling of being abandoned, so I abandoned him instead. It does not sound like much of an epiphany, but when I understood what I had done, I ran along the sea wall to the point where I could make out the length of his barge slicing through the water. I stared without blinking for what seemed like seconds, but must have been quite long, because when I came to my senses the barge was nowhere in sight.

I say came to my senses because, though I was entirely alone on the sea wall, I felt your father reach out to touch me. His hands delicately caressed every part of me, and the sublime pleasure I experienced when with him transformed into something profound. Our skin has a memory, Harun, and, while facing the sea, I was being ravished by emotions far deeper than simple love. Inconsolable sadness mixed with forbidden pleasure until I was trembling all over. I believe my soul was reassembling itself so it finally could be immersed in what was human, and stop aspiring to what was divine.

So the men on the beach turned out to be correct. The war did make me better, stronger, perhaps even master of my universe. War has its good points, sad to say. From that day, I never feared my emotions again. I forgave my father for abandoning my love, and my mother for resenting me. I forgave your father for leaving, and the Germans for taking him from me. But mostly I forgave myself for all that had come before. I did not know as I stood on the sea wall you had already begun your journey inside me. I received a wonderful gift from the universe that day, and I will always equate the beginning of your new life with the beginning of mine.

With all my love,

Your mother

⚏

Eldridge stood very close and shouted into Harun's face. There was an accusation that Harun didn't understand English. An indictment against the security police for barbarically arresting Alice during cocktail hour. A cheeky suggestion that Alice Miss Pierce Alexandra—for heaven's sake, make up your mind—might be an unsavory character with a seedy background. And, because this was Eldridge, a last-minute pitch for his "first-class run" rooming house.

Grow a cock, you cocksucker. Tell the arse to piss off! the little prisoner railed at Harun, who asked Sayeed to retrieve Alexandra's personnel file.

A chaos of words bubbled at the surface. Harun had a linguistic question he wanted to ask a native English speaker—*Is English particularly suited to having genitalia act as a form of chastisement, or is it in the nature of English speakers in general to be crude?*—frothing right beside his response to Eldridge's outrage. "Mr. Whitby . . . I am certain Alexandra's detention was a mistake. Syrian authorities must make a show of everything, even when it means nothing."

"Alice is in your charge. Your assessment of the situation is of no interest to me. Your obligation is to take immediate action, Lakhosh!"

It didn't matter that Harun was the interim director of a cultural, not a political institution. It didn't matter that he was Egyptian and not privy to the inner workings of the Syrian state. Eldridge still thumped on Harun's desk. Eldridge had been thumping since the seminary. He'd practiced on his worm-eaten student desk. Practiced on the village bar with a pint of beer. And especially practiced on the Bible. No point in being an army chaplain if you can't thump a Bible during battle. Not everyone got a pulpit to thwack. "If this mistake, as you call it THUMP, is not resolved to my satisfaction THUMP, the British embassy will be informed of your negligence THUMP. After that, no western rooming house will assist you in the future THUMP."

Sayeed returned with Alexandra's file, sidestepping Eldridge as he stormed out.

Harun riffled through Alexandra's internship application and visa papers. "Why do you think they are questioning Alexandra but not you?"

"By detaining her first, they probably want to frighten me."

"Is it working?"

Sayeed half-smiled. Harun tucked the file under his arm and moved toward the door. "I will try the interior ministry before alerting the American embassy. No reason to create a crisis. If anyone asks, do not say where I am or why."

Sayeed entered the makeshift darkroom he'd created in what was once a gunpowder vault. Crevices in the stone were etched with a fine black residue. The room was a catalog of his related interests: stereoscopic viewers, tattered movie posters, old cameras. Among the recent photos of Ebla hanging up to dry was a candid profile of Alexandra near Ishtar's temple. Sayeed cropped everything around her face until the picture was the size of a cigarette pack. He slid the photo into his shirt pocket and ducked out of the room, running straight into Dr. Arman.

"Ah, Sayeed . . . The very man I am looking for."

Sayeed realized the top of Alexandra's photo was sticking out.

"When you have time, I need you to rephotograph some tablets." Dr. Arman walked on, calling back over his shoulder, "Does she know you carry a photo of her near your heart?"

"I printed this for her, not me."

"That is too bad."

Sayeed returned to his office and pulled out the copy he'd made of Alexandra's internship application. He wanted to read through the details of her life: Born in Indiana, raised in Oregon, schooled in California, mother's name Mary, father deceased. Sayeed paused. Why did Alexandra lie about her father on her application? If she had lied about that, what else was untrue?

Harun cursed under his breath *oboe shithouse* as the minister's aide entered, exited, and reentered the minister's office without a word about how much longer Harun must wait. It was distressing to be forced back to the very office he'd fled a week earlier, especially since the little prisoner now tortured him in earnest. Accompanying the relentless pressure behind his ribs was a steady stream of vitriol.

Women . . . ! Masters of the universe . . . fuck no . . . pains in the arse!

For once Harun agreed with his tormentor, if not with "his" choice of language.

Cunts. Real cunts. You hear me? Cunt times two. No, times four. We invented arithmetic so we can say that.

Harun leapt to his feet. Twice he'd heard that word in English pubs and it had shocked him. That word was simply off limits. No excuse ever to use it. Ever! The little prisoner was way out of line, and now "he" wouldn't shut up, spewing the word with poetic mania, incessantly repeating *we* and *cunt,* implicating Harun in his coarse rant.

"Stop it!" Harun hissed, well aware the voice was nothing but self-loathing, and he wished he'd never begun to converse with it. But it had been the only way to deal with his excruciating loneliness at Oxford after Sana stopped writing. He'd always been alone, not because he wanted it, as he'd convinced himself, but because he'd come to believe there simply wasn't the possibility of a life with others. People who thought otherwise were fools. Yet he had loved Sana, and wanted to marry her from the moment they'd met as students on an archaeological dig in Greece. He never quite understood what went wrong between them, and was surprised after twelve years how much her memory filled him with a sense of longing and concern for her safety in Beirut. He suspected the chaos in Lebanon, along with what had happened at Ebla and his mother's letters, had resurrected the fucker.

The minister's aide waved Harun in. He handed over Alexandra's file and explained the situation. The minister had his aide telephone a man whose name Harun made a point to instantly forget. Do not be curious, forget everything, was his motto for living in Syria. His talent for appearing incurious had gotten Harun promoted to his current position over other equally qualified people when his predecessor died. The promotion was meant to be temporary, but his unobtrusive competence allowed those in power to forget about him, and so Harun was furious that an American intern, a foreign female with multiple names and disreputable rubber bouncy condom things, was disrupting his carefully constructed existence.

⁘

7 August 1975

My Dearest Adjo,

It has been years since I called you that. At first you loved it, then it wounded you. I suppose boys do not want to be known of as "treasures." You are my grief and my happiness. My grief because you refuse to open your heart. My happiness because you are love itself to me. This is strange for a mother to say, but I would feel better if you were more of a sinner. Despite what some scriptures say, I am not sure deities smile on those who are merely good. There has always seemed something silent and inert about the good, not in their actions, but in their soul.

When I am unable to sleep, my thoughts turn to you as a baby. From your first day, your skin was the color of new honey from a hive. The neighborhood women called you "tiny bee." Before you were born I did not know bees were so revered in ancient times. Honey buried with our pharaohs millennia ago is still edible today. There is barely a sarcophagus, obelisk, pillar, tomb, or temple where bee or honey hieroglyphs are not found. I suppose we historians and archaeologists, in our quest to seek the new and different, overlook what is everywhere.

I had planned to tell you the truth about your father, but naively assumed I could control the moment when you would first ask about him. I imagined you would be fifteen. I was off by nine years. On your sixth birthday, the gang of older boys that so frightened you, convinced you that children without fathers came from eggs. The look in your eyes when you asked me where your father was made me want to weep. So I said what I felt a six-year-old could understand with every intention of correcting the facts later. As it turns out, nine years of lying is hard to undo.

My young doctor just dropped by to check on me. The interruption gave me time to reconsider what I wrote. The story we tell others becomes the story we tell ourselves, until we cannot separate the truth from what our heart surely knows is false. I think I lied to you about your father because part of me believed killing him off would bind us closer together. My beautiful son and I cradled in a cocoon against the world.

My actions did not help you to become a man. For that I am sorry. By turning myself into a widow, I closed my heart to someone new, and you never witnessed what it means for two souls to delight in each other. I fear your indifferent heart is a result of my foolish nostalgia. Love is a feast, not only of mind and body, but also of the soul, and marks us forever.

It is late and the man across the hall died a minute ago. Not everyone on this ward wants to live. Illness causes unwanted memories to flood back. For some, they are too painful. I, on the other hand, have enjoyed how the mundane details stand out. I remember begging you to stop saying, "Qaleelan" when you were nine. A boy cannot go through life wanting "just a little" or soon that is all he expects as a man. Then there was the time when you pretended to be a crocodile. I would wake to find you on my bedroom floor, eyelids half closed, your eyes fixed on what only you could see. I would touch the tip of your nose and tell you I loved you. You then touched the same spot, and later, when you finally spoke again, you said that your nose loved me too.

I hope what I am sharing interests you. At some point we all must find a way to live only in the present even when we think all we have left is the past. I pray to hear from you soon.

■■
■■

Harun returned to work astonished to find Alexandra in his office. She showed no adverse signs from her night in custody. Beside her stood a very short man in a suit, though his slight frame could have carried off a dress just as well. With his oversized head, delicate nose, dainty though prodigiously hairy hands, he was definitely a primate, but of some crossbred genus. He struck Harun as the perfect hermaphrodite, belonging more to the circus than to Syria's bureaucratic class.

Though grateful to see Alexandra, Harun was disturbed by the speed of her release. As if her detention wasn't really a detention, but a calculated test. He barely registered her complaint about not being permitted to contact the American embassy, curious to know more about the short man, who addressed Harun in English, accented by way of Algeria. He introduced himself as Leopold, then launched a salvo whose subtext Harun couldn't fail to grasp—he was being watched.

"It is nice you have the leisure to walk to work, Dr. Lakhosh. Walking lets us notice how a city changes. On foot it is hard to miss all the Lebanese refugees. It is one thing to be forced out of your country because of drought. Quite another for political reasons. Of course, most of the refugees are men. Women and children being quite beneath politics."

Alexandra snorted. Before she could do anything else that might aggravate the situation, Harun asked her to phone her landlord to let him know she was all right.

After she left, Harun busied himself at the hotplate so he could study the man from behind. His long arms, large ears, and squat neck resembled a chimpanzee's. Harun set Leopold's cup of tea on a ceramic coaster, then sat behind his desk, which made him 6 inches shorter than his visitor. It wasn't the choice a man who wants to gain the upper hand would take, and Harun hoped it would be read as a sign he had nothing to fear or hide.

The muezzin's call to prayer permeated the silence. With Alexandra gone, Harun picked up the man's odd rosewater scent. Harun expected Leopold to excuse himself to pray, but he lit a cigarette and, when the muezzin had finished, returned to the refugee problem, still talking in English.

"What kind of man leaves his wife and children behind . . . and for what . . . ? To protect their country? These men deceive themselves.

Lebanon is not a country. It is Syria's younger brother. And what brother does not wish to protect his weaker sibling?"

Harun leaned forward. "Brothers always protect one another."

"Yet you have no brothers, Dr. Lakhosh." Leopold drew heavily on his cigarette. "The Americans believe in Lebanon and so Lebanon believes in itself. When will we Arabs learn?"

Harun watched Leopold's cigarette ash bend precariously toward his expensive Egyptian-wool carpet. He slid an ashtray across his desk. Leopold let the ash fall.

"But this is nothing new. Egypt has had her trouble with Americans too. That is why we must never come under their spell. They seek our destruction." Harun gently pushed the ashtray closer. "Americans are an unfeeling, dangerous people. When they baptize their young, did you know they nearly drown them?"

Leopold droned on about America's turpitude. Harun nodded, leaned forward, rested his chin on his hands—a dance the light from his desk lamp captured in shadow. Harun's head grew large, then small. His nose stretched, then flattened. He became completely caught up in his mutable features. Only after Leopold struck a match to light another cigarette did Harun realize the subject had shifted to the effect of radical campus groups on college students. Leopold wanted to know to which groups Alexandra had belonged.

Harun needed time alone to clear his head. He knew the answer to this question wasn't in Alexandra's file, but excused himself, suggesting a quick glance through her internship essay might yield something he'd overlooked. To anyone in the corridor, Harun appeared to be a man on a mission, eyes fixed ahead, purposeful stride. He had never seen a play or opera, so he didn't recognize himself as the character whose calculated self-assurance imperils all.

On his circuitous path back to his office, he spotted Sayeed and Alexandra conferring through the half-open darkroom door. They stood close together, studying an unspooled roll of photo negatives that Sayeed held up to the light. Harun couldn't make out the images, but was intrigued by the pair's ease with one another and watched them until he felt he must get back. By then, Harun assumed Leopold would have searched his office. In fact, leaving the circus creature alone suddenly seemed to have been a shrewd move. A man guilty of something would never take such a chance.

Harun was impressed by how he'd managed the situation. His mother always said he was diplomatic, delicately balancing between people and ideologies while evading the quicksand himself. He'd never accepted her assessment, suspecting she meant something negative by it. She was forever urging him to plunge into things, to take a stand when he preferred to wait. Now he understood her motivations, and while it disturbed him to think she may have subconsciously wished he'd make a life-altering mistake on the scale of hers, he finally valued her judgment. She'd misunderstood so much about him that he didn't mind granting her this concession. Tonight he'd write to her. A gesture he could offer without really forgiving her. That was important. He couldn't forgive what she'd done. Her weakness had made him a bastard. No. A half-Jewish bastard. Even worse.

Harun froze, remembering his mother's letters in his desk drawer. Leopold was sure to have found them by now. If the Syrian government knew the truth, they would never allow him to retain his post. He'd be fired, humiliated, deported back to Egypt. His colleagues would shun him, his mosque exile him, and that would just be the beginning.

He entered his outer office and it hit him. The Syrians could arrest him as a Jewish spy. They'd executed people for far less. Harun considered escape. But where would he go? The basin of the bearded men was his life's work. Everything would unravel without it.

This was the cost of trying to protect his American charge. He would be punished. Destroyed. Career and life over. His stomach churned and he was instantly back, face down in the dirt, the neighbor boy who pulled cats' legs off crushing him. Every time he was frightened, the same memory, the shitting in his pants and, after that, huddled alone, never part of anything.

His legs refused to move. He forced each foot forward and pushed open the door to be met by Leopold's disagreeable face. Leopold was in the precise spot Harun had left him, which was so preposterous it was evidence the man had been up to no good. Harun was furious with his mother. For all her talk of love, she was remarkably cruel. The warmth of her last few letters had softened him, and he'd considered taking time off to visit her, but those feelings were dead.

His voice quavered as he explained that there was nothing of relevance in Alexandra's application. He opened his desk's bottom drawer, and pretending to retrieve a pen, was relieved to see his mother's letters hadn't been disturbed; the residue of sprinkled disinfectant remained.

His unwanted guest jotted down something in a notebook, then fixed his eyes on Harun's. The man's large head and bulging eyes lacked symmetry or balance. Completely grotesque from an aesthetic perspective. He should not be permitted to enter museums and foist his garishness on visually attuned people, Harun thought. He should not be allowed any profession outside the circus, with his insect-like features. Only animals could endure such a monster.

"Dr. Lakhosh . . . I need your help. Can I count on your assistance?"

"Of course."

"Your assistant and Miss Pierce . . . Keep an eye on them, report anything suspicious."

Harun's muscles unwound. "I know Miss Pierce is much more forward than any Syrian woman, but I believe she understands and respects our traditions. And my assistant is deeply religious. He would never be intimate with a woman he had not married."

"I could not care less who Miss Pierce is *intimate* with, Dr. Lakhosh. She and your assistant are Lebanese spies."

■■
■■

14 August 1975

Dear Harun,

So my love is cruel. I believe men often accuse women of that. They

93

say it is part of our nature, but it is men who weaken and exhaust their hearts at Friday prayers.

When I was a girl, I wanted to accompany my father to the mosque and be part of a collective sea of faith. Crowds made me feel wonderfully dizzy. Sometimes I would spin around until I fainted. I do not know why I felt most alive before losing consciousness. Perhaps it was because everything became black or white in those last few seconds.

My sisters and I were close as children, and despite our long years of silence, they have visited since I began these treatments. They probably want to clear their consciences for abandoning me after I became pregnant. They are fatalists who do not believe in fate. Often their sentences begin "We should have stopped time when . . ." If they get in touch after I am gone, you will hear a steady stream of ends to that thought applied to me because I chose to leave Cairo. They see this as the origin of my ruin, but actually I was insulating them from the deep anger I felt towards them. They were always moralizing, but when I was younger I mistook their advice for wisdom and not the fear of living life I see it for now. Your aunts made "good" marriages, but they were both loveless, and they insisted I do the same. I am telling you this because I want you to understand that anger is sometimes a good thing. When it visits you, let it happen.

Have you ever been swept away by a word? Mine is CENOTAPH. I did not know its meaning when I was first drawn to it, but now I see my affinity for something that describes a ceremonial tomb never intended to receive a corpse as yet another sign I will survive this disease. Your father loved words too. I know he had a favorite, and I almost discovered what it was when he taught me a word game popular with children in America. It involved a hanging man, but I lost the game and your father's secret stayed hidden.

A nurse just replaced the bandage on my breast. The doctor took a sample three days ago to see if the medicine is working. He will not know whether it is good or bad news for another ten days. Unlike other people here, I am never anxious to hear test results. They are what they are, and with them come emotions that can scatter the mind away from what it needs to focus on.

The daily newspapers here are full of the Egyptian-Israeli disengagement talks. Mr. Kissinger assures us that America does not consider this agreement an end in itself, but one step in a process toward peace. I have never thought of President Sadat as handsome, but beside Mr. Kissinger almost any man becomes a prince. From his raspy voice croaking out slow sentences never varying in tone, to his nonexistent neck and middle bulge, he could be a toad squatting on a lily pad.

Though President Sadat is quite capable of being ruthless, I am not sure he is shrewd enough to negotiate with the genius toad. Perhaps I should have more faith. He did reopen the Suez Canal in June, which took real courage. Our president does seem genuinely tired of war, and for a life-long soldier that cannot be an easy thing to let go of.

I am not sure how I drifted off on that tangent. Drugs have a way of encouraging the mind to skip about. It is not an unpleasant sensation, though occasionally my dreams are full of characters one might read about in a frightening tale.

The only thing I cannot tolerate is how the drugs affect my nose. Everything stinks of garbage. Even perfume smells of rotted lamb and festering wounds. I saw such wounds during the war as a hospital volunteer, and the stench of a boy about to lose a limb is a memory not forgotten.

Your father spoke of a wounded German soldier his unit found in the desert. He was alive though his intestines were no longer in his body. Your father recounted the story, staring straight past me, as if part of him had been lost forever along with the boy's soul. The smell of that German really shook him. Despite your father's love of words, he could not find ones to accurately describe what the smell was like. He said it was beyond human perception.

I am sad you no longer have time to come visit me. I hope this is genuinely because you are busy at work, not because you now think me cruel.

It is two in the morning and the hospital staff moves silently through the corridors as if gliding on a film of water. I do not pray any more, but I do discuss my hopes and fears with the universe during this time of night. I believe it to be a living organism capable of listening to whatever burdens or excites our consciences. Tonight I will tell it what you said about my love being cruel and see how it responds. People are never wholly wrong when they make an observation like that, and so I will try to be kinder in the future. That is all I can promise.

Your mother

∷

20 August 1975

Mother,

You asked me to tell you if I want you to stop writing. How can I do that? It is like asking me to tell you to stop breathing. No matter how much I might wish not to hear your words, I cannot be the one who silences you.

Because of your present situation, I understand your desire to rid yourself of secrets, but as many scriptures teach, desire can lead one down false paths. Regrettably, the result of your revelations is that you have made me feel eight again. That was not a pleasant age for me. It has taken all of my faith to guide me to where I am today, so, yes, I think your love is cruel, not because you are a woman and I am a man, but because you are my mother and I am your son. That relationship is inviolate. You became pregnant, gave birth, and by doing that you took an oath to protect me. That oath did not stop five, ten, or twenty years ago. It never stops.

My work here is very demanding right now. However, since truth is now your religion, even if I were not so busy, I do not think I would visit you. In your effort to expose my father to me, a mere junk man from what I can tell, you have ironically left a mound of debris in his wake. Did you ever consider the harm you might cause from your actions? I no longer sleep through the night. Food uninterests me. Sensations long buried have resurfaced only to torment me. In spite of this, I do want to know the result of your recent biopsy. Contrary to what you often imply in your letters, I am not without feeling.

I think you should know that when your letters arrive I hesitate before opening them. I never know if their contents will cause me to feel merely queasy, or as if I have contracted the plague. Also, when you share such personal details about the past, especially when they are not explicitly about me, you make me feel as if I am your confessor, or a female friend you would gossip with. One thing I am curious about is, since you had already committed so many sins, would it have really been so difficult to just go on lying to me?

I also find your catalog of truths profoundly selfish, your behavior not so different from Kahlil's, the bully from our old neighborhood who dismembered cats. Your words have that same crude power. Most people equate words with knives, but that metaphor does not work in your case. Your words are not sharp. They do not cut cleanly. Your tongue, your pen, is more like a gun fired indiscriminately, without regard for the wounds it inflicts. In that, you remind me of the Americans I have met. I have one under my charge right now. A young intern I am certain you would like. She does not belong here, yet here she is. Her carelessness is not unlike yours, and may yet cause her to be arrested and me to lose my job.

So as you can see, Mother, I have a great many burdens confronting me right now. Despite them, I am continuing my research on water basins, but have had to push back the completion of my abstract to some time next year. Consequently, I will not make my deadline, and will soon have to break the news to the editors at the journal.

I really must conclude this letter as I am pressed for time. Do not concern yourself about whether your sisters, my aunts, will contact me in the future. They have been in touch with me for some time. They usually send a note around Ramadan wishing me a long life. Everyone in the family signs it, so I do know my cousins' names, despite your never taking me to visit them.

Again, please let me know the results of your tests.

Harun

---

26 August 1975

My dear son,

I applaud your last letter. I know how hard it must have been for you to say those things. I have never quite thought of motherhood as taking an oath before, but I can see how a child might. While I respect your point of view, I still believe from the moment each of us enters the world we are, and always will be, alone, without a protector, earthly or divine.

I regret adding to your problems right now, though I will risk causing one more by asking if it is your good fortune, or just revealing, that your list of disturbances includes nothing about love? I ask because I remember a time when you were not inclined to be troubled by sleepless nights or childhood torments. It was after the excavation in Greece. On your way back to Oxford we spent time together, and though you never said anything, I was certain you must be in love. I may have been wrong, but mothers can usually tell these things. You see . . . love is not always tragic.

I know you prefer to move quietly through life, but occasionally a person must declare himself. Perhaps this is why the young American under your charge so irritates you. I can imagine any woman who speaks her mind is hard for you to take, but since I have never been careless, and do not consider it fair for you to label me that merely because I fell in love and had you, I wonder whether this American girl deserves the description either. I am sure whoever wishes to arrest her will soon come to their senses. American girls are easy targets. They never seem to do what is expected, so men in authority feel unbalanced when dealing with them. But men who react like this would do better to look in the mirror.

I have tried to avoid talking about your father in this letter, but it feels unnatural. You are similar to him in many ways, and so even if I want to confine myself to telling you things about your childhood, it is still reflected through him. I do not know how to separate my love for the two of you. His heart is part of yours, and your heart has always kept his beating for me.

When you were in my womb you were so still the neighborhood midwives insisted you were a girl. But I knew I was carrying a boy. None of these women had ever met your father. What they did not know was how still he could be. When he slept he never moved, not so much as a finger. And when he looked through the book he bought, I never heard the pages turn.

You asked if it would have been difficult for me to go on lying. Yes. You have no idea what a struggle it has been to stay silent this long. Do not forget, you are the one who asked me to write about your father. I warned you about Pandora's box. I will keep this letter brief in order not to stray back towards Aaron. It is strange to write his name. I have only done that once with you. But his name is always on my lips, and has been for as long as you have been alive.

Your mother

Harun threw off his sheet and padded back and forth from bedroom to kitchen, parsing Leopold's words. Did the man really believe Sayeed and Alexandra were Lebanese spies? At 3 a.m. the pressure behind his ribs flared and the little prisoner exploded: *you weak fuckin' bastard!* Harun ignored the voice until dawn, when the call to prayer inspired him to drag a chair into his bedroom closet, take down the white djellabah he never wore, and stuff it into his briefcase.

For three days he rushed out of the museum just before closing and hid behind the scruffy fan palms near the entrance. The djellabah, which at first seemed like a brilliant disguise, was oppressive over his suit. Each day he followed Sayeed in the same direction to the same café, only to discover his assistant had many friends to meet for coffee before evening prayers.

On the fourth day, a mangy dog skulked over, hoping for a morsel. Its ribs protruded through scabrous gray skin. Harun moved to pet it, but it jumped back and snarled, revealing a mouth nearly devoid of teeth. Since the animal was too young to have lost so many naturally, either disease or cruelty had claimed them. Harun offered his open hand, and after a few minutes the skittish animal approached to lick the salt from his fingers. Its tongue was dry, its nose warm. Harun would've liked to get it something to eat, but he didn't dare abandon his post. It would be a form of death not to follow through on what he had already agreed to, no matter how futile.

Harun shielded himself in the foliage as employees exited the museum. Sayeed appeared, deep in conversation with the mail clerk, who, Harun suddenly suspected, might be a mole for state security, given his access to all incoming and outgoing correspondence. How naive not to have thought of this earlier. And then there were the guards, with their truncheons and keys and thick-lipped frowns, any one of whom could have been purposefully placed to gather information.

Sayeed laughed at something the mail clerk said before the two men parted and Sayeed walked off in a direction he hadn't before. Harun followed at a discreet distance, joining a current of white djellabahs. His joints loosened, his stride eased, his chin rose—an unconscious effect of being part of a collective swarm.

Sayeed led Harun into a part of the city he'd ventured into only once, while searching for a mechanical carpet sweeper that turned out not to exist. He looked back on the escapade as a thing utterly foreign to him. What bewildered state of mind did Syria put him in that he'd embark on such a useless errand?

The storefronts were smaller, unkempt, selling a jumble of poorly constructed products it would depress Harun to own. To satisfy his archeo-anthropologic impulse, he would have liked to stop and ask a shopkeeper to profile the typical customer, but Sayeed angled into a derelict alley, forcing Harun to duck behind a mountain of dinged pots. The mangy dog flopped on the ground beside him and rolled onto its back for a belly scratch. How could Harun have been so oblivious as to let a dog follow him? His mother would surely laugh if he described the scene to her. Laugh and applaud his spontaneous compassion, which was why he'd never tell her. Once something touches your heart, she'd remind him, you can no longer control it.

Sayeed used no key or signal to enter a rundown building with blacked-out windows at the end of the alley. Harun was surprised he took no precautions to cover his path nor once glanced back to see if he was being followed. If he was a spy, he was certainly a careless one.

Harun approached the same door, eased it open. The smell of tobacco coated the darkness and drew him inside. Muffled voices led him to a wooden staircase, where a faint glow and a whirring noise spilled from the landing above. The voices belonged to a couple speaking German. Abruptly, another voice intruded, speaking Arabic, first as a man, and then imitating a woman. Harun crept up the stairs until the Arabic man said, "Happiness isn't always fun."

The phrase jolted him. The perfect counterpoint to his mother's remark about love not always being tragic. He sat on the step and thought about his parents' affair. He hadn't done that yet. Not in the physical sense of imagining his mother's body lying beside a man's. Maybe it was because of the dark and the phrases drifting down from above, the man and the woman talking about love and prejudice, while other voices, less friendly and crueler intruded on their tenderness.

Harun never lay with Sana during that long summer in Greece, or the next year either, though she encouraged him. He assumed it was because she was Maronite. A Muslim girl would never bring dishonor on herself by suggesting such a thing. However, he did kiss Sana beneath the constellation Hercules on several occasions as they stood between the rows of small wooden stakes that divided their archaeological plots. He wasn't an experienced kisser. Sana's lips were the first and only he'd ever tasted, the touch of her tongue almost more than he could bear. He'd been tempted once to stray beyond what his integrity told him was permissible, when he held her close enough to feel the curves of her body through their dusty work clothes.

"German master, Arab dog!" the man upstairs shouted, startling Harun. Groans of disapproval followed. Whatever was going on up there, Harun couldn't interpret it from where he was, so he ventured further up the stairs toward the fog of tobacco smoke and a doorway of flickering light.

He hung back, uncertain what to make of the film playing on the wall. He hadn't seen a movie since his mother had dragged him to silly musicals as a child. It was embarrassing to sit beside her, watching people her age shamelessly flirt. This film was completely different. On screen, an older pale, unattractive woman sat on a bed beside a young dark-skinned man in a clean but graceless apartment. The man appeared to be from North Africa or Turkey. Harun tried to tune out the man who was translating for the dozen others crowded in the small space.

Surely the film was politically subversive. Why else view it clandestinely? Yet as Harun focused on the quiet scenes of yearning between the German cleaning woman and the Arabic day laborer, the only thing subversive he discovered in the plot was society's inability to accept that these two people were deeply in love and wanted to marry.

When the lights came on and someone began changing the reels, Harun noiselessly retreated down the stairs, though he was desperate to know how the story ended. Would the couple persevere, or would their friends and neighbors succeed in destroying what existed between them?

Lost in thought, he stepped into the alley, where the mangy dog waited. He paid no attention to it as he ran home, fleeing an ominous despair that had clung to him since Leopold's visit. Darting erratically through traffic, he replayed the film's scenes of intolerance and filial cruelty, his heart tight with fear for the couple's happiness. And then he was with Sana, sieving dirt under the relentless Greek sun. His muscles ached with loss. He couldn't catch his breath but staggered on, appearing quite mad in his flapping djellabah. Unobserved, Leopold kept pace, his cracked lips fixed in a smile.

■

1 September 1975

Dear Adjo,

Last night I died. Do not worry. I am fine now and was never frightened. The experience was oddly serene. Slowly things began to slip away. I could not feel my feet, though I could see them, but not remember what they were called. I was light and heavy at the same time. No longer in hospital, but still able to hear my doctor's questions. I knew not to answer. Death was that fragile. Talking about it would have destroyed it. Even thinking about it made me heavier, a stone falling and falling. It was good not to feel my feet. I might have tried to stop falling and land somewhere, but I was not supposed to stop. Everything happens at the right time, the right speed, if we let it.

I could see where I had been and where I was going. A jumble of images, past and future, no division between the two, just as it was meant to be. It was easier than I thought to give in to lost gravity, that endless falling through space. Whatever had bound me to the world was forgotten, but not gone. Transposed into something beyond language or sensation.

This morning I woke to poetry. The granddaughter of the woman I share this room with was reading Cavafy. I have always liked him— what Egyptian does not?—while still finding some of his work overly sentimental. The poem's simple truth struck me, and I realized how many words of encouragement and warning I have written you these past weeks trying to convey what Cavafy does eloquently in just six lines:

> *Like beautiful bodies of the dead who had not grown old*
> *and they shut them, with tears, in a magnificent mausoleum,*

with roses at the head and jasmine at the feet—
this is how desires look that have passed
without fulfillment; without one of them having achieved
a night of sensual delight, or a moonlit morn.

As you can see, I am very much my old self. Dying is not as hard as people think. Please do not feel like you need to come to me. I am fine. I mean that sincerely. However, the experience has provoked me to do something I never imagined.

I have a favor to ask. I am writing your father a letter and will mail it to you tomorrow, along with the photo I have of him. After I am dead, please find out if he is still alive. You do not need to meet him. Merely send him the letter. I could ask someone else to do this, but if I ask you, it will happen. I hope you do not see this as just one more in my string of follies. Never underestimate love, Adjo. It is stronger than all the natural forces in the universe.

Your mother

Harun stared in dismay at the photo Sayeed had taken of Ebla's limestone basin of the bearded men atop its basalt-offering table. What he'd previously found fascinating—the bull-men with their braided tails and sharp ears alert to the negotiation between the bearded men in embrace—seemed irrelevant, even dull, and the point he'd planned to make about the uniqueness of this water basin, groundless. The crucial theme of his abstract, having lost its center of gravity, collapsed. Harun picked up the sheaf of papers, two years' worth of research, and tossed them into the trash.

All he cared about was the film he'd stumbled upon. Why did the young Arab man's stark insignificant life so fiercely appeal to him? He had no urge to *fuck an ole hag,* as the little prisoner sneered, though he did inexplicably desire the couple's unadorned walls, threadbare curtains, and worn-out sheets. Harun sensed it was not primal simplicity he craved, but something tangibly raw, a thing he could hold in his hands and squeeze the life out of.

His gaze drifted back to the photo of the water basin. Still nothing. Over the years he'd grown accustomed to a persistent feeling of emptiness, but he'd never been without professional purpose before. He wondered what it would be like to walk out of the museum and never come back. Where would he go? Back to where he saw the film. That was what he yearned for.

Sayeed paused in the doorway and rustled the pages in his hand to get Harun's attention.

"Yes, yes, come in, what is it?"

"The grant we received from the Ministry of Culture . . . you must sign the papers."

Sayeed also laid an air-letter envelope on his desk. "Another letter from Alexandria."

Harun grimaced, tucked it into his breast pocket, then gestured to the photo of the bearded men. "Do you ever photograph things besides ruins?"

"I photograph people all the time."

"Have you photographed me?"

"Yes. I hope you do not mind. In fact, you photograph well. In profile you look like Jean-Pierre Léaud. A famous French film actor."

Harun tensed in excitement. "I never go to the cinema."

Sayeed drew nearer, lowered his voice. "The films he is in are banned here."

"Why? Are they politically subversive?"

Sayeed laughed. "All foreign films are banned here, except Soviet or eastern-bloc films." He picked up the signed papers as the midday call to prayer softly echoed through the museum.

"Yet you still managed to see it."

"I love the cinema. And when you love something, you always find a way."

Harun was desperate to find out more about the film he'd seen, but also wanted to tell Sayeed he admired his passion and courage. Yet the words didn't come and the moment was lost.

The ache behind his ribs ebbed, only to be replaced by the feeling of a stone in his stomach, worse in some ways since it was unfamiliar. The stone felt remarkably heavy, and as Harun stepped from behind his desk, his legs trembled. He stumbled to the courtyard for fresh air, and found Alexandra standing in the blazing sun among the cracked tiles and weeds.

"Sometimes the archive feels like a refrigerator. After two minutes out here it's a relief to go back." She checked her watch. "I didn't think my being here would disturb anyone right now."

Harun evaded her obvious reference to midday prayers by glancing at her wrist. "Is that a mouse on your watch?" He leaned forward for a better look.

Alexandra held out her arm, embarrassed. "Yes, that's Mickey . . . a silly cartoon character. I've had this since I was seven. I don't know why I still wear it."

"Because someone important gave it to you."

Alexandra had never considered the watch in that way before, and it made her want to rip it off. "If you came out here to pray, I can leave."

Harun peered over his shoulder. "I know it is wrong, but I do not feel like praying today."

"It's good to play hooky occasionally."

"Hooky?"

"It means to take off from work. Do something secretive, fun. I know it doesn't sound very daring, but I used to sneak off to a coffee shop and stuff myself with glazed doughnuts."

"I have no idea what a glazed doughnut is, but since I want to talk to you about your translations, if you would like to join me while I play hooky, I would happily buy you coffee."

Harun knew it was forward to ask, but Alexandra was American and made a wonderful alibi should someone notice him leave. He asked which café she'd like to go to, pleased she picked the Al-Nawfara, a perfectly proper place with its coffee served on gleaming silver trays.

In deference to Harun, Alexandra covered her hair with the scarf she kept in her purse. Still, the proprietor sat them away from the street, where men arriving from prayers would settle in for tea and a smoke. The small raised stage remained as Alexandra had first seen it, a stool beside a wooden box where the hakawati kept his props. After a waiter took their order, Alexandra leaned across the table to whisper, "It's been 112 days since the hakawati was silenced."

"What a strange fact to know."

"Not really. I came here the day I arrived in Damascus. My advisor told me about Antar and Abla, but the reading was stopped on the 158th day."

"It is the usual story. A tale of virtue and sacrifice."

"No, it's a story about love."

The waiter returned, having donned a red fez and embroidered vest. After he served their coffee, Alexandra groaned. "I can't believe they always put that getup on for me."

"To him you are a tourist. He must play his part."

"Well, I liked him better without it."

"Then I fear the hakawati's clothes would not appeal to you either."

"That is entirely different. That's tradition for a reason."

"I am not sure I understand the difference, but no matter."

Alexandra tasted the coffee. I was strong and acrid, not at all how she liked it. She was grateful when a plate of baklava arrived and quickly took a bite.

"Arabic coffee is an acquired taste."

"Not for my mother it wouldn't be. This is how she likes it, black and bitter."

"Then you must take after your father."

"I certainly hope not."

As they sat in silence Alexandra realized her father had introduced her to coffee. He'd warm sweetened milk in a pot for the two of them and mix it with half a cup of coffee. That was how he drank it, and how Alexandra preferred it to this day. She nodded in the direction of the raised stage to blunt the memory. "I feel as if Antar and Abla's love is trapped in suspended animation. How much longer do they have to wait until President Assad lets them live again?"

"They are Syria's Romeo and Juliet. Just pretend they are sleeping."

He smiled, pleased with his comparative analysis, and took a bite of pastry. There was something sly in his look that Alexandra hadn't noticed before, and without thinking she blurted, "You suddenly strike me as a bit of a Romeo. A buttoned-up one for sure, but still a Romeo."

"I am definitely no Romeo. Shakespeare did not write parts for people like me. Audiences want heroes to learn from their mistakes. I merely acknowledge my wrongdoing on rare occasions, and then repeat the error twice-fold the next time."

Alexandra laughed. "I don't believe a word of that."

"Talk to my mother. She will confirm it."

Boisterous men filled the café. One group arrived, speaking English. Alexandra glanced over, catching the eye of the American from the shawarma stand. He excused himself and approached. "I wondered if I'd ever see you again. I thought you may have left Damascus."

"This is my boss, Dr. Lakhosh. I'm sorry but I don't know your name."

The man shook hands with Harun. "Richard Poole."

"We almost met at a shawarma stand," Alexandra explained.

Richard laughed. "But instead I infuriated one of the people she was sitting with."

"Dr. Lakhosh has had the *pleasure* of meeting Eldridge."

"So that's his name. Well, that explains a lot."

Alexandra chuckled. She'd forgotten how easy it was for Americans to make small talk.

"And now before I rejoin my boss, and lose all sight of you again, what is your name?"

"Oh, how stupid of me. I'm Alexandra Pierce."

"Well, goodbye, Alexandra Pierce. It was a pleasure to meet you . . . again." Richard turned to Dr. Lakhosh. "And you too, sir."

Harun stared after the man in his perfect western clothes, with his perfect western manners.

"Hmm . . . Never thought I'd see him again. I wonder why he's in Syria."

Harun had seen the type before. Richard Poole was either a diplomat or a spy.

"So . . . What translations did you want to talk about?"

Harun was briefly confused, having forgotten his original lie. "Nothing in particular. I merely wanted you to know I think you are doing a splendid job."

"Thank you."

"And . . . to be fair . . . my mother agrees with you about Antar and Abla being a love story."

Harun had never sounded so sincere or candid with her. She smiled and he half-smiled back in an oddly familiar way.

The café bustled with men huddled around wooden tables inlaid with mother-of-pearl, their voices rising between long draws on ornate brass argilas. Harun knew there were security people mixed in with the crowd, but the noise level was such that he felt he could take a chance.

"I saw a film the other day that may deal with the same theme as Antar and Abla's story."

"What was it? I'd like to see it."

"I only saw the middle. It was a German film about a young dark-skinned Arab man and an older white cleaning woman. They wanted to marry, but their families couldn't accept this."

"Oh, I saw it last year in Berkeley. It's great. It won some huge award. I think it was called . . ." Alexandra's brow furrowed.

Harun shifted to the edge of his chair, willing her to remember.

"*Fear Eats the Soul.* What a great title. Where was it playing?"

Harun was flooded with a warmth he'd not experienced since Sana. He had dozens of questions to ask her about the film. "Shall we play hooky a while longer?"

"That is the whole point of hooky."

He turned to signal the waiter and was horrified to spot Leopold watching them from a corner table. The stone in Harun's stomach returned with a vengeance. He leaned forward. "We have to go. Right away. Act as if our leaving now is completely normal."

"Why? What's happened?"

"I will explain outside." He followed Alexandra into the street. "Try not to look over your shoulder. Try to walk slowly."

She did as he asked, despite an overwhelming urge to see who was behind them. Harun waited until they entered a busy street full of shoppers before he spoke. "The night you were detained . . . The man who came with you to my office the next morning . . . He thinks you are a Lebanese spy."

"That's ridiculous."

"Of course it is, but this is Syria. All foreigners are mistrusted."

"You're a foreigner."

"Yes. I have just begun to remember that. Tell me . . . no matter how inconsequential it seems . . . have you done anything that might lead the authorities to suspect you?"

"No. Absolutely nothing."

"Then we must figure out why they might want to make an example of you."

They returned to the museum at a steady pace. Once inside, Alexandra was at a loss. "Return to the archive. Go on with your work as if nothing has happened. In the meantime, I will see what I can find out."

Alexandra walked off. Halfway down the hall, she glanced back with a girlish frightened look, and for a moment Harun felt an overwhelming urge to protect her. The sensation was new to him, and as he went in search of Sayeed the stone in his stomach vanished.

The DO NOT ENTER sign hung on the door to the makeshift darkroom. Harun barged in, startling Sayeed. In the dim light he couldn't see the determination on Harun's face and wanted to set him at ease. "Do not worry. Everything is in the fix. Nothing is ruined."

Harun grabbed a stack of photos and searched them. Clay tablet after clay tablet flew past.

"What are looking for? I can help."

"I think you have done enough of that already."

Sayeed was shocked by Harun's tone and perplexed when he launched into a second pile. Near the bottom, he found a photo of Alexandra mixed in among the tablets and set it aside.

"I did nothing disrespectful by photographing her."

Harun riffled through other piles, discovering only photos of himself, Dr. Arman, and Alexandra among Ebla's ruins. In frustration he glared at Sayeed. "Where are the men?"

"What men?"

"The men you meet with."

"What are you talking about?"

"You see films that are banned. Take photos of who and what you want. What else do you do that is subversive? I am not oblivious. I have watched you and Alexandra together."

Sayeed ignored him and reached for the doorknob.

"If you care for her, Sayeed, stop whatever it is you are doing."

Sayeed whipped around. Toe to toe, he and Harun were the same height, though Sayeed's more muscular build made him appear much larger.

"Are you a Lebanese spy?"

Sayeed laughed in his face.

"This is not a joke. I know you are involved in something because I have followed you."

The admission blindsided Sayeed. This was betrayal. He had worked for Harun for five years, doing any task, no matter how menial. He was far from being the nervous twenty-two-year-old Harun had initially hired, yet he was often still treated with condescension. Sayeed locked eyes with him. "Why did you follow me?"

Harun coolly scanned Sayeed's face as a biologist would a specimen. When he returned to Sayeed's eyes, he saw a man capable of anything. Leopold must be right.

Harun's silence incensed Sayeed and he shoved Harun against the workbench. "Why?"

"Because the security people asked me to."

"Did they give you evidence, a reason why they think I am a spy?"

"No."

"So you did it on blind faith, believing the worst of me."

"Yes. I followed you into the alley. I saw what you did there. There must be more."

The sudden blow to Harun's face sent him reeling. Sayeed punched him twice more before he collapsed. Harun protected his head as Sayeed knelt beside him.

"I belong to a cinema club. The films we see are not subversive. They are about love or freedom or the struggle to lead a life worth living. They are not about country or nation. They are about people, so they are banned."

Harun was overcome by shame.

"And, yes, I do care about Alexandra, but I know it is impossible to get involved with her. Nothing good can come from it. So I take my photos, that is all."

"They think you are both Lebanese spies."

"They think everyone is a spy."

"I do not understand . . . Why do you risk everything for a film?"

Sayeed sighed. "Because to be Syrian now is to be small. And a man who settles for a small life is really no man at all."

Harun stared at him blankly, still unable to grasp the implication of Sayeed's words.

"Prison is not what frightens me most, Dr. Lakhosh. Perhaps not even torture. There are worst things men do to themselves. God is indifferent to our situation, and yet I still pray to him. Where is the logic in that?"

"God is not indifferent. He is merely asleep."

"Well when he wakes and sees what a mess we have made of his universe, that will be something to behold."

Harun rested his bloody bruised cheek in his hand. When he finally spoke, his voice was full of anguish. "I watched part of *Fear Eats the Soul* . . . I need to know . . . How does it end?"

"As all love stories should."

The feeling of love was so distant, Harun wasn't sure what that meant. "So they stayed together despite everything?"

"Yes, though the director let us know it would not be easy. Hope, but with suffering."

As Sayeed helped Harun to his feet the door burst open. In strolled Leopold flanked by two security police. He smirked at seeing Harun's bloody face.

"You have made a terrible mistake," Harun declared, but Leopold raised a hand for him to be silent.

Sayeed stepped forward, resigned to go quietly, but Leopold faced Harun. "Dr. Lakhosh . . ."

The words were so unexpected they had no impact. Sayeed continued to walk forward, a man condemned, while Harun stood utterly still, his strength focused on how to aid in Sayeed's defense.

Leopold was forced to grab Harun's shirtsleeve. "Dr. Lakhosh . . . please . . . do not make your case worse."

Only then did it sink in that the innocuous uneventful life he had labored so hard to cultivate was over.

Harun was led to a side entrance that opened onto the delivery alley. Outside, the mangy dog rushed to greet him, wagging its tail, dragging its new leash. Harun had forgotten all about the animal and was touched that it had waited right where he'd left it.

"Just a moment," Harun pleaded, but the men forced him into a closed canvas truck.

Sayeed bolted into the alley and heard Harun cry, "Someone . . . anyone . . . Please feed the dog!"

Sayeed lunged for the leash as the truck lumbered off. The dog strained at its collar then circled Sayeed, panic-stricken. He dragged the poor creature into the museum and rushed to the archive. Alexandra would know how to care for it. But when he opened the door, Dr. Arman was working on a translation.

"What is that dog doing in here?!"

"They have arrested Dr. Lakhosh."

"What?! Why?!"

"I cannot explain right now. I need you to take care of this dog." He handed Dr. Arman the leash and darted back into the hallway.

"Sayeed! Come back!"

Sayeed followed a circuitous route to the derelict alley, but this time he didn't approach the building with the blacked-out windows. Nearby, a stack of rusted grillwork lay in a heap, chained to iron beams. Above the far left beam, he removed a brick and flipped it around, revealing a faint yellow mark to anyone who knew to look. Within ten seconds he was back on the main street, keeping pace with the crowd. Harun's arrest was either a tremendous stroke of luck or a sly and calculated distraction by the authorities. Either way Sayeed had to warn the others that the group, and perhaps their plan, had been compromised.

2 September 1975

Dear Aaron,

After so many years I should explain who I am, but I will trust my heart that, since the war, I am not forgotten. When you receive this, I will already be dead. I am sorry to be so blunt. I have something else to say, and it is also best said quickly. We have a son. He is an archeologist, handsome like you, very responsible, perhaps overly so, and much to my surprise quite pious. His name is Harun, the Arabic form of your name. Whenever I said it, I was always reminded of you.

There. It is done. I hope you are not angry to find this out so late. I do not wish to cause distress, merely to let you know that a piece of you remains here, in this volatile part of the world where so much goes wrong, but in this case went right. I have no good excuses for why I kept this from you until now, just bad ones I have slowly come to understand.

Until recently I believed love existed to help us endure life. I also believed admitting to love exposed our fears and desires. For a long time I did not want to confront either. Fear and desire can be such uncontrollable and destructive emotions. Now I think love exists so we can discover who we really are.

I have many regrets. When you left Alexandria I did not know I was pregnant. If I had had more courage, I might have tried to find you after the war. I am certain you cared for me as deeply as I did for you, so my largest regret is the days, hours, months, and years I have missed spending with you. Also, by sealing my love for you inside a box, our son never learned what love truly means. I have spent these last months trying to undo that mistake, and have revealed everything. Whether Harun ever accepts the truth of us I will never know. If he seeks you out, then there is the answer.

I hope your life has been a good one. I believe mine was, though always missing a certain energy I could never quite define. Now of course it is all so obvious, but for decades I convinced myself it was my melancholic nature, and not losing you, that made me restless. Why we need another person, why we love them, remains a mystery to me. Perhaps it is the way our souls are made, slightly imperfect, so that we must seek a lover to make us whole.

It is soothing at this point to look back contentedly at the one truly important thing I did in life. By all measures of that time and place I did something disgraceful. But by all measures of my heart and spirit I was rewarded a hundredfold. The day we met I was handed a gift. That I chose to open it is completely because of you. I remember the exact moment I fell in love, and since that day my feelings for you have never wavered. I am sorry that the frightened little girl in me decided to freeze that moment, destroying what chance we might have had. I do not mind being alone now, but I do mind not seeing your smile one last time.

In my memory I carry a picture of you, ironically from a moment I never actually saw. It is of the day your barge left Alexandria. I imagine you sitting on deck in the army coat you hated except for all of its pockets, where you kept your keys. Around you there is nothing but light, sea, and sky. No other people, little motion. As if you were not rooted to anything at all. You look concentrated yet serene, and you never grow older. It is a lovely image, and I hope it will be the one I see just as I die.

All my love,

Farah

Part 3

Harun could bear the blindfold, darkness fueled his other senses, but the loss of his shoes caused him distress. Even as a child he'd refused to go barefoot, and still found it difficult to remove his shoes for Friday prayers. He had no idea where he was in the city. He should've listened for cues as the truck rattled through Damascus. Instead, he'd obsessed about the mangy dog. He'd been with it for less than a day and, while he'd forgotten about it in the chaos, it hadn't forgotten him. Harun had fed it, bathed it, applied ointment to its sores, and when it refused to leave his side in the morning, he'd purchased a collar and leash, never imagining that loyalty could be so easily bought.

A key clanked in the door. Harun detected Leopold's rosewater scent. When a guard removed his blindfold, there were his confiscated shoes on Leopold's feet.

"The leather is extremely supple," Leopold taunted, sitting opposite Harun at a metal folding table. Leopold lit a slender cigarette, which made his oversized knuckles appear more absurd. He smoked it down before pulling out Harun's pocket watch. "What is inside here?"

"A clock, I imagine. I was never given the key."

"Yet you still carry it."

"It is a family heirloom."

Leopold turned it over in his hand. "Now that Egypt has signed a treaty with the Israeli devil, what further humiliations does Sadat have in store for Assad?"

"How would I know?"

"Does Egypt intend to intrude in Lebanon and disregard Syria's sovereign rights?"

"I am completely apolitical and have not lived in Egypt for years."

"Have you ever advocated treason, Dr. Lakhosh?"

"I would not know how."

"It is quite simple, really."

"I disagree. Treason is too subjective to be simple. I would wager you see Mohammed not as a religious leader, but as a great Arab figure.

Maybe even a nationalist one. Is that not a form of treason to some?"

Leopold took a long draw on his cigarette then laughed. "I see you enjoy games. I must keep you around to amuse me." He signaled the guard, who yanked Harun to his feet.

Harun glanced at his pocket watch. "May I have it back? Since the key is lost I will not be able to use the springs to tunnel my way out."

Leopold slid the watch across the table.

"You never thought Miss Pierce was a Lebanese spy, did you?"

Leopold's devious smile was answer enough.

"You never suspected my assistant either. Yet you still got me to follow him."

"Yes."

"Then you also must know I am not an Egyptian or Lebanese spy."

Harun was led away, still with no idea about why he was detained.

■■
■■

Nestled among a profusion of cement manufacturing plants, two abandoned warehouses were home to a colony of feral cats and Sayeed's cinema club. Twelve men, from eighteen to eighty, saw the yellow mark on the brick in the alley and made their way there at the prearranged time. The younger members were furious that an outsider had breached their film sanctuary. The oldest, Ghazwan, reminded them that this was precisely why they met in a crowded district with no locked doors. The best way to deflect attention from one's real purpose was to hide in plain sight. Ghazwan was not concerned about their project, only Sayeed's safety.

"But what if they arrest Sayeed? He knows everything," Tarek, the youngest, countered.

Ghazwan cradled his withered left hand in his right. "Even if Sayeed tells them every detail, they will laugh, thinking he must be lying. Now let us read through the revised sections."

Adil, the Arabic translator of the movie Harun witnessed, handed out the rewritten opening to their picaresque film script, *The Adven-*

tures of the Ingenious Gentleman Ad-Ass al Fez-Ha of the Moon, an episodic parody with their president as a stand-in for well-known characters in Arabic and western literature. This short scene followed a hapless Othello unable to consummate his marriage, having bored his bride to death with the interminable tale of his suffering. With subtle references to the setbacks Assad had endured as an insecure general from an impoverished backwater, the comparison between Othello and Assad would not be lost on the public.

The men read through the scene. Discussed possible locations. As cinematographer, Sayeed suggested the Khan As'ad Pasha dome in homage to Orson Welles. Others couldn't envision transitioning from there to the woods where the second adventure would take place. The film's director sketched out an expressionist approach, with Othello rising from his unconsummated wedding night wearing a lion's skin in the middle of a paper forest. Adil challenged the idea as too obvious since everyone over the age of three knew al-Assad meant "the lion." Ghazwan interrupted everyone, intent on reviving an old debate—to forego *Othello* in favor of a satiric *Tempest.*

Tarek exploded. "It is stupid and cowardly to include Shakespeare at all. We are not British. Our film should be about Syria, how it is now, and how the government corrupts people's lives. Why must we hide our metaphors behind theirs? Why must we make a spoof at all?"

Ghazwan glared at him. "Because your film will never get past the censor."

"That is your opinion."

"No, that is my experience. None of my scripts has cleared the censor in eighteen years."

Sayeed, who respected the old man like a father, whispered to Tarek, "I want what you want. But it is not possible right now. We are young. He is not. Let it go."

Ghazwan seized on Harun's arrest to illustrate the parallels between Assad and Prospero's subjective justice, hoping to persuade the others it would be the more potent farce. Sayeed agreed they could conceive an episode aligning the two men's manipulative misuse of power, but suddenly imagined something bolder. To make Miranda the key. Shoot the episode entirely from her point of view.

There was a rush of disapproval, but then the room quieted, the others' curiosity piqued. Sayeed confessed that he didn't know exactly how to do it, but sensed it could be modern, amusing, and subtly more political than their *Othello*.

"Then it would not dig at Assad," Ghazwan protested.

"But it will," Sayeed countered. "Assad is Prospero personified, controlling everyone's fate, terrorizing and imprisoning whomever he wishes. Prospero is an embittered magician, but above all a hypocrite, tyrant, and irresponsible father, if not the actual pimp, orchestrating his daughter's own violation. Let us have Miranda condemn her father for us and bring an end to his unjust reign."

Harun kept his distance from the other barefoot men in the cell. He assumed they were Lebanese refugees, though some could be beggars. The cell's floor was thick with reddish-brown grime that might have been blood or something fouler. There was nowhere to sit, so the men squatted against the walls. Harun was desperate to urinate, but a bald, middle-aged man had been eyeing him for an hour. Harun wished he could muster the little prisoner's outrage and tell the guy, "Fuck off."

The men's toilet was a battered bucket, nearly full, with yellowish turds floating on the surface. Harun tried to piss slowly, but the pressure was so great it came out in a torrent. A few drops sloshed over the rim, but he didn't disgrace himself or foul the space. Still, he felt like an animal as he returned to his solitary spot at the other end of the cell.

"Are you Christian?" a voice quietly asked.

Harun spun to see the middle-aged man, who up close had a fleshy, kind face.

The man eyed Harun's left hand jammed deep into his trouser pocket. "I thought you might have a rosary in there. You have not said a word, and have not let go of whatever that is."

Harun relaxed his grip on his great-grandfather's watch. "No, I am not Christian."

"It is all right if you are." The man pointed to three men near the sink. "The one in the middle is Christian. The other two insist they are atheists, but when it is time to pray, they join us."

"How long have you been here?"

"Nineteen days. Some were here before. Others are gone. It is better now, less crowded."

Harun couldn't imagine how more had squeezed in. "Are you all refugees?"

"No, I am Syrian, and so are those four men over there."

Harun was curious about one of the men, whose nonstop head bobbing struck him as deranged. It turned out he was an imam, counting seconds to keep track of minutes, so they'd know when to pray. Harun confessed that he'd thought the person was crazy, and the man chuckled. His wide, cheerful smile calmed Harun. They stood in silence another minute before the man gestured to Harun's cheek. "Did the small man with the large head do that to your face?"

So much had happened since Sayeed had punched him in the darkroom that Harun hadn't given his swollen cheek a second thought. "No. A colleague did this. But I deserved it."

The man nodded toward the only inmate sitting on the floor, his leg ineptly splinted by a piece of woolen blanket wrapped with a shirt. "The small man broke his leg with a metal pipe a week ago. I tried to set it, but I am not a doctor."

"What do you do?"

"Bake bread."

"How does a baker end up in prison?"

"What do you do?"

"I am an archeologist."

"How does an archeologist end up in prison?"

"I am not exactly sure."

The imam called the man over. He and the others knelt on the floor. Harun silently prayed for the dog and Sayeed, hoping they were safe and together. He also prayed for his mother's recovery. Only then did he remember her letter was still in his breast pocket. It was so thin, the guard who patted him down missed it. Harun opened the envelope to read, "Last night I died."

■■

Sayeed had volunteered to come up with a *Tempest* outline by tomorrow, but as he pondered the psyche of a teenage girl at the mercy of her father's whims, his confidence waned. He would've liked his sisters' input, but didn't dare go home. Instead, he walked toward the Barada River to think. On the bank, a dog lapped the murky water, reminding him that he'd left Harun's dog with Dr. Arman.

Sayeed stopped at a bakery, but his peace offering of dessert did nothing to quell Dr. Arman's fury about Harun's arrest. After three hours with the security police he knew nothing more than Alexandra had already related when she took the dog off his hands. An account so preposterous Dr. Arman knew there must be more. As a child he was taught that nothing is inevitable, everything knowable . . . but this?

Sayeed held out the bag of pastries. "Taj al-malik, pistachio and cashew."

Mikha'il swatted it away. "How you made them think Alexandra was a Lebanese spy is beyond me! But your implicating poor Harun is unconscionable!"

Sayeed explained that Harun had followed him and seen something. Nothing treasonous. Something Dr. Arman would in fact applaud, but when asked to divulge what it was, Sayeed refused in order to protect Dr. Arman from detention too.

Mikha'il considered the situation. "Very well. It is better if I do not know. I can appeal again to the authorities like a real fool without pretense." He snatched the bag of pastries from Sayeed and laid them on two plates. "Save me from myself and eat one of these."

Sayeed had never been inside Dr. Arman's apartment and was struck by how organized it was compared to his office. He scoured a crammed bookcase in the hallway just off the kitchen.

Dr. Arman glanced over his shoulder while he made tea. "What are you looking for?"

"In *The Tempest,* do you think Prospero is complicit in Caliban's rape of Miranda?"

"So you think she was raped?"

"I don't know, but I think it is more interesting to leave the question open."

Dr. Arman retrieved his paperback of *The Tempest.* "Shakespeare was very cunning about that point. After all, who encourages Miranda to teach the brutish Caliban language . . . ? Her father, Prospero, of course. Does he chaperone them during these lessons . . . ? Of course not."

Dr. Arman pour Sayeed a cup of tea, gestured for him to sit. "Think about this . . . Father leaves precious daughter alone for years with an uncivilized beast and, in all those years, on a single day he stumbles upon a single incident, and believes he has stopped the foul deed." He joined Sayeed at the table. "But we have to remember Miranda is an innocent. Can she discern the difference between savage gropes and true violation? And are we really expected to believe Prospero is like an American superhero arriving just in time? I think there is much more between the lines. Miranda's honor may have been saved that day, but I wonder about all the days before."

Sayeed's mind reeled. He flipped through the book, noting Dr. Arman's comments in the margins. Mikha'il leaned back in his chair. "It has always troubled me that Prospero was still in his sexual prime when he was banished from Milan. It must have been a torture to be stuck on an island watching the only female around blossom into a beautiful woman."

"But she is his daughter."

"Oh, please." Dr. Arman grabbed Sayeed's empty plate and headed to the sink.

Sayeed flipped to a random page. "Would you mind if I read through your notes?"

"Keep it. It is yours."

"If you had the choice between seeing a more modern and satirically tinged version of *Othello* or *The Tempest,* which would you choose?"

"*The Tempest.* It is morally ambiguous and the characters' motivations less clear. Yet it is still a love story, and at this point in my life, I prefer happy endings."

Sayeed laughed. Dr. Arman was one of the most entertaining men he'd ever met. As Sayeed left to retrieve the dog, he wished Mikha'il could play a part in the film.

■■

Sayeed reached the Collinwood Arms after ten and strolled through the patio gate, frightening Mrs. August and the other residents who were trying to cool off. After Alexandra introduced Sayeed to everyone, Mrs. August heaved a sigh. "I thought you were one of those horrible refugees. I've heard what they're doing to people."

Alexandra stroked the dog's ears. "I'm sure whatever you've heard has been exaggerated."

"No. I have it on very good authority."

Sayeed had hoped to talk to Alexandra alone, but now that seemed impossible. "I am sorry I startled everyone. I came to get the dog."

"I'd like to keep her for the night, if you don't mind."

Eldridge pitched out of his chair. "I told you . . . No dogs! I will not have fleas in my home."

Alexandra tickled the dog's belly, then reluctantly handed Sayeed the leash.

Nicole Fouquet, the only Collinwood tenant who sensed Sayeed's desire to be with Alexandra, signaled Jean-Paul to follow her. She stopped in front of Mrs. August to reach for her glass. "Let me fix you another before we start playing."

"You're such a dear." Mrs. August rocked back and forth, gathering momentum to lift her heft out of the sagging chair.

Nicole glanced back. "Come on, Rafi. You said you'd be our fourth tonight."

Rafi closed his book. "I am very tired. I think Eldridge should take my spot."

Jean-Paul snorted. "Eldridge is not a bridge partner. He is a curse."

The women laughed and headed inside, Eldridge nipping at their heels. "I resent that."

Once everyone was gone, Alexandra beckoned Sayeed to follow her around to the side of the building where no one could hear them. She was disturbed that the police had divulged nothing to Dr. Arman, and that Sayeed seemed to know less than she did. She hoisted herself onto a low wall that had once enclosed the small garden. "Do you think they'll come back for me?"

"I doubt it. I suspect you are being used to confuse the rest of us."

"Do you think they'll come for you?"

"Eventually . . . That is why I am not going home."

"Where will you sleep tonight?"

"Actually, I have a lot of work to do."

"Museum work?"

Sayeed sat on the wall beside her. "No. A project I am involved in. I wanted my sisters' help, but yours might be even better since you are . . . divided from your father."

"I'm not divided. He just doesn't exist for me."

"Have you read Shakespeare's *Tempest*?"

"Ages ago."

Sayeed lied about the cinema club. Said he was part of an experimental theater group looking to challenge classic texts. He sketched out what he and Dr. Arman had already discussed about Miranda, neglecting to mention his group's interest in political subversion.

Alexandra laughed. "My God . . . you're a feminist." She gave him an affectionate nudge and jumped off the wall. "I'll get paper and pencil. We can work out here."

"We . . . ?"

"Someone has to help you write Miranda."

Two guards brought a bucket of soup, but no bowls. They set it in the center of the cell. The men were forbidden to approach until their defecation bucket was emptied. A guard ordered the imam to pick it up. The baker interceded, which upset the others. They were hungry and knew the outcome of this ritual, with the imam doing what he must.

The soup and defecation buckets were identical. Harun imagined the guards exchanged them each day out of morbid pleasure. When the imam returned, the men were given spoons. Harun hung back, despite having eaten only two apricots and a bite of baklava. He was still rattled by reading that his mother had briefly died, only to live and have the nerve to ask him to deliver a letter to his father.

The baker approached Harun. "Everyone feels sick at first."

"Tomorrow I will eat."

"Tomorrow there may be no soup."

It never occurred to Harun they might not be fed, but he preferred starvation to this. The imam joined them and the baker took his turn at the bucket.

"If you would ever like to talk, I will listen."

"My imam says that too."

"So you are one of us."

"Not any more. Why are you here?"

"During Friday prayers I said Beirut should never be ruled from Damascus."

"Is everyone here a political prisoner?"

"No, six are refugees, most caught stealing food because they were starving. That man over there is a Palestinian journalist who crossed the border illegally. And then there is Hakeem." The imam pointed to the baker. "He counts for me when I get tired."

"I could not be as pleasant as he is if I had been here for nineteen days."

"Is that what he said? He has been here for three years."

"Three years! What for?"

"Murder. He killed his business partner."

Harun felt queasy. How could he so misjudge someone? When did he lose the ability to gauge friend from foe, right from wrong? How could he have allowed such pernicious ignorance to invade his system? He tried to focus on the imam's tranquil voice, but it faded as the little prisoner erupted in panic: *Get me out of this fuckhole!*

Alexandra tapped a pen against her thigh. She and Sayeed had sketched out two possibilities. In the first, Caliban unambiguously raped Miranda. In the second, the rape was left vague, while Prospero's ardor for his daughter appeared certain. Both lacked irony. It was impossible to satirize something as despicable as rape, especially when one writer had no idea as to the real purpose of the scene.

Sayeed regretted that he'd lied about the project, but felt he'd glimpsed a different Alexandra. Her anger at her father had seeped into the text, but instead of inflicting damage on Miranda, the wounds steadily gave her a power and eloquence Sayeed never could've achieved himself. It made him think about his parents, and all the marriages good and bad he'd seen in films. He never was sure what made one work better than another, but suspected it had something to do with knowing oneself so well that your partner felt safe yet free. Alexandra made him question that. It was her willingness to flail and fail, to be hurt and loved, that energized the scenes. Miranda was a mess, and that allowed her to expose the truth. Sayeed took the pages from Alexandra and paced as he read.

"What are you thinking?"

"I think my theater group will not know what to think."

"You said they wanted to turn Shakespeare on his head."

"I'm just not sure they, or a Syrian audience, can be upside down for this long."

"There is nothing quite like blood rushing to the brain."

"Or out of it."

"I don't think critics shoot to kill."

"It is not the critics that worry me." He hated that he was now censoring himself. No need for the government to do it any more. He felt like a coward compared to her.

"You are getting cold feet, aren't you?"

"What?"

"It's a popular American phr—"

"I am familiar with it."

Alexandra had thought Sayeed was done with being curt to her. In writing these scenes they'd discussed personal things that couples who are intimate often never share. She'd divulged more than she had to her last boyfriend, but then Damascus had changed her in many ways. Witnessing everyone's enthusiasm for the Ebla tablets showed her that her heart didn't crave deciphering the mysteries of ancient intent. She felt no exhilaration about unearthing the nuances of the dead. Not in the way Dr. Arman or Dr. Lakhosh did. A place's physical attributes, people's expressions, history she could see right on the surface was what made her pulse jump. It perplexed her how she could have missed this about herself for so many years.

"Give it to your theater group. See what they like and dislike. Then we can make changes from an informed position. If you'd like me to come and take notes . . ."

"No, really, thank you, but that would not be a good idea."

"Okay. I can see when I'm not wanted."

"It is not that."

Alexandra checked her watch. "My God . . . It's 3 a.m.!"

"I am sorry to have kept you so late."

"Don't apologize. I enjoyed it. But I really need to get some sleep before work."

"Good night then."

Wandering through Damascus, Sayeed wondered if the authorities were even after him. No black Volgas were suspiciously parked on his street. No shadows lurked in doorways.

The city seemed lax and formless after his time spent writing with Alexandra. One line in particular haunted him. A line he would've never dared to write. "That thing inside me as he smiled brutishly then dripped his vile fluids on the sand . . . which I once loved for its purity." Only a woman could risk pitting rape against beauty so seamlessly in the same breath.

As the empty hours drifted by, Sayeed unexpectedly felt a tremendous affinity for Tarek, the cinema club's young anti-Shakespeare holdout. Something shockingly bold was truly the only thing worth doing. It took a teenage boy and an American girl to show him he wasn't a rebel at all, but had only deluded himself into thinking his fervent interests made him one.

The dog nuzzled his leg. "I am a fraud, dog." The dog rolled onto its back for a belly rub. "Again? It is always the same with you. You are just like your master. Predictable and consistent."

The observation shocked like lightning. In the day's confusion, Sayeed assumed the authorities had made yet another of their idiotic blunders. He'd never considered what Harun might have done to make them suspicious. Now it struck Sayeed that Harun's very consistency was the provocation.

He hurried across town with the dog in time to interrupt Dr. Arman's breakfast. He characterized Dr. Lakhosh as a man you could set your watch to, and then recounted his recent erratic behavior. "He locked himself in his office, skipped prayers to take Alexandra for coffee, picked up this stray dog, followed me, and was seen running through the streets in a djellabah by our mail clerk. And that is only what we know. For years his behavior, his entire life in Damascus, has never varied until all those letters from his mother began to arrive."

"She has written before."

"Not this often."

Dr. Arman grabbed his briefcase. "You are playing amateur detective."

"Please . . . Come with me to the museum before you go to the police. The answer is there. I know it." Sayeed opened the door for him. "Besides . . . It is on the way."

"If it will get you to stop pestering me."

Sayeed now understood why Harun had stopped walking to work with Dr. Arman. At every block he became distracted by what others would ignore. Sayeed didn't try to hurry him. Their pace projected the ideal aura of indifference if they were being observed. After Dr. Arman slowed yet again, this time to point out a tourist's loud striped shirt—provoking a discourse on the sordid history of stripes in western art and thought—Sayeed joked, "It must be a burden to know so much."

"With all your talk of Shakespeare last night it may interest you to know, in *Othello,* Iago's character is often costumed with one trouser leg audaciously striped."

"Why?"

"It began with the Carmelites striped robes and the unsophisticated medieval eye, but even in modern times stripes still have a checkered connotation." Dr. Arman chuckled at his unintended pun. "In many countries servants and prisoners still wear stripes."

"What was wrong with the medieval eye?"

"When you and I look at an image we discern foreground from background quite easily. Even when an artist plays with perspective, and we have to work a bit harder, we do not get upset. But people in the Middle Ages did. Stripes were reserved for jesters, errant knights, fools, prostitutes, and of course, the devil. It was a recognized symbol, a standard uniform of evil or the powerless, and worn in our century by the most powerless of all, Jews in concentration camps."

When they arrived at the museum, the staff was already filing in. A few stopped to pet the dog, but all seemed unaware of their director's situation. Sayeed secured the leash to a jujube sprouting through a crack in the concrete, then followed Dr. Arman to Harun's office.

Sayeed searched the drawers until he discovered the disinfectant-covered envelopes. He held out the pile to Dr. Arman, who backed away. "I cannot read them."

"You must! You are the only one who can."

"This is ludicrous. I have let your newly inspired dramatic impulses influence me."

"The letters are the key to Dr. Lakhosh's arrest. I am certain of it."

"If you are so certain, you read them."

Sayeed unfolded one. His eyes raced over the sentences. "Dr. Lakhosh's father was American."

"He was not American. He was British."

Sayeed held out the letter. "I do not think so. And his parents were never married."

Dr. Arman snatched the letter. Refolded it. "That is enough. This is none of our business. And as we agreed last night, the less I know the better when I talk to the authorities."

"Perhaps they think he is an American spy. That would explain his arrest."

"If these letters had been read by them first, Harun would have known. There is no way to open an air-letter envelope and reseal it since the envelope is the letter."

"They could have found out about his father some other way."

"You are guessing again."

"Unless you read the letters that is all we have."

Dr. Arman picked up his briefcase. On his way out, his glance back was unmistakable. Sayeed was not to read the letters. And yet Sayeed was convinced that Harun's survival hinged on his reading them, and decided to ask Mohammed for guidance during prayer.

When the mail clerk arrived, Sayeed sifted through the pile, hoping there would be another air-letter envelope from Alexandria. Instead, there was a normal one. This envelope could be steamed open and resealed without anyone knowing, and perhaps it already had been.

Harun picked up the defecation bucket. The guard ordered him to put it down. Harun didn't. Instead, he took a threatening step toward the guard. The step, quite unconscious, had no intention behind it at all. Harun took the step because he was trying to remember a quote an Oxford professor used to spout when situations became untenable. Not as succinct or stirring as "Give me liberty, or give me death," but more

English, wordier, less definitive. Before losing consciousness, Harun had a vague feeling the little prisoner was cheering him on.

He came to, not where he fell, but on the floor of the interrogation room. Harun's face was puffier, his shirt bloodier, the pressure behind his broken ribs altered. The feeling of chaos replaced now by uncontrollable fear, an emotion the little prisoner had never exposed before.

Harun dragged himself to his feet. His body had left an imprint on the grimy floor. It reminded him of an archaeological find and his thoughts drifted to Ebla's basin of the bearded men. A pang of regret washed over him for discarding his research, though he still believed his overemphasis on the basin's use in ritual purifications neglected its emotional possibilities. He was too easily influenced by others' conclusions that the bearded men's pose—each with one hand locked in embrace while the other touched his partner's face—depicted a historical event or treaty agreement. Now Harun suspected it meant much more. The sacred and historical emotionally bound in a way that transcended simple worldly affairs. Perhaps the basin was part of a funerary moment, and the men were brothers reunited in the afterlife. Harun was excited to return to Ebla and meditate on this further.

Footsteps approached. The little prisoner whined in a distant garbled voice. Harun had briefly forgotten the little shit existed, and was surprised how fear had weakened it. The door opened and a guard entered. Leopold followed in a cloud of cigarette smoke.

"Did you sleep well?" Leopold took out a pack of Nefretiti 100s and offered Harun one.

"Thank you, but I never smoke."

"I have seen you smoke a pipe."

"I had quite forgotten."

"Since you like games, let us play a new one. I ask a question and you answer it. Why have you received so many letters from Egypt?"

"Because my mother is unable to censor herself."

"What is she doing in Egypt right now?"

"Dying."

Leopold sneered. "We are all dying."

"I have a letter of hers with me." Harun reached into his breast pocket. "Do not be angry with your men for missing it. It is very thin." He laid the air-letter envelope on the table.

Leopold unfolded it.

"Her description of death is very soothing, is it not?"

"Where is your father?"

"I have no idea."

"What does he do?"

"Collects trash, I think."

Harun watched Leopold's eyes search the letter again for a secret that wasn't there. His oversized features were unfit to project nuance. Harun imagined Leopold's childhood: the blows, the skulking away, the slipping back among others as if nothing had happened. No choice for someone like that but to cultivate depravity. No chance of love. Nothing to temper or starve his innate cruelty.

Harun had a sudden urge to know how Leopold lived. What direction did his bedroom face? What did he see first in the morning? Did he read the Bible, the Koran, or dismiss both? Had a woman ever kissed him? Instead he asked, "May I know why you arrested the imam?"

"Because he is a traitor?"

"And the baker?"

"A traitor too?"

"Am I a traitor?"

"Everyone is a traitor. It is easier that way."

"Can you tell me why I am really here?"

"Because someone has to be."

Harun nodded. Everyone needed a reason to exist, even Leopold. "May I offer advice?"

Leopold gestured with his slender cigarette for Harun to continue.

"Never wear another man's shoes."

What made him say that? He didn't even mean it. Not in the way it sounded. Aristocratic. Slightly threatening. As if he and Leopold were enacting a scene from a stodgy British drama. Harun didn't even care about the shoes. Just loathed going barefoot. If they had given him leaves to strap onto his feet, he would have been satisfied.

Harun had heard about the easily concealed weapons the security police kept in their pockets, the special rings they wore to mar their victims. The Syrian equivalent of brass knuckles was how he imagined them, never expecting to taste their effect.

⣿

Sayeed felt absurd waiting in the darkroom to be instructed by Mohammed about steaming open the envelope. The characters Sayeed disliked most in films behaved like this. Men who ended up dead or forgotten, frame wasters. He slipped out to drop off the dog at a friend's and, when it came time to pray, asked Mohammed nothing.

He mounted two nearly identical photos of Alexandra side by side on the stereoscope. The viewpoint was perfect, foreground and background distinct. He could make out the drawing of Dr. Arman emerging on Alexandra's sketchpad and also her subject dozing against Ebla's crumbling wall.

She was now his Miranda. He had no other muse from which to construct the role. The cinema club expected him to show up with a plan. He'd never failed them, but he knew nothing about his subject. How could he possibly understand Miranda when he judged and analyzed everything and everyone in the context of films he'd seen?

Alexandra watched him from the doorway for a beat, wishing she had half his ability to focus that fiercely. "I have an idea."

Sayeed lowered the stereoscopic viewer.

"What if we combined the drafts before you show it to your theater group? If they're going to hate it, give them something to really hate. Then maybe you can get away with more."

Sayeed laughed. "Did you learn that in graduate school?"

"No. Whenever I was really excited about something, my mother never let me do it. It took a while, but I learned if I added something outrageous to the mix, the original thing seemed okay by comparison. People like saying no. So give them something to say no to."

"That actually makes sense."

"What were you looking at?"

He handed her the viewer. Alexandra was flattered to be the subject of his fixation.

"Wow . . . I've seen old-fashioned prints like this a couple of times. How did you do it?"

"With a lot of a practice. When I take the two photographs they must be offset perfectly, trying to duplicate what our right and left eyes distinctly see."

"I wondered how it worked. I assumed it was magic."

"No, not magic. It is how we see the world. The spacing between our eyes gives us the illusion of depth. I just re-create that."

"You're brilliant." She ran her hand along the viewer's polished wood.

"My father bought it in England. He studied there before the war."

She glanced around the darkroom. "Do you have any more of these?"

Sayeed got down a box and mounted two more photographs. Alexandra was unsettled to see Dr. Lakhosh stirring the goat stew over Ebla's fire pit, the encampment's tents behind him.

She handed back the viewer. "What do you think is taking Dr. Arman so long?"

"He is sitting in some official's waiting room, or being shunted from office to office."

"What did you do with the dog?"

"I left it with a friend. I'll pick it up later."

"Doesn't it have a name yet? It really needs one. Everything deserves a name."

"What would you like to call it?"

Alexandra considered all the pet names she kept lists of as a child. "How about Olivia?"

"That is a dramatic name for such a sad-looking dog."

"Maybe it's just what she needs."

"Like the name Alexandra."

"Exactly. I should get back to the archive, but please let me know when Dr. Arman returns. And if you'd like to work more on your *Tempest* later, I'm free."

▓

Harun counted his cellmates. Still thirteen. No one had been taken or added. He asked the imam how long he had been gone and was surprised to hear it had been three prayer cycles. The imam brushed dirt from Harun's forehead and mouth. "Your wounds must be cleaned. Hakeem and I are happy to share our water ration, but I am not sure the others will."

Hakeem tore a strip from his shirt and dabbed at Harun's split lip, then at a cut under his eye, picking off the coagulated blood with his long fingernails. "Did you find out why you are here?"

"I am a traitor."

"We are all equal in the eyes of the little man with the big head."

"My mother is dying," Harun murmured.

"Do not be sad. When it happens, her heart will fly to heaven."

Harun closed his eyes. Before his mother had started writing, his memories of childhood were vague, just a handful of negative episodes that acted like buoys to navigate around.

"Do you have a wife?" Hakeem asked. Harun shook his head. "Brothers or sisters?" Another head shake. "Is your father still alive?"

"No. Perhaps. I do not know."

"I am sorry. When your mother dies, you will be alone."

Two guards brought the soup, and again no bowls. The daily ritual was reenacted, though this time Harun was ordered to empty the defecation bucket. He held his ribs to suppress the pain and distracted himself by picturing the wondrous public baths in ancient Rome that Sana had so expertly described. He thought of her curves in his embrace, her wet tongue inside his mouth, her love of water basins and purification rituals, almost as deep as his own. He scarcely remembered where he was until shoved into a putrid room with a slimy floor, a small opening at its center the size of a golf green's hole. The only way to reach it meant walking through excrement that had slopped over from previous buckets inmates tried to empty from the doorway. But like an insidious golf green designed by a master, the incline back toward the door doomed any attempt.

Harun summoned the image of the mummified crocodile raised on its wooden bier, reminding himself that it had once skulked the Nile's fetid muck during the dry season. It knew how to attack, how to survive, pouncing with such intent its prey had no chance. He followed the crocodile's example, surging into the room, one barefoot step after another, waste browning his toes. Only after he'd dumped the bucket did he realize the little prisoner wasn't showering him with abuse, but was utterly silent, and had been since Harun had challenged Leopold.

Alexandra pressed her palms against a cuneiform tablet, trying to sense the energy Sayeed had captured in his photos. After working on *The Tempest,* she'd begun to think he possessed a wizard-like quality that allowed him to extract something eternal from molecules of cold stone, landscapes, or faces. She wondered if he'd found a way to project all that he is and had been onto the object within his view at the moment the shutter clicked, giving his images the collective force of many lives lived.

She'd felt a similar effect from Dr. Arman, an amassed energy that effortlessly flowed, allowing him to discern complex connections among seemingly discordant concepts. Her instincts on the plane to Damascus had been correct. She didn't belong here, not because she wasn't ready, but because she was here for the wrong reason. It was a city's lines, a logogram's shape, a language's patterns—the way things were enclosed in space and the space between—that fueled her daydreams.

Daydream was a word she'd been taught to distrust until she audited a history of architecture class. The instructor spoke vividly about the space between conception and execution as daydreaming's most dynamic ground. Alexandra often sat in the back of the lecture hall, eyes closed, absorbing words and ideas never heard in her own field. She considered it time off from the rigors of her regular courses, never understanding that she was in fact doing deep work, daydreaming her way into an alliance of ideas, until a fellow student pointed it out.

Her fingertip traced a chiseled dog at the cuneiform tablet's edge. What was its story? Where was it headed? What drew it to the space beyond the tablet? These questions interested her more than recording the precise translation did. Her imagination ran wild with possible answers until Sayeed barged into the archive. He set the manila envelope from Egypt in front of her, laying out what he suspected from what little he knew.

"Are you looking for my advice, Sayeed, or an accomplice?"

He shrugged. "There is a teakettle in Dr. Lakhosh's office, if we decide to open it."

Alexandra noticed the hospital's return address, then asked Sayeed why the letters might've prompted Harun's arrest. Sayeed admitted to knowing nothing except that Harun's father was American.

"If this were my letter, I'd be furious someone had opened it, unless it saved me from disaster. Then I'd be grateful. But if we do open it, we shouldn't pretend we didn't but take the consequences."

She stared at the envelope for a beat, then tore it open. "It's better if Dr. Lakhosh gets angry at someone he can't fire. Besides, he doesn't have a high opinion of Americans to begin with." She reached inside the envelope to find a smaller, sealed, unaddressed envelope inside. "Oh, that's a bummer." Alexandra held the envelope up to the light. "There may be a photograph in here."

Sayeed flopped onto a stool. "Dr. Arman warned me not to pry."

"If you really think the answer lies with his mother, instead of prying, let's ask her. I'll place a call to Victoria Hospital at the post office. If that doesn't work, I'll send a telegram."

"You know all international calls and telegrams are monitored."

"I'll be careful."

"Should I go with you?"

"No. Let me appear like a stupid American. What can they do?"

"Detain you again."

"Yes, but I always have the American embassy. You don't." Alexandra grabbed her purse. "Let me know how it goes with your theater group."

En route to the post office, she rehearsed what to say but, when faced with a two-hour wait to place international calls, was forced to telegram cryptically in Arabic. She agonized over the message, tearing up form after form until hitting on one tantalizingly simple sentence.

She rushed home in case Dr. Lakhosh's mother decided to phone. Eldridge was furious that she'd given out the Collinwood's number, even though she explained it was an emergency. Her detention had shaken Eldridge more than she'd realized. The way he shouted and threatened to throw her out—someone might have thought his future in Syria was at stake, not hers.

Amid his tirade, the phone rang. Eldridge thrust the receiver at her. There were distinct clicking noises, then a woman's raspy voice came on the line. Alexandra didn't know if the short man had staged the call, but the clicking meant someone surely was listening. The woman claimed to be Farah Lakhosh and there was nothing to be gained by distrusting her.

Eldridge and Mrs. August gasped when Alexandra explained that Dr. Lakhosh was suspected of being a spy. This was, of course, ridiculous, she added, but since arriving in Damascus she'd been surprised by how the most innocuous things were misinterpreted by the authorities. She explained that she herself had been suspected of involvement in completely preposterous events. Alexandra admitted to Farah that telegramming may have been an overreaction, but, being American, she was the only one who could risk getting in touch. She asked if there was anything Farah could tell her that might clear up this misunderstanding, or if there was something in her recent letters that had confused the authorities.

Farah's ragged breathing stretched the uneasy silence. Alexandra had to stop herself from filling it with promises she couldn't keep. The silence felt unendurable. She had no capacity for another's uncertainty because she had no capacity for her own. Alexandra was sure this trait was her father's fault. His silences, even during their treasured hangman games, had always rattled her as a child. And so she talked and talked until she began to think that her voice was what was keeping her alive. Finally, she offered to telegram Farah each day with news, but Farah insisted that she'd come to Damascus immediately, and asked Alexandra to meet her tomorrow at the train station.

▒

Harun moistened his lips with his water ration, three finger dips into the communal cup. He didn't mind the thirst or dehydration—the less he urinated, the better—but seeing blood in his piss made him anxious. As the others prayed he half dozed, lulled by their soft whispers.

Shortly after prayers, the guards returned, prodding Harun down the long corridor filled with moans reminiscent of the mangy dog's after he'd bathed it and left it to dry in the bathroom. He'd assumed the dog was scared to be shut up in a small room, so he'd put it into the kitchen, but when he'd left to change clothes, the moans had resumed. Just as the German cleaning woman clung to her Arab love and he to his German hausfrau, the dog had tasted real companionship and needed Harun in sight.

Leopold appeared more agitated when Harun arrived at the interrogation room. He circled around to Harun's back. "Miss Pierce sent a telegram to Egypt. Why would she do that?"

"You will have to ask her."

"What she wrote seems harmless enough." Harun heard paper crinkling. "Your son did not get the letter. Please call me. The American's emphasis on *the* letter is what intrigues me."

Harun willed himself to relax.

"There are many such seemingly innocuous communiqués that move between Syria and its enemies in just this way. Do you know the contents of this letter?"

"Yes . . . and no."

A fist slammed into Harun's kidney, catching him by surprise. He dropped to his knees.

"What is in this specific letter? One so important the American girl knows about it."

"You know as much as I do, and even more than the American girl, but you do not have the ability to add two and two together."

The next blow landed between his shoulder blades, knocking the breath out of him. Harun curled onto his side.

"Do the math for me."

"I showed you my mother's last letter," Harun panted. "So obviously, this letter, *the* letter in question, is to my father."

Leopold stepped over him. "You said you do not know where your father is."

"That is right."

"Yet you think you will find him."

"No. My mother thinks I will find him. I will do nothing."

Leopold thrust his hands into his pockets. The shoulders of his suit rode up toward his ears. Again, Harun was struck by how much the man resembled an oversized chimpanzee.

"Your story makes no sense. Why else would the American girl be involved?"

Harun laughed. "You clearly know nothing about American females."

"I need no one's permission to execute you."

Harun called what he hoped was a bluff. "Do as you will."

"Is your father also Egyptian?"

Harun flinched. The chimpanzee was finally on the right track. "I do not know."

"You are lying. Is he Lebanese?"

Harun hesitated. Was it worse for Leopold to think he was half-Lebanese or half-American? He rose to his knees. He could almost feel the facts and misperceptions piling up one on top of the other, the truth condemned to sink under the weight of Leopold's need for a conspiracy.

"Very well. I will take this up with your mother."

"My mother . . . ?"

"Oh, yes . . . She and the American girl have spoken. Your mother is coming to Syria."

Sayeed combined their *Tempest* drafts as Alexandra had suggested. He had only one copy when the cinema club members arrived at the abandoned warehouse, so Sayeed asked Tarek and Adil to read the two other parts with him for the group. The scene was a bold beginning and, as Tarek preferred, not a spoof, but it was still Shakespeare. Adil, with his deep voice, played Prospero to Tarek's Miranda. Sayeed read the staged action and took on the role of Caliban. The three men stood shoulder to shoulder under a dim bulb, their voices assaulting the darkness.

ACT 1 SCENE 1. A FIGURE sleeps under a blanket. Strands of blonde wavy hair drape across a pillow. PROSPERO furtively approaches. Leans over the figure he thinks is his daughter, Miranda.

PROSPERO: Sweet eyes, gentle smile, gave me strength to steer that wretched bark safely to these shores . . . Now fourteen years hence, same eyes, lips, burn into me, something base and depraved.

Thunder CLAPS. Prospero peels back the blanket. Finds his slave, CALIBAN. Deformed, nearly naked, human, yet somehow not, Caliban's wavy hair is but a crude wig of woven reeds.

Caliban snickers. Strikes a seductive schoolgirl come-hither pose, mocking Prospero, who shakes his fist at the sky. Thunder CLAPS. Caliban spreads his legs. A jagged bolt of lightning descends from the rafters. Strikes the bed right between them. He looks at the audience, wide-eyed.

CALIBAN: That was close.

MIRANDA, Prospero's daughter, rushes in, her wavy blonde hair tousled. Seeing Caliban in her bed, she looks to her father to explain. Prospero strikes Caliban with a stick that magically appears in his hand. As Caliban flees, Miranda yanks off his wig, revealing a tangled mass of filthy hair.

MIRANDA: What was Caliban doing in my bed . . . again?

PROSPERO: I have done nothing but in the care of thee, my dear one, my daughter.

MIRANDA: Were you caring for me when I was raped by your creature, your slave, Caliban? Was this with your connivance or your negligence? The difference is small, though important. I don't get to ask these questions in the other play.

PROSPERO: You are not the protagonist, and Caliban merely a slave.

MIRANDA: To help you dominate him with your magic you made me tutor him. Your daughter, tutor to her rapist. Teaching him the language he had not when atop me, flailing and pounding. That thing inside me as he smiled brutishly then dripped his vile fluids on the sand . . . which I once loved for its purity.

PROSPERO: Stop speaking, my child, and take a breath. Your words flow so swiftly you are apt to drown.

MIRANDA: I will go on speaking to hear what I say for the first time. You robbed me of my speeches in that other play. I'll take back as much time on this stage now as you took from me with your treacherous blather repeated throughout the globe.

PROSPERO (helplessly to the audience): What is this globe of which she speaks? Besides this isle, I've never stepped foot outside Milan.

His jest inflames Miranda's fury. Prospero grabs her as she stalks off.

PROSPERO: Forgive me, I see 'tis time to inform thee further. Lend thy hand and pluck thy magic garment from me. I will tell you the tale. The hour has now come. Obey and be attentive.

MIRANDA (pulls away from Prospero): Poor Ariel. Poor Caliban. All those you rule over. I know now how they suffer from your manipulation as much as I do. Your powers are warped through fear, Father.

PROSPERO: Miranda . . . Please listen . . .

MIRANDA: No, Father . . . You have brought this tempest on yourself!

The pages trembled in Sayeed's hand during the tense silence. He apologized for straying so far from the group's aims, but suggested that what he'd written could be used as a template for a bold attack on Assad. One serious vignette nestled among nine satires might just slide past the censor. Tarek and Adil remained at his side as the room erupted in disagreement. Some members were offended by Miranda's language, others now feared their title—*The Adventures of the Ingenious Gentleman Ad-Ass al Fez-Ha of the Moon*—would doom their project outright.

Tarek jumped onto a chair and shouted above the others. "Sayeed has given us an opportunity to expand our focus. We can do both *Othello* and *The Tempest* if everyone still wants to, but why not include satires about tyrannical goatherds, despotic village chiefs, imperious censors desperately trying to hold on to their pathetic little fiefdoms? We can have a train conductor who declares his train car his kingdom and will not let passengers disembark until they swear allegiance to him. An authoritarian policeman whose empire consists of a mouse cage at the zoo, and whose sole job is to guard the mouse so it does not scare the lion to death. Each main character can have one quality or fact that is essentially, though obliquely, Assad. And perhaps it will slide past the censors if we return to our original title, *The Bastard Kings.*"

Ghazwan sat, a quizzical expression on his face as more arguments flared. Sayeed desperately wanted the old man's approval, but he seemed lost in his own world. Soon, however, he rose.

Sayeed bolted after him. "I know what I wrote is impossible. That it can never get made."

"I must go. My youngest daughter is in hospital giving birth. This will be my tenth grandchild."

"Mabrouk!" the others exclaimed, then quieted as Adil approached their eldest member. "Before you go . . . What do you think about this *Tempest?*"

Ghazwan licked his dry lips. "It should be longer, more of a political fable. Miranda must ultimately stand in for Syria. Let us build on what Sayeed bravely gave us and, if possible, keep his words." He then turned to face Tarek. "And let us listen to our young friend and follow his advice, for who is Assad if not the perfect bastard king?"

Harun paced in a corner of the cell, anxious for the day's interrogation to begin. It was past midday prayers and the guards still hadn't come for him. He had spent all night constructing a story. Now he must tell it before Leopold got to his mother. He turned and bumped into Hakeem, who had raked his bald scalp with his fingernails into a mass of crisscrossing welts.

"No more counting. The imam has asked me to stop," Hakeem lamented.

"He probably wants to give you a rest."

"No. I have lost a number. The one that comes between twenty-nine and thirty-one."

"You mean thirty."

"That is what the imam said, but you are both wrong." His kind face contorted in anguish. "It is half of sixty, you know, the number that is lost."

"Maybe if we count together we can find it," Harun suggested.

Hakeem bowed his head. "No. I cannot. It has been forbidden."

Harun took out his pocket watch. "Inside here is a clock. If we can get this open, no one will have to count any more."

Hakeem's eyes brightened and he reached out his hand for the watch. Harun reluctantly laid it in his palm. "It is very special to me. Please take care with it."

Hakeem's fingers delicately ran over the watch until a fingernail caught on the lock. He gazed in fascination at the tiny keyhole. "It looks like a small cross will open it."

"Should we try to make one?"

Hakeem smiled and gave back the watch, eager to search for something to fashion into a cross. Harun went over to talk to the imam. "Why did you forbid Hakeem to count? It is all he has."

"I did not forbid him. It is in his head. This has happened twice before."

"Has he gone crazy?"

The imam shrugged. "Hopefully this episode will pass quickly . . . without incident."

"That sounds ominous."

"During the first episode he broke Bashir's leg."

Harun glanced at the inmate whose leg was splinted. "He told me Leopold did that."

"I am sure he believes that. Three years is a long time to be in here."

Footsteps reverberated down the corridor. The men burrowed

deeper into the corners, as if melting into the grime would protect them from interrogation. One guard leveled his gun at the prisoners. The other unlocked the cell. Harun stepped forward as a surname was barked out, but it wasn't his. No one responded and the guards shouted the name again. The imam glanced at Hakeem, who continued his search, oblivious to the guards' warnings for him to stop moving.

"He is unwell," the imam explained. "Come back in an hour. I will prepare him."

Hakeem retrieved something from under the sink, then turned excitedly toward Harun. The guards cocked their guns and ordered Hakeem to the floor, but he walked on, palm held out, a child intent on sharing his discovery. The inmates' pleas were drowned out by the guards' frenzied commands as their authority gave way to panic. The younger guard burst into the cell and leveled his gun at Hakeem's chest. Harun's memory flashed to an archeological student at Oxford—blue-eyed, copper-headed, the perfect chap, always good for a round at the pub, never let the cricket team down, the first to volunteer to be lowered into the hole above a cave-in. His funeral was attended by hundreds. After Sana stopped writing, Harun wanted to die like that to show her what she'd given up.

Harun stepped in front of the gun, "Please calm down. He does not understand."

The guard pushed Harun to his knees. Rammed the gun barrel against his neck. Harun considered praying, but was facing north, and since he didn't know all the words to any Jewish prayer, decided this wasn't the moment to mess with the wrathful Jewish God. He hadn't read much about Him, just enough to sense He was a God to be feared, not loved. A God that thought nothing of killing firstborns or inflicting plagues. So instead, Harun mumbled the text on the yellowing label beneath his beloved crocodile. "Symbol of the cult of Sobek, son of Set, god of turmoil and thunder. Sobek rose from the dark water to create the universe, but allied himself with the forces of . . .

. . . chaos" rolled off his tongue as the shot rang out.

▞▞

Alexandra braved Mrs. August's nonstop chatter in the courtyard for hours to avoid Eldridge, and because she expected Sayeed would drop by with news. He still hadn't appeared when Nicole and Jean-Paul returned from a soirée at the French embassy, interrupting a story Alexandra had already heard twice. Nicole, in evening gown and heels, struggled to steer a drunken Jean-Paul across the uneven tiles toward the front door.

Mrs. August raised her glass to Nicole. "Like crossing a minefield, ma chère." Nicole nodded and pushed Jean-Paul through the front door.

"That was me twenty years ago. I adored my Bertie, but . . ." Mrs. August knocked back the rest of the drink, then reached out her hand so that Alexandra could help her up. "If you're waiting for that young man to visit again, my dear, I'd advise you to go to bed."

"Why?"

Mrs. August gave a benevolent smile and patted Alexandra on the head on her way inside. "Because he is Arab and you are American."

Alexandra curled up in the rattan chair, grateful to be born in an era when people didn't think like that any more. That whole generation needed to die for something better to take hold, and Alexandra would be part of the renaissance. It was nice to have the patio to herself. Listen to the city. Sounds she could recognize, but that would never be truly familiar. She was anxious to know if Dr. Arman had learned anything, and how Sayeed's theater group had received their *Tempest*. Sayeed would come, she knew it, so she was genuinely surprised when Richard Poole strolled through the gate.

"How did you find me?"

"I'm a pretty resourceful guy. And when you work at the American embassy it's easy to find out where every American in Damascus is. Especially ancient language scholars."

"I may be the only one here."

"Surprisingly, you're not. But the other is sixty-eight."

"Would you like a drink or anything?"

"No, thank you. I was on my way home and thought, why not walk in the completely wrong direction for a change and ask that lovely Alexandra Pierce out to dinner?"

"What did she say?"

"I think she said yes."

"Well, she's not a stupid girl, you know."

"Saturday all right? Pick you up at seven?"

"Seven is good. Do you mind leaving your phone number?"

"In case you want to cancel?"

"No. Something happened and it would've been good to have had your number, not that they let me phone anyone."

"What are you talking about?"

"The Syrian authorities detained me overnight. They thought I might be a Lebanese spy."

"And they didn't allow you to phone the embassy?"

"No. And remember the man I introduced you too . . . My boss . . . Now they've arrested him. In fact, I thought you were someone else coming with news."

Richard handed her his phone number. "Drop by the embassy tomorrow to make a report."

"If you think that's necessary."

"It's necessary."

Alexandra waited another hour for Sayeed before heading to bed. She left a note for him tacked to the front door in case he showed up in the middle of the night. She wanted him to know she'd be meeting Farah at the train station tomorrow, and then would bring her straight to the museum.

Mikha'il was hunched over his desk, absorbed in writing to a culture ministry friend about interceding on Harun's behalf, when Sayeed rushed into his office and gave him Alexandra's note.

Dr. Arman looked up in disbelief. Sayeed dropped the cache of Farah's letters in front of him. "The security police surely know his mother is here. They will eventually pick her up, and when they do not find these on her, they will come here."

"First, you want me to read them. Now you want me to hide them."

"That. Or we should destroy them."

"We have no idea what they say. They may be innocuous."

"Do you really want to take that chance?"

Dr. Arman swept up the stack. "Why would Alexandra do something so foolish?"

"I am equally responsible. I did not stop her from contacting Dr. Lakhosh's mother. I just never thought she would come here."

Dr. Arman scanned his chaotic office. Sayeed was right. It was the perfect place to temporarily stash a half-dozen letters. As he laid them between heavy abstracts piled behind heaps of folders, he noticed the unaddressed, sealed envelope. "What is this?"

"It came inside another envelope from his mother. There was no letter. Just that."

As Dr. Arman hid it, Sayeed noticed the sketch Alexandra had started of him at Ebla.

"She took your advice. My head is more oblong. Please . . . do not be embarrassed. You have an excellent eye." Dr. Arman returned his attention to finishing his plea for help, then sealed the letter and set off for the ministry.

Sayeed returned to Harun's office to wait for Alexandra and Farah. He closed the office door and sat in the vestibule beneath his Ebla photographs, consumed by fear. Not the fear he'd experienced as a boy when he thought about life without his parents, but one that stemmed entirely from doubt. He thought he'd come to terms with certain failures of his personality. So he wasn't the rebel he'd hoped, but why did he so quickly insist to Ghazwan that his and Alexandra's *Tempest* could never get made? For all his criticism of Harun's lack of boldness, Sayeed realized he was the one disengaging from life. Adept at thrusting himself into things or explicating ideas just far enough to appear radical. But even his thrusts were sloppy and backed up by nothing but imperious wind.

Alexandra and Farah entered, accompanied by Leopold and two men. Leopold barged into Harun's office and gestured for Sayeed to follow. Instead, Sayeed introduced himself to Farah. Up close, her sallow skin seemed almost transparent in spots, and though her eyes were cloudy, they were the only part of her that resembled Harun.

"It is a pleasure to meet you, Sayeed. I am sorry for this trouble."

Her voice had nothing of Dr. Lakhosh's studied cultivation. Sayeed would have liked to say more, but Leopold thrust him inside the office and closed the door.

"According to Farah Lakhosh . . . I have arrested the wrong man. But I am inclined to think I have arrested the right man, but for the wrong reason."

"I did not know you needed a reason to arrest anyone."

Leopold flashed a sly smile. "What film will you and your friends view next?"

"I have no idea."

"And this film your group intends to make . . . Do you think that will happen?"

Sayeed forced himself to remain composed. This could mean only one thing. Someone in the cinema club was an informant. "Yes. Some day."

"Then you are not as intelligent as I imagined."

"If you have arrested Dr. Lakhosh for the wrong reason, what is the right one?"

Leopold glanced around the room. "So . . . where are the rest of the letters? I have already read the one Dr. Lakhosh had with him. He showed it to me quite freely."

"Apparently it did not give you what you need."

"I need very little."

"What did his mother say was in her letters?"

"Nothing but foolish memories."

"That sounds right."

151

"So you have read these letters?"
"No. But I did burn them."

The cell was silent, motionless. Guards and prisoners, tableau-like, bodies and expressions fixed in surprise and horror, reminiscent of doomed Pompeians. The only sign of life was the small rivulet of Hakeem's blood, trickling across the uneven floor. He didn't so much fall as buckle, knees landing first so that he dropped backwards between them, feet beside his waist, like a female gymnast warming up.

The imam was already praying before he reached the body. A few others joined in, a ragged chorus. Harun mumbled the prayer unconsciously, having recited it dozens of times outside the British cemetery in Alexandria, convinced his father was buried there.

The guards soundlessly retreated as the cellmates focused on Hakeem's body, marred only by the hole through his forehead. He showed no other signs of distress, asleep more than dead, his palms lying open to heaven.

The imam sat cross-legged next to the cooling body. Harun adopted the same pose on the opposite side, realizing he'd soon be doing this beside his mother. Her letters had so infuriated him that he didn't follow their thread to its logical end. He may have told Leopold that his mother's depiction of death was soothing, but those were words unattached to his body.

Bashir, whose leg Hakeem had broken, dragged himself over and unwrapped the splint Hakeem had made for him. He used the tattered blanket to cover Hakeem's body, but parts of it remained hopelessly exposed. When he tucked Hakeem's hand underneath a corner, Harun spotted a sliver lying in the dead baker's palm. It was cross-shaped, small enough to fit in the watch's keyhole, but far too brittle. The instant Harun picked it up, it broke in two. That was why Hakeem had ignored the guards. He'd needed to open the watch, stop the counting, put an end to missing numbers.

No soup arrived. No one demanded they empty the defecation bucket. Hours slipped by before two different guards came in with a stretcher and ordered Harun and the imam to load the body. They couldn't straighten Hakeem's rigor-mortised legs, so they rolled him onto his stomach and let his bent knees drop over the sides. He might have been an ancient Greek deity—half human, half grasshopper.

They carried the stretcher into a distant part of the prison. Doors flanked both sides of the corridor, the layout similar to old photos Harun had seen of British sanitariums. He wondered if the prison had once been an insane asylum, but the idea that the Syrian state would jail and feed someone they could just as easily make disappear seemed absurd. The wing was eerily silent. Perhaps this area was the morgue. Harun hoped Hakeem's body would be returned to his family, but feared it'd be lost forever in the prison's vast nothingness, another victim of morbid Leopold.

The guard leading the way opened a door. Harun swung the front end of the stretcher through the opening, not surprised to see Leopold waiting inside. As usual his suit was impeccably pressed, and though the room was sweltering, no perspiration dotted his brow. He gestured for them to set the stretcher on the only piece of furniture, an empty desk from a bygone era, and then he examined the hole left by the bullet where it had exited through the back of Hakeem's head. "A good clean shot," he observed with satisfaction, then poked at the stiff, bent legs. "But a ridiculous pose to die in."

The guards escorted the imam out. Harun followed, but the door was shut in his face. "Your mother is a pleasant woman. A terrible liar, but pleasant."

Harun fixed his expression before he turned, mimicking a painting he'd seen in London of Winston Churchill. Though Churchill usually appeared steely, sometimes grim and wily, this painting captured something different. It reminded Harun of the mummified crocodile, fierce but without a conscience, and with eyes that had never glimpsed the sun. A look that, if Hitler had ever seen it, might have given him pause. "Yes. My mother is a terrible liar."

"Your assistant is a terrible liar too. He says he burned your mother's letters."

"There, you are wrong. Sayeed is quite capable of that."

"We shall see if his story changes by morning."

"So he has been arrested?"

"Yes. Along with your mother."

Stone-faced, Harun approached Hakeem's body. "This man was mentally ill."

"He was a murderer. That is all that matters."

"I thought he was a traitor." For a second Leopold appeared perturbed. "So we are all more nuanced than you let on."

"Would you like to see your mother?"

Harun shrugged.

Leopold studied him with the same thoroughness he'd shown Hakeem's wound. "You, on the other hand, are a very good liar."

Harun likewise scrutinized Leopold with an intensity he had formerly reserved for water basins. "I have finally pieced together who you remind me of."

Leopold took out a cigarette and, after lighting it, set the spent match on Hakeem's back.

"There was a short man in Alexandria I walked past every day on my way to school. He sold postcards. No one ever bought any because he had already written messages on them. When I asked him why, he said it was easier for people to have someone else do their lying."

Leopold let out a dry, barking laugh.

"The more we lie, the easier it is for you to do your job. You are not really interested in the truth. Just the outcome." Harun ignored Leopold's condescending grin. "If you were interested in the truth, you would have asked me what my mother had written in her other letters instead of focusing on the one I could not possibly have read."

"I see. Now you wish to tell me what was in those letters. What do you want in return?"

"Deport my mother to Egypt. It will be such a nuisance if she dies here."

"How do I know that what you will tell me will be worth it?"

Harun took a deep breath. "Take me to my mother and I will prove it."

Leopold nodded to a waiting guard.

"One piece of information. That is all you will get. Since I know you will not be disappointed, I will want proof my mother has been set free."

"Agreed."

"For the second piece of information, you will release Sayeed. And he will escort my mother back to Egypt."

"That I cannot do. He is a traitor."

"No. He is an impetuous but harmless young man interested in movies and photography."

"He is planning to make a clandestine film critical of Assad by way of mockery."

Harun couldn't contain his laughter. "Syria is on the brink of war—unemployment high, Lebanon slipping away, Israel making inroads with former allies—and you are telling me this regime is so fragile it cannot withstand what will surely be an amateur piece of work that hardly anyone will see. Assad should welcome such efforts. Better malcontents throw themselves into politics by way of art and not revolt."

"They have broken the law and must be punished."

"You are a smart man, but there are some things you do not understand, so you must take my word for this. Art never happens quickly. Consensus is nearly impossible to reach. This film of theirs will take years to finish, and disagreements will prolong it at every turn. By then the laws, and maybe even this regime, will change."

Leopold considered Harun's analysis. "I will think about your proposal after I hear what this valuable piece of information is."

The door opened. Farah unsteadily entered. Though alarmingly thin and very pale, she was still elegant, and Harun had to restrain himself from going to her. She didn't see him at first, only the dead body, and thinking it might be her son, her anguish filled the room.

Harun forced himself to remain as emotionless as possible. "How are you, Mother?"

Farah stumbled toward him, relieved, though shocked to see his deplorable state. Harun backed away in that peculiar way she hadn't seen since he was a child. Her heart tightened to think that even under such extreme circumstances he was still afraid to accept her love.

"Mother . . . My father was American, correct?"

Farah shook her head. Gave Harun a severe look, imploring him to stop.

"I need you to tell this man the truth, Mother."

"Why?"

"Because I have promised."

"I do not care what they do to me. I am dying anyway."

"Please . . . for me . . . tell him. If you do, they will let me go."

Farah's eyes drifted from Harun to Hakeem. Would this happen to her son if she lied? "Yes. Your father was American."

Harun turned toward Leopold. "What I tell you next will interest you even more."

Farah lunged toward him before the guard caught her by the arm. "Harun . . . no!"

Leopold's twitchy fingers came to his chin, reflexively stroking it like an adolescent searching for that first peachy stubble. "Goodbye, Mrs. Lakhosh. It has been a pleasure."

With that, Farah was swept out. She craned her neck for a final glance of Harun. He felt Leopold's eyes on him. No beginnings, no endings, he repeated to himself as he burned the image of her exit into his memory. At the last moment, he touched the tip of his nose, his last gesture of love.

What had Alexandra done? She used to lie in bed at night and tell herself, Don't fall asleep. If I do, I'll stop breathing. I'll choke to death on my dreams. I'll wake up in another bed, far, far away. I won't recognize anyone. There won't be someone to take me to school. Then, between the ages of fourteen and eighteen, she had slept peacefully while everyone else her age was besieged by sleepless adolescent angst. But after camping in Death Valley, it started again. If she dozed off, she dreamt of mutilated cacti or haunted mesas. Her teeth regularly fell out between 3 and 4 a.m. Driving the nauseating snakeback from Big Sur to Carmel made her head wobbly, her legs shake, her palms sweat fog. Would a highway crew even bother to retrieve her body?

Don't close your eyes, she told herself. The police have sent you home like a naughty child. You got Harun's mother and Sayeed arrested. If you fall asleep, they'll vanish forever.

There was a knock at her bedroom door. Alexandra sprang out of bed. Rafi stood in the hallway. "The woman from Egypt is here. The police dropped her off. She is quite ill."

Downstairs, Nicole sat on a sofa beside Farah holding a glass of water to her lips. Alexandra knelt in front of her. "Thank God they let you go. Should we call a doctor?"

"That would be pointless."

Nicole put down the glass. "Mrs. Lakhosh . . . let us help you up to Alice's room."

"Thank you. And please call me Farah."

Once Farah was settled in bed, Alexandra was left alone with the dying woman.

"I am a bit confused. Is your name Alice or Alexandra?"

"Both, but I prefer Alexandra. I'm so sorry about everything. I never should've telegrammed."

"I am so happy you did. I saw my son one last time."

"What was it like to see him?"

"Painful yet beautiful. I have caused him much heartache these past few months, but I can see he has changed. No one else would notice, but I can. He is being obstinate and foolish, but also brave, and though it is frightening to think what might happen, I cannot help but be proud." Farah took Alexandra's hand. "Harun wrote to me about you. I can see I was right to defend you."

"Whatever he said was true. I'm sure I'm to blame for what has happened."

"I very much doubt that." Farah rested her head back against the pillow and closed her eyes.

Alexandra was desperate for any news about Sayeed, but couldn't bring herself to ask. Instead, she watched Farah labor to breathe. Her hand was cold, her skin slightly blue. Alexandra was grateful when her eyes opened.

"Are you in love with my son's assistant?"

"I don't know. I might be. We've just begun to know each other."

"Do not think about the future when you think about love. It interferes with your heart."

"I'm not an optimist like you. I spend every day deciphering dead languages and hieroglyphics. It must mean something that I've never come upon a depiction of love."

"Maybe not as we expect it, but look harder. It is surely there."

Alexandra wished that were true. What a relief it would be to stumble upon a cuneiform love letter. To know the heart has always been buoyed or burdened.

▓▓

A dreadful silence had fallen over the cell. A distant moaning settled in the air. Harun became convinced it must be Sayeed. Surely a man like that could survive one night's torture. Or perhaps it was a dog whining. The security apparatus must have reasons to arrest them too.

The imam hadn't counted or prayed since they took Hakeem's body away. He appeared to have gotten shorter too, faith or guilt chipping away at its agent. Who was to say the gray coat, the skullcap, the endless counting and praying wasn't part of a disguise, and underneath lay a murderous thief or a police informant playing at confessor? All this carrying of piss and shit may have been part of Leopold's game. Shooting Hakeem part of it too.

Harun inspected the imam's face as he approached. It was ugly in the way a baby's can be until it settles into the world. Nose squashed, lips puckered from too much sucking on the brass nipple. The imam took Harun's hand. "What you did for Hakeem took faith."

"I was trying to impress an old girlfriend. To show her what she had lost."

The imam's lips parted in an odd smile that showed off his very small teeth, teeth meant for a frog or an even tinier amphibian. "Why did you say you were no longer Muslim?" The imam bobbed his head as if he'd begun counting again. "If you want to pray, I will pray with you now."

Harun placed the imam's hand against his ribs. "There is this rude thing that lives right here, right behind this rib. It recently woke up, but now I think I have killed it."

"I will start and you join me, silently if you wish."

The imam turned his back to Harun and toward Mecca.

Hands tied, face bruised, Sayeed stumbled out of a steel door into a trash-strewn courtyard. The men who'd arrested him and Farah yesterday shoved him forward. Surrounded by windowless brick walls, concealing any sign of the city beyond, Sayeed assumed this was to be his execution. Within seconds, though, he was bundled into the back of a waiting sedan and warned to remain silent.

As they arrived at the Collinwood Arms, one of the men freed his hands. "You will escort Mrs. Lakhosh back to Egypt and remain there on photographic assignment for one month. In the trunk there is a suitcase. Inside is a change of clothes, a passport, a visa, and a camera. Play your part and nothing will happen to the woman."

Alexandra was half-asleep on the sofa when the doorbell rang. She answered it, shocked to see Sayeed with one of the men from yesterday. The man pushed past her, saying they were there to pick up Mrs. Lakhosh. Sayeed explained that he would be escorting Farah back to Egypt.

"Egypt! She isn't well enough to travel to this door. She's upstairs in my room."

The man pointed a gun at Sayeed and told Alexandra to take them to her room. Farah was semi-conscious, her breathing uneven. When the guard stepped forward for a closer look, Alexandra gently touched Sayeed's bruised face. "Are you okay?"

"Yes."

"How long will you be gone?"

"At least a month. You will be back in America by then."

"Maybe I'll stay and be a tour guide."

Sayeed pulled her close. "Dr. Arman has the letters."

"You!" the man shouted at Alexandra. "Wake her."

"I can't wake her. She is dying."

The guard gave Farah a violent shake, to no effect.

Sayeed stepped forward. "Clearly, they will not let her on the plane like this."

The guard glared at Farah for a long time, then grabbed Sayeed and dragged him out. Alexandra chased them downstairs, still shouting Sayeed's name as the sedan squealed away.

■■
■■

Harun flinched as a jet roared overhead. He was grateful his mother wasn't leaving by train. The quicker she returned to hospital, the better. The midday sun baked the sedan's interior, but Leopold insisted the windows remain closed. The driver stepped out for air and Harun glimpsed how close they were to the tarmac. He hoped Sayeed and his mother were booked on a commercial flight, and not one arranged by the security police. The swiftness with which Leopold had obtained Sayeed a visa concerned Harun, but so far Leopold had been good to his word.

Minutes ticked by. The temperature climbed. Sweat finally dripped from Leopold's temples onto his shirt collar. Harun leaned toward him. "There are limits to self-preservation."

"You so enjoy philosophizing, you should write a book. Show everyone what you know."

"I will be thirty-two soon and know almost nothing."

A loud rap on the window interrupted them. Leopold leapt out and slammed the door. Harun let his mind drift, imagining the next few minutes; his mother and Sayeed walking together across the tarmac; their steady climb up the boarding steps to the plane; the car door opening for him to verify their departure. That was how it would happen. His last look of his mother would be from behind as she ducked through the jet's doorway.

The car door flung open. Leopold's large head filled the opening. "Your mother is not coming. She is too sick to travel. If this is a trick, I will kill you both."

"Is Sayeed with her?"

"No. He is here."

"Let him board the plane and I will tell you what I promised."

The words tumbled out. His mother's life was nearly over, and his of no consequence. Sayeed, though, had courage. When they fought in the darkroom five days ago, Sayeed had said, "A man who settles for a small life is really no man at all." Harun had settled long ago. Sayeed never would.

Leopold weighed the situation, then whipped around. "Release him." He yanked Harun out of the car. Harun's bare feet hit the scorching asphalt. Sayeed stood about fifteen meters away. Harun was thankful for the distance between them. Neither could make out the details of the other, so they'd part not knowing what each had been through.

Passengers walked across the tarmac toward the waiting jet, mothers in hijabs, children clinging to their hands, men in djellabahs or business suits. They moved slowly in the sun, each step sinking into the soft asphalt. Harun felt he was drowning in sunlight, the people, apparitions gliding in the distance. Sayeed moved toward them, now among them, entering a wondrously askew world. The boarding steps wavered. The steel frame vanished in the heat. Soon the stairs were gone, and the people floated upward on nothing. Was this hunger, Harun thought, or a new way to see?

The plane taxied, its nose bobbing as if searching the air for food. It didn't strike Harun as a noble creature, its plumage downright dull, and as it hurtled down the runway its awkwardness made it seem irrevocably earthbound. He turned to Leopold. "Where is that plane going?"

"Where it should."

Harun's hunger accelerated the friction inside him. "My father was not only American, but also a Jew."

"So you are a spy for Israel."

Harun laughed. "I do not think I have ever met an Israeli in my life."

Leopold's cheeks darkened. "We had a deal. You have not kept your end of the bargain."

"I said you would find what I had to tell you interesting, not enlightening or definitive."

Harun's tone was haughty, spiteful, and he recognized it as the little prisoner through and through. So the uncouth scoundrel really was a part of him, and now that the inner chaos and voice were silent, Harun realized what remained was a pugnacity he could summon at will.

⋮

Alexandra rang Dr. Arman and asked him to bring the letters to the American embassy. If Harun's father was American, wasn't Harun? It was a long shot, but Alexandra wanted Farah to know her son would be okay before she died.

Except for the clacking of a typewriter, the embassy was hushed. Alexandra waited in the lobby reading the trust papers her father's lawyer had sent. Talking to Sayeed, working on *The Tempest*, watching Farah endure so much to see her son one last time made Alexandra question her actions. If her father died without her showing a single act of acceptance, would she regret it? She didn't want his money, but she wanted to be the type of person capable of an overture of kindness.

She turned to the signature page and clicked the pen top. At some point you need to move on, she told herself. Her mother's hurt had become as damaging as her father's silence. She might not be ready, but it was time. A loopy "A l e" flowed from the pen, when she suddenly stopped to convert the "e" to an "i." The "c" and "e" that followed felt foreign to her hand. She barely recognized her own signature, which seemed appropriate to the moment. It was done. She slid the papers back into the manila envelope as Dr. Arman joined her. He wasn't confident her idea would work, but together they read the letters, looking for anything that might prove their case.

Plunged into Harun's parents' love story, Alexandra and Dr. Arman were forced to confront their own failures of heart. Neither had come close to experiencing such pain or pleasure. For the last few years, while Alexandra had considered a diet of one-night stands, Dr. Arman had contemplated the idea of an arranged marriage. Alexandra suspected it might be the most feminist thing she'd do in life, while Dr. Arman imagined inevitable disaster. Still, unlike Alexandra, he'd recently acted on this impulse. Any woman he spotted on the street who had a chance of being a Copt provoked him to reverse course to follow his potential wife on her errands.

The cigarette tasting list was not the only item recorded in his black notebook. Had Alexandra perused further she would have discovered an array of observations that began in honeyed adulation but ended in desolation after his dream Copt was discourteous to a shop worker or exhibited any imperfection. He was incapable of compassion when he viewed the slightest intolerance, an idiosyncrasy he'd had since childhood.

Yesterday, after failing to induce his Ministry of Culture friend to intercede in Harun's case, Dr. Arman had felt his old despair rise to the surface. Everywhere he looked he saw corruption and contempt, but the truth of Farah's letters revived him. Maronite, Copt, what was he thinking? A woman of his faith wasn't required. Love was all that mattered.

Too sick to travel . . . Was it true, Harun wondered, or was his mother up to some mischief? The guards didn't return him to the cell, but locked him in isolation on the lonely corridor, the sole occupant of the forgotten wing. A rectangular cement sink protruded from a wall. Its dimensions were obscenely pleasing. Harun used his shirt sleeve to measure the distance between the spout and the trough, the trough and the base, the midpoint and the corners. The basin was a perfect example of Pythagoras's golden ratio. It comforted Harun to know that an architect had bothered to infuse beauty in such a place.

He sketched a mental image of the sink to later duplicate on paper if he were ever released. He wanted to send the drawing to Sana. To share its ideal proportions with the one other person who truly appreciated water basins. He crouched against the wall and constructed the letter he'd write to accompany the sketch. The fact that she was probably married and a mother by now crossed his mind, but didn't stop him. The letter was simply his only way forward. He finally grasped the compulsion that had seized his mother. He didn't feel near death like her, but close to the end of something, and writing the letter would push him irrevocably toward it.

Dear Sana,

Twelve years is a long time. My last letter to you was more than unkind; it was unjustified. It has taken me until now to understand why you said you could not love me any more. A man who thwarts desire does not deserve someone else's heart. It is indecent to destroy another person's love, as I did yours. Perhaps it is even a crime. If so, I am paying for it.

Enclosed is a sketch I made of the other passion we once shared. The basin in real life is handsome, flawless, a perfection few can hope to attain. As I stare at it I realize the obvious: birth is not just our beginning, but also the beginning of our end. I know that statement is embarrassingly sophomoric, but the simple truth of it escaped me before today. I have been leading a double life, though unaware of it. If someone had asked me two months ago whether I still loved you, I would have laughed and struggled to re-create our time together. Now, without warning, every moment I spent with you seems etched in copper, no detail too small to remember. It has forced me to ask myself, what is the purpose of love? What is a human being? I think the answer to both is the same.

One particular day we spent together in Greece still torments me. We were sent to the village to buy bread and olives. It was a long walk, and, on the way, you found a headless mouse in the scrub. Its limbs and tail were undamaged, and since there was no blood, you insisted its head must be nearby. You wanted to bury the creature, but would not until we found the head. It was late and I got upset, all the more because by then we cared deeply for one another and I could not understand why that mouse meant more to you at that moment than my happiness. I do not remember my exact words, but they were cruel and insensitive, and we left the mouse, headless and unburied, in the dirt. You behaved with love. You were the human being.

That mouse's ghost has hovered about me for weeks, giving off a queasy stench of death. But it is my own ignorance and arrogance I smell. Though the mouse torments me, it does bring me closer to memories of you, which is a small price to pay for that privilege.

I will send this letter to your parents' address. It is the only one I still have. I pray Lebanon's current crisis does not last long and spares your family. Do not feel obligated to respond to this letter. The writing of it has been healing for me. I hope receiving it has not distressed you. I know it is not an eloquent letter, but it is from my heart. I wish you all the happiness and goodness of the universe.

Sayeed had hoped the plane was bound for Egypt, but as northern, not southern, Damascus passed below, he wasn't surprised to hear their destination was Aleppo. He hadn't really expected that Leopold would let him just walk away, even to escort a dying woman home. Still, he had such a deep desire to visit Egypt that he'd let himself believe it. He was grateful that Harun's mother was too ill to travel. Whatever happened next, at least he wouldn't be responsible for her life too.

Now that he knew the flight would be short, he slid his pencil and Dr. Arman's copy of *The Tempest* into his kurta pocket, and settled back to listen to the whimpering children who'd convinced their parents to let them fast on this first day of Ramadan. He'd done the same when he was their age, wanting desperately to be strong like his father. Then came mid-afternoon, the long hours preceding sunset, when the feeling of unbearable hunger and thirst left a hollow ache in him deep as a well.

Across the aisle, a child too large to be on his mother's lap, yet too disabled to sit alone, drooled on his mother's headscarf. Sayeed listened to his unintelligible gurgles, which seemed to make up a complex language. The boy's fists were in constant motion, his right thumb the only thing he could free from his clenched fingers. When his thumb found its way into his mouth, he quieted for a few minutes, but soon he pulled it out to ramble at it, sounding like other children, mystified and uncomprehending. Occasionally, he found the strength to lift his head on his rubbery neck to gaze at his mother. It was unclear what he saw, but his face brightened each time, and his mother pulled him close in a way that told him he was the most precious thing on earth.

Sayeed closed his eyes to stop the tears. At first he'd pitied the boy, but he now pitied himself. He wasn't sure when he had begun to feel something that might be love for Alexandra. It was agony to realize he'd have no memory of holding her close or tasting her lips.

The whine of the landing gear jarred him. This was his first bird's-eye glimpse of Aleppo. He'd never seen the city from the air before, though, as a boy, he'd been excited to spot the rare plane flying over his grandfather's house. He regretted not taking the time to drive by the old place while he was in the city with Alexandra. He could've shown her the thriving olive tree he'd planted when he was five.

Sayeed stepped aside to let the other passengers exit. A soldier milled about on the tarmac; a few more stood near the terminal. He assumed one of Leopold's men must be on the flight, but no one waited for him to get off. The only other passenger not rushing to depart was the mother with the disabled boy. She calmly adjusted her headscarf as her son's flailing hands repeatedly pulled it off. Sayeed wanted to help her carry the boy down the stairs, but sensed any offer would be rejected.

She lifted her son and made her way one slow step after another. The effort was evident, but without burden. She carried the boy, not as a cross to bear, but with a purpose and pride that bolstered Sayeed. He slowly followed her down the steps, staying close in case she needed him.

The air outside was hot but pristine. Sayeed took long deep breaths as he approached the terminal. The soldier on the tarmac didn't fall in behind him, and after Sayeed opened the door for the woman, the soldiers at the entrance didn't follow him inside. He considered the possibility he truly was no one in the scheme of things, and chuckled at the idea he'd ever thought otherwise. But just ahead, the clean-shaven officer from Ebla leaned lazily against a counter, alone and strangely unarmed, beckoning Sayeed with his smile.

The letters' impact on Richard Poole was profound. As if the sentences before his eyes allowed him to let go of his official body. When he slit open the last unaddressed envelope, and had a photo to accompany the words, he became the kind of American Alexandra saw on television when the national anthem was played. Those were the people who looked adept and clear in purpose, two things utterly alien to her. They were qualities that made her particularly suspicious, partly because of Vietnam, but mostly because she'd never met a genuinely thoughtful person who possessed them.

Richard escorted Alexandra and Dr. Arman into the ambassador's outer office and asked them to wait while the ambassador read through the letters. Alexandra was grateful that Dr. Arman was such a convincing advocate. On the strength of his personality and Richard's advice, the ambassador was willing to examine the evidence to see if there might be a chance that Harun was half-American.

Dr. Arman had feared that, without absolute proof, the Americans would never risk involvement. He longed to smash open Syria's tiresome stupidity so his country could be part of something extraordinary. Why not call it humanity? he had thought, sitting beside Alexandra and feeling very much like Othello on the brink of oblivion.

At the ambassador's signal, Richard brought them back into the main office. The ambassador thanked them for bringing the matter to the embassy's attention, but his confidence was restrained. "Our ability to help will depend on corroborating the information in these letters. Washington will know whether this unit existed. The picture will go a long way toward supporting the claim if this soldier ends up being one of those five men. However, he must still be alive and able to confirm this woman's statements. Regrettably, many women have claimed paternity of their children by elderly American G.I.s."

Dr. Arman and Alexandra nodded. There was nothing more they could do. The ambassador promised to have everything sent on to Washington by diplomatic pouch that day. As Richard stepped forward to usher them out, the ambassador asked Alexandra why she hadn't filed a report yet about being detained. "Richard informs me of everything, Miss Pierce. You are my responsibility as long as you are here."

"I'm sorry, sir. The woman who wrote those letters is now lying in my bed near death. It is my fault she's here, and I haven't wanted to leave her side."

The ambassador accepted Alexandra's reason and extended his hand. Alexandra reached forward, her gaze drifting to the photograph Farah had enclosed. One hand snatched it up. The other came to her mouth.

Dr. Arman stepped forward. "What is it?"

Alexandra shook her head in disbelief. "I think I know this man."

Everyone shared incredulous looks. Richard reached for the photo to take it from her, but she wouldn't release it. He spoke softly, as if to a child. "We understand. You are upset about your friend and want to help, but it isn't likely you could recognize the man in this photo."

Alexandra looked from man to man, and their doubt spread to her. She examined the photo again. It was so old and tattered, but the eyes and mouth were unmistakable. She knew how it would sound. They would take her for a liar, but she had to say it. "This is my father."

Harun grew fond of the isolation cell. It seemed to hold a nostalgic value for Leopold too, who returned every hour to ask some unanswerable question about America's relationship with Israel. Initially, Harun had speculated that Leopold might have murdered a prisoner here, and perversely enjoyed returning to the scene of his crime. But after the third banal visit he concluded that the man's superiors were pressuring him to make progress. An idiom Harun had heard in England described their circuitous conversations, and he told Leopold, "You are fishing."

Leopold was flummoxed by the phrase, and Harun realized that the man was shrewd but had no flexibility of mind. He reminded Harun of himself. How threatened he felt when he didn't understand something straightaway, and how important it was not to admit it.

"At some point you will have to remove your mask," Harun taunted as Leopold stepped into the cell for the fourth time. "Otherwise you will get sick like my mother."

"I was told by a fortuneteller I would lead a long and prosperous life."

"Mazel tov, as they say."

Leopold struck a match to light a cigarette. The curl of sulfur lingered between them.

Harun leaned back against the wall. "You are a little like God, I realize."

"Yes, I am."

"Not the Christian one, though. You are strictly Old Testament. Perhaps one of your ancestors was also Jewish."

Leopold laughed, his head bobbing on top of his squat neck. From Harun's angle on the floor, Leopold's head didn't look securely attached.

"May I have some paper and something to write with?"

"You wish to make a confession?"

"Yes, in a way, but not the kind you are looking for."

"I will give you blank paper, if you sign the confession I have already written for you."

"I will not sign something absurd that makes me look like a fool."

"So your reputation as a traitor concerns you."

Harun exploded, his body jerking forward. "Since I am not a Syrian citizen, I cannot be a traitor! Find another word! Call me a spy! I do not care! For pity's sake, use some imagination!"

Leopold swayed backwards at the propulsive force of Harun's fury. Not that it mattered, but he was beginning to think Harun might be telling the truth. Leopold crouched so he could look Harun in the eye. "Do you know what day it is?"

"September 6th. Ramadan."

"It is near sunset. Are you hungry?"

"Very."

"Then we will break saym together."

Harun didn't know if Leopold was sincere, but his circus-like features for once appeared almost normal. "You have no one else to spend iftar with, do you? Bring the confession you wrote, and I will consider it."

"It is ironic, but tonight is also the end of the Jewish New Year."

"Then we can celebrate that too."

Leopold chuckled.

"The crime you are going to accuse me of . . . what is its sentence?"

"The sentence is always the same, and quite incidental to the crime."

Sayeed came to, face down in the dirt, unsure where he was or how he'd gotten there. He tried to roll over, but a shockwave of pain shot through his body. His left arm and both legs were broken. He thought he was also blind, but as his eyes adjusted to the dark he realized he was below ground.

His right arm and shoulder were viciously sore but miraculously intact. Discovering this helped stifle the panic overtaking him. That lone appendage, and the familiar smell of the place kept him tethered to reality. He turned his head, trying to make out the shadowy details illuminated by faint pinpricks of light. He spotted the outline of what appeared to be a large rock and crept his right hand toward it. His knuckles searched the rough surface, similar to limestone. He inched closer, his right fingers clawing the dirt, his belly dragging until he was beneath the rock. His hand reached up to graze carved fingers, a wrist, two arms. It was the basin of the bearded men. He was at Ebla.

He hooked his two middle fingers into a notch in the relief and used his shoulder to creep up the limestone. Each move required a negotiation with pain until he was half leaning against the basin. He rested his head against the bearded men's intertwined arms to catch his breath and saw that the illuminated pinpricks came from starlight falling through cracks in the ceiling above. If it weren't for the new moon, he might've realized where he was sooner.

He remembered only a few of the clean-shaven officer's blows. They had come so quickly, and with such destructive precision that he must've lost consciousness right away. He still couldn't comprehend why the officer had asked no questions. If the intention wasn't to extract information, why not kill him outright? Or had he infuriated Leopold so much during their last encounter that the malevolent man just wanted him to suffer before he died?

Sayeed closed his eyes to apologize to the Prophet. There would be no bowing, no outspread arms, no prostrating in submission during his Ramadan prayers. He wouldn't be able to recite the first thirtieth of the Koran. This Ramadan would be like no other.

He daydreamed about Alexandra, reliving their time together in Aleppo. That was when his feelings for her shifted, and he realized he'd misjudged her. Her intelligence, curiosity, and openness were the things he wanted most in a wife. It was comforting to know she might stay in Syria, and he convinced himself their *Tempest* would be the beginning of a collaboration to challenge the status quo. He wished they'd had time to finish it, and wondered how it would end if left in her hands. Would Miranda forgive her father's flaws and restore the play's harmony?

A pack of jackals let loose spine-chilling howls. He might soon be carrion for them. They'd be drawn into the ruins by the smell of a creature succumbing to death. They'd approach when he was at his weakest, and their hunger would dictate whether they'd wait for him to die before they pounced. If their stomachs were empty, he'd be just an injured animal to tear apart.

Sayeed prayed out loud until the jackals quieted. In the silence, he mistook the wind whistling along the ramparts of the upper town for voices and cried for help. He buoyed his spirits by fantasizing that tomorrow the site's guards would abandon their post in the shade near the concrete building and venture this far into the ruins, though he knew they'd conserve their energy since they were fasting. Probably one would sleep while one stood guard, taking turns every few hours, only waking the other when it was time to pray.

Sayeed glanced around the dark temple room. He knew the precise configuration of the basalt offering table with its base of bull-men. Ritualistic sacrifices had been done here for millennia. He would die on ancient sacred land. Through the darkness, he saw what looked like a brick near where the steep stairs led up to the town, though a brick had never been there before. It would be smarter to wait for morning to find out what it was, but he needed a distraction. If he moved slowly, he might be able to make it.

He recited the part of the Koran he'd memorized at eight years old. It wasn't much, but saying the words brought him closer to his father, though strangely more afraid. He didn't want to die among jackals. He'd always wanted to die in someone's arms. Not a man's death, but a woman's, and only now could he admit that to himself. The image was very clear in his mind, a crisp photograph really, nothing blurred at the edges.

Sayeed was puzzled about why Leopold wanted him killed in this way and not another. Officers crave efficiency, clarity, and this death lacked both. He refocused his attention on the words of the Koran, but his mind kept sliding into recesses. He wanted a piece of bread, one bite would do, anything to break the fast, ground him to the earth. When he was young, and he'd seen something remarkable, his description would tumble out in an anarchic stream he couldn't control. His mother would listen patiently, then bake him a pot of root vegetables, her remedy for ungroundedness.

He reached the bottom of the staircase and discovered the brick was Dr. Arman's copy of *The Tempest*. It must've fallen from his pocket when they tossed him down there. He pulled it closer and rested his cheek on the cover. It was too dark to reread the play's last act, so he envisioned an end that Alexandra would admire and Dr. Arman enjoy. When dawn came, maybe he'd be able to roll over. Then he could attempt to write the final scene of his and Alexandra's unfinished *Tempest* in whatever blank margins were left. That would be his last and only act of love to her.

Alexandra had never seen a dead body. Especially one in her own bed. Downstairs, Rafi handled the details with the Egyptian embassy. The phone call to her father had undone her. For years she'd hated him for abandoning her, but knowing he'd abandoned this dead woman too caused something else to collapse within her. Were there more women he'd impregnated and betrayed? Did she have half-siblings all over the world? And now he was en route to Damascus courtesy of the state department, expecting to see the only woman he'd ever truly loved. The one who had caused him to leave so much of himself behind in Egypt that there wasn't enough left for her or her mother. Richard Poole had told Aaron that Farah was still alive. Now Alexandra would watch her father experience the emptiness she'd felt as a child.

No one at the embassy had believed Alexandra recognized the photograph until Richard, in an effort to calm her, woke up Aaron in Indiana. Richard asked Alexandra to listen in on an extension, just to verify that it was him. Her father's voice became warm and expansive when he was asked whether he'd met a woman during the war and what her name was. It was a tone completely foreign to Alexandra and painful to hear. Richard asked question after question until finally Aaron spun out the story himself, his words tumbling over each other, so eager he was to relive the memory.

When Richard explained that Aaron might have a son, Alexandra hung up the phone, unprepared to hear how happy that would make him. She joined Dr. Arman in the hallway, and he apologized for doubting her.

"Why would anyone believe me? I hardly believe it myself."

"It is a lot to assimilate."

"I had always thought I was an only child."

Dr. Arman leaned in. "I will share something I've never told anyone. When I was young, I wanted to be the only person in the world. I got very upset when I saw other children."

"You . . . on earth alone . . . ? You are the kindest, smartest man I have ever met. What a terrible thing it would be for you to be the only one around with no one to appreciate you."

Dr. Arman pulled out his black notebook and handed it to Alexandra. "Look in the back."

She rifled the pages until she came upon the description of a woman—florid images dissolving into cruel judgments. She turned page after page, reading each entry. "Is this your poetry?"

"No. It is my folly. My embarrassing attempts to find a wife by recording on-the-spot impressions of every marriageable-age woman I see around the city who might be Christian."

"They all can't be this flawed."

"Exactly. This is my problem, not theirs."

"So you think because I'm hurt, I'm behaving like a child?"

"All I know is, no matter the reason, I would be thrilled to discover someone I share a past with."

Harun and Leopold ate quietly, sharing a small wooden table brought in for the occasion. If it weren't for the setting, they might have been friends enjoying a meal along a quaint European road. Continental Sunday motorists, who didn't picnic the way Americans do with a blanket spread on the ground, but with tables set near the roadway, replete with glassware and white linen.

The food was exceptional. Harun chewed each bite until it became paste on his tongue. He'd barely eaten for five days, and his taste buds reacted by discerning every grain and spice, each mouthful overwhelming his senses. Meticulous chewing gave him time to study Leopold's fetishistic table manners. He wiped his mouth after each bite, first touching the right side of his lips, then the left, then above, in small strokes reminiscent of a rodent cleaning itself. He never varied the order, and finished one item on his plate before starting another. He seemed unaware that his obsessive ritual prolonged the meal, but Harun didn't mind. Strangely, he'd grown used to the man's company, and even felt some empathy for his isolation and his sense of being professionally unappreciated.

Within his tiny fiefdom, Leopold was king. Outside it, Harun suspected, his superiors treated him as a jester. And the peril of all jesters is that they are amusing to their sovereigns until they are suddenly not. Harun felt sorry for the peculiar man, whose tenuous power and strange physiognomy provoked him to constantly overcompensate, to cast his net wide because in numbers there was safety. Leopold admitted as much when they moved on to dessert, Harun's favorite, basbousa soaked in rosewater syrup. "If you disrupt enough lives, you are bound to find one legitimate traitor," he explained between bites of cake.

"You think like a gambler. But the odds are not in your favor."

Leopold leaned toward Harun, interested in his reasoning. "You have based your calculation on the wrong criterion: difference. And by that measure you should arrest yourself. You would qualify as a superb candidate."

"Inconsistency, or difference, as you like to say, is the perfect criterion, and you are the perfect example, Dr. Lakhosh. You are not a traitor, but you are up to something."

"I am eager to know what you think it is. May I see my confession?"

Leopold handed Harun a single sheet of paper. The writing was succinct yet nuanced, stating point by point what had been behind his recent odd behavior. No single item seemed egregious, but taken as a whole it became a tale of purposeful deceit. An Egyptian in a prominent cultural position seeking to embarrass the Syrian regime. The document reeked of paranoia, yet was peculiarly cogent, and before Harun reached the end, he decided he would sign it.

He glanced up to glimpse Leopold drag his finger through the rosewater syrup and lick it slowly, savoring the distinctive sweetness. Harun was taken aback at how the man's uneven features transformed when suffused with delight. This was what he must have looked like as a child, when his satisfaction could begin and end on a dessert plate.

Harun returned to the confession. He turned over the page to see if there was more written on the back, but it was blank. Surely something was missing. He hadn't been accused of anything subversive. What was the logic behind building a case of foreign intrigue if it didn't lead to a definitive crime? Apparently, someone had forced Leopold's hand. The real purpose of this document was to allow him to save face, it seemed. Harun wondered what on earth his mother had done, or Sayeed had sacrificed, to accomplish this.

Leopold set a pen on the table, then called a guard to clear away the dishes. Harun signed the confession and, as agreed, was given a few sheets of blank paper.

"Will my sentence still be incidental to my crime?"

Leopold paused in the doorway, his back to Harun. It was hard to tell if he was seriously considering the question, or deciding whether to answer at all.

From behind, his authority appeared to crumble by the second, his elfin body contracting further within his suit. Harun began to transcribe the letter he'd already written to Sana in his head, but his eyes kept drifting to the stooped man, whose fate now looked as bleak as the mangy dog's. The strange little man stood motionless, unwilling to look back or move forward, and Harun realized this had been their last supper. He would not see Leopold again.

He felt the urge to bolster the man's ego. It was the same urge that had made him rub salve on the mangy dog's raw sores. No words came to him, though, and as Leopold finally shuffled away, Harun muttered under his breath, "The king is dead."

Sayeed woke before dawn. His broken limbs had swelled overnight and he struggled to roll onto his side to relieve himself. The pain sapped his strength, but he was grateful for a change in position.

Dusty light crept down the staircase as the sun rose. Determined ants scurried up the steps on their queen's mission. Mesmerized by their effortless movements, he imagined being Ganesh, or Vishnu, or Shiva, with arms enough to splint his injured limbs.

The silence of the place made him feel slightly deaf, as if his senses were already failing. Dawn was supposed to quell terror, but the unrelenting solitude enhanced it. Last night he understood he was likely to die, and yet he slept—the sleep of resignation, he'd assumed, but it was merely exhaustion. Now the ants, the assassin jackals, the flesh-burrowing flies filled him with rage and sadness. He was furious for not letting life's real magic enter his heart. In the end, he was no different from the characters in *The Tempest*. He had never allowed himself to be truly free.

He cursed in a fit of anger and release, then called for help again, despite knowing the guards would never hear his hoarse cries, even if they were to enter the upper town. He wormed his way closer to the staircase in the vain hope of dragging himself up the steps, but a coughing fit defeated him. Tasting salt, he brought his fingers to his mouth. Blood. So the clean-shaven officer's blows did more than break his bones.

Sayeed drifted in and out of consciousness for hours until the sun's golden light illuminated the familiar altar. He gazed at the carved relief, and for the first time truly appreciated Harun's obsession with its unique allure. It was finally light enough to read. Time for him to tackle rewriting the last scene of *The Tempest*.

Many of the margins in the last act were still blank, free of Dr. Arman's notations. Sayeed read through the closing pages in frustration, having forgotten what a paltry part Miranda had at the end of the play. A daughter more of connivance and convenience than of flesh and blood.

He must back away from what Shakespeare had done, and from what he and Alexandra had rewritten. Miranda couldn't mete out justice the way Prospero did, through manipulation and fear; she had to be better than that. And it couldn't be left to her father to pick her future husband, or to the audience to release her from her fate. Unlike Prospero's epilogue, Miranda's words mustn't request applause that would grant her leave to exit the stage.

Sayeed wanted his scene to open with Miranda's demand that her father return what he had taken. "I want my story back!" But as he began her soliloquy, her words gave way to his.

Dear Alexandra,

Home coddles the delusion of immortality. It strokes our hollow self, our unchanging rhythms, until we break out of our captivity, and find we are all alone. "Truth or dare?" you asked, and I picked truth. What other questions will forever lie between us? When it was my turn I should have asked your question back to you: "What is it about me that makes you dislike me so much?" It would have been interesting to hear your answer then . . . and hear it again now.

Some men only wish to feel a woman's body, but I crave more. I want to swallow a woman whole. Each morning the sun rises and we give it no more thought than we might a yawn. Sometimes we pray. Sometimes we curse. Our sleep meaning more to us than the new day.

Truth: You were my new day. The closer to midnight it comes the more I know that. Another truth: I was not completely honest when I said that I did not dislike you in particular, but people like you in general. I did dislike you, in particular, and in general. Men are frightened of women's expectations. It is much easier to dislike than to love, as it is easier to forget than to forgive.

You were right about Miranda. She must take hold of the reins or be doomed to remain on the island, a victim of her father's tempest, more than the sea's. But when you write her, try to make her ire less shrill so her father can see the damage he has wrought, and be given a chance to change. I am going to spend the time I have left imagining us together, not growing so much as changing.

Dare: I dare you to be happy. It is something I have never known. It is embarrassing to admit I am textbook Freud, my ego hopelessly enlarged. When I think about all the stereoscopic prints I took, trying to capture people's dualities so I could cancel them out and make the person whole, I can only shake my head.

The wind is getting stronger. I can see particles swirling in the patches of sunlight at the top of the stairs. Out there it probably feels like fire, but it is not too bad down here. I want to tell you that I love you, but I cannot. I do not know love well enough to be sure. What I feel for you, though, is beyond myself, and if that is love, then I do love you.

At the end of *The Tempest* Prospero says, "Every third thought shall be my grave." I fear he is right in his calculation. I wonder how long it takes to die in the desert.

How was it that her father's body could grow so brittle in seventeen years, while his face had changed so little? And in it, Alexandra could now see Harun. It was hard to grasp that he was her half-brother. Except for their interest in things ancient and ruined, Harun was the epitome of everything she wasn't. He had never challenged the status quo or acted spontaneously.

She felt abandoned or betrayed by all the men in her life, including Richard Poole, who refused to request any information about Sayeed. Richard tried to explain that, by even asking, he would likely make matters worse. But Alexandra pleaded until his patience snapped and he raised his voice. "After all that has happened, how can you still not grasp where you are?" Then he excused himself to retrieve some paperwork.

Alexandra expected her father to take Richard's side, but he remained silent, staying true to what he'd written about having forfeited the right to butt into her life. When he broke the silence it was only to say, "I hope you'll sign the paperwork for the trust."

"You know, it's a bit late for that kind of stuff."

"Yeah, I know. But the money's still yours. Do whatever you want with it."

Richard returned, files tucked under his arm, outlining the course that events would take. Alexandra was grateful to hear that Farah's body had been moved to the Egyptian embassy. Up until that moment her father hadn't reacted to the news of Farah's death, as if it might not be true, but now he looked stricken. Alexandra didn't really mind that he was suffering. She only wondered what it would have been like to travel thousands of miles to discover that the person she'd hoped to kiss once more was already dead?

Richard plowed on, explaining that Harun would arrive shortly, but that Richard alone would question Harun to see if the facts lined up. He asked them both to wait in his office.

Alexandra busied herself examining the plaques and photos on the wall to avoid her father. There was a picture of the ambassador and President Ford with Richard off to one side, a diploma from Georgetown Law School, and what looked like a recent family photograph, Richard with his parents and sisters, all tall.

"Hard to believe I came all this way to be kicked in the head. Can't say I don't deserve it. Still, it would've been nice to hold her one last time. But I bet that's every bastard's plea."

Alexandra spun on him. "If she meant that much to you, why didn't you come back after the war and look for her?"

"I've got no good reason except the war dragged on and I forgot who I was. There's a lot I'm not proud of."

"Harun looks like you."

"And you look just like your mother. Same eyes, nose, and mouth. Never thought I'd see that face again."

"You don't sound too happy about it."

Aaron sighed. "No one likes to be reminded of the damage they've wrought."

■■
■■

All Harun wanted was to take a shower, change his clothes, find his mother. That was what he wanted when a prison guard escorted him to the Ministry of Culture, and what he wanted again after the minister's aide shuttled him off to another department. No one seemed interested in what he wanted, though, and he began to worry this was another of Leopold's games.

He'd never really believed Leopold would execute him outright in any traditional way, but feared he might still end up dead. This feeling intensified when a different aide handed him a pair of ridiculously large shoes, then bundled him into a dilapidated car. Neither the car's driver nor the perspiring soldier in the backseat beside him would divulge their destination, so Harun suspected his torn clothes and outlandish shoes were a setup. The perfect costume for a hapless victim of an "accident."

Two days earlier he had given in to death, willing to sacrifice himself to protect Sayeed, but now he desperately wanted to post his letter to Sana. Not because he expected to hear back, but because writing it had aroused desires long dormant, especially the desire to live.

He slid closer to the door, preparing to jump out the moment the car slowed, though when he reached for the handle, there wasn't one. Given the car's decrepit state, he didn't know if this was another malevolent sign, or merely the status quo of the ministry's motor pool. His sleep-deprived brain groped for another escape plan, but before one materialized, the car turned onto Al-Mansour Street and stopped in front of the American embassy's massive gate.

To Harun's left hung the seal of the United States. He'd seen the bald eagle before, wings spread wide, with its flag-striped torso of red and white, a blue bar in place of its neck. From a design standpoint, he found the image unsophisticated and clunky, not fluid like those carved on ancient water basins. Until this moment, though, he'd never focused on the constellation of stars behind the bald bird's head. For some reason that stellar halo gave him a measure of hope.

The large gate swung open. A marine ushered him into the building and down a characterless hallway into a windowless room painted a bland yellow. It was furnished with one Formica-topped table and two folding chairs. Its banality made it the ideal bureaucratic space, inspiring neither confidence nor dread.

Harun tensed when the door opened, still half expecting Leopold to appear. In strolled Richard Poole, gesturing with a clipboard for Harun to sit. "I have a few questions I need to ask."

"I am sorry to interrupt, but I am confused."

"Yes, I imagine so. Please bear with me and all will come to light."

Richard's steady voice put Harun at ease, and he answered his questions, until Richard asked if he had a photograph of his father.

"No. Well, maybe." Harun handed Richard his great-grandfather's pocket watch. "There might be a picture of someone in here, but I have never forced it open. It requires a key."

Richard turned the watch over in his hand, studying it carefully. Engraved in a corner on the back was an indecipherable design, or a series of scratches.

"It belonged to my father. He left it with my mother during the war."

"I see . . ." The words were innocuous, but Richard's body language showed how much this fact particularly interested him. He set the watch on the table and stood. "Thank you for your forbearance. That was very helpful. Don't worry. I won't leave you here much longer. Hungry?"

"Yes, but I am fasting."

"Of course. Stupid of me."

Richard strolled out, leaving the door ajar. Embassy personnel quietly scurried by in their identical blue or gray suits. Harun watched, struck by how even the Americans' strides seemed unvarying and unnecessarily quick, the way Londoners walked. Harun had learned to walk that way too, but now these people reminded him of bees, a little too industrious for their own good.

Richard asked Aaron if he had ever owned a pocket watch. When Aaron said yes, Richard handed him the clipboard and asked him to draw a detailed picture of it. Aaron set to work delineating height, width, and the exact location of some scratches that had happened during the war.

"That's very good, sir. I can see exactly what type of watch that is. I believe it has a clasp on the side to open it."

"Young man, you don't know the first thing about watches. This one requires a key."

"Do you still have it?"

"Haven't seen that watch since '43, and the key since '57."

Alexandra sheepishly pulled the gold chain from inside her shirt. "I stole this from your box when I was six. I hated that you loved your keys more than me." She unclasped the gold chain and laid the necklace on the table.

"It couldn't have been in better hands."

Richard slid the key from the chain. "I've just spoken to Dr. Lakhosh. His watch matches your description, sir . . . And if this key opens it . . ."

Alexandra looked up at Richard. "Can we please have a minute?"

"Absolutely. I'll wait in the hall."

Once Richard was gone, Alexandra picked up the key. "You know there is a good chance Harun will hate you for abandoning his mother."

"Yeah. I know that."

"And it is kind of late to find out I have a brother. Maybe I don't want one."

Aaron nodded. "Could be."

Alexandra didn't know why she was delaying what would inevitably happen?

"Look, Alexandra . . . It's something I owe Farah. You don't have to be a part of it."

▓

Sayeed had always disliked incantations and magic spells. The props many writers rely on so that their lovers wind up together. He also disliked that most stories end before the lovers are tested. One kiss, one vow, one night together foretells nothing. To him, endings are the true beginning.

He tore out the pages of *The Tempest* he had written Alexandra's letter on, added her name and the Collinwood's address, then tucked them under a rock, safely away from the jackals. He hoped whoever discovered what was left of his body would find them, and that the person could read. Otherwise, the letter would eventually go up in smoke in a goatherd's fire.

The day crawled by. He dreaded nightfall, but still wished the minutes felt less like hours. Marooned in despair and famished, he passed the time searching for the ideal word to describe his favorite flavors. He wasn't interested in obvious adjectives, or even what his taste buds might actually experience, but rather the perfect word to capture the sensation of what it was like to eat certain foods. Words like "luscious," "tangy," "squishy." English words his father had taught him, and that you needed your entire mouth to say.

Outside, the wind grew fierce. Rivulets of sand spilled down the stone steps. Not enough to seal Sayeed off or protect him from the jackals, but enough to distract him. Toward sunset the wind calmed. He didn't realize what a soothing companion it had been. He thought about what his family would be doing right now. His father's broad hands ceremonially laying out the dates. His sisters and mother woozy from fasting, anticipating that first flash of sweetness. Or, stricken with worry about him, they would forego every ritual.

Sayeed dozed off. When he woke a pair of green-brown eyes gleamed at him in the darkness. A jackal stood a meter away. There was nowhere for Sayeed to retreat to, even if he could have. The jackal didn't move for a long time, then sat down and began to groom itself.

Except for its pointy nose, it looked nothing like the statue of Anubis in the museum. With its burnished headdress and loincloth, that golden jackal looked less like the Egyptian god of death than a half-man, half-beast servant fetching its master a cool drink. It was hard to imagine that this creature, contentedly licking its coat, would eventually eat him. Initially, he stayed vigilant, but as night deepened, he relaxed, comforted by the jackal's companionship. Its soft breathing accompanied his Ramadan prayers, and as it lay prostrate, head touching the ground, Sayeed felt at least one of them was honoring Allah.

A distant howl provoked the jackal to raise its head, sniff the air. It stood and marked the bottom step of the temple's entrance with urine. It turned its back to Sayeed, listening for the next howl. When it came, the jackal answered. Inside the temple, the howl exploded, the pitch shocking, like nothing Sayeed had heard before. The jackal straddled the temple stairs, silhouetted in the starlight. Sayeed could see that it wasn't large, probably a young female.

"Waiting for your lover?" Sayeed asked. The jackal turned its head in his direction. "May you have better luck than me." Coughs wracked Sayeed's body. Again, blood filled his mouth.

The jackal anxiously strode up and down the stairs.

"I can tell you have not experienced love yet. Better to let him ambush your heart than give it away straight out. But do not wait forever, or you are liable to lose all."

The jackal craned its neck, its large ears twitching. A soft yowl caused it to back away.

"Do not be cruel," Sayeed warned. "And do not be frightened. He has crossed so much of the desert to find you. It is your scent that draws him, no other."

The jackal leapt forward with a soft whine, throwing itself at its would-be mate. Sayeed watched new life beginning and wept. He couldn't remember the last time he had cried. Through his tears, he glimpsed the jackals locked in an awkward embrace. He coughed again. His lungs felt heavy, and he pined for the female jackal's return. He wanted to look into her feral eyes again. Not because he believed in something beyond the Prophet, but he was in an ancient temple, where gods, often disguised as animals, came down to walk among men.

More than the sun or the day, he wanted to see his family and Alexandra once more.

The jackals released each other and stood together at the top of the staircase. They were majestic in that light, perhaps more so because of what they'd just shared. Sayeed hoped it would be this couple that would come back for him. That he would be part of sustaining them through her pregnancy. In death he would join their family, his blood part of theirs, and through them be joined to the desert forever.

■■

Richard returned with the clipboard to the windowless office, apologizing to Harun for having a few more questions. "Are you a member of a political organization that meets regularly?"

"Yes, classical archeologists are a political bunch. If they were not, meetings would go far more smoothly."

Richard laughed. "I mean a dissident organization."

"I am beginning to think I am the most subversive man in all of Syria. I live alone, have no friends to speak of, no woman in my life, never miss a day of work unless I am arrested, and, up until six days ago, faithfully prayed five times a day. I certainly hope, for any organization's sake, there is not another dissident like me. I did nothing illegal."

"We know that."

"Why are the Americans interested in all this?"

Richard sighed. "The Ministry of Culture would like you to leave Syria voluntarily. Your arrest and treatment have been embarrassing for everyone. We—the Americans, that is—are interested because of the unusual situation between your mother and father. May I see your watch again?"

Harun set it on the table. Richard opened the door for Alexandra. She was horrified to see Harun's bruised and swollen face. Richard gave Alexandra a look. "If you wouldn't mind."

Harun watched in disbelief as Alexandra took the key resting in her palm and inserted it into the watch's lock. The cover instantly popped open. She held the watch out to Harun, but he was too stunned to take it.

Richard silently ducked into the hallway. Alexandra could hear hushed voices on the other side of the door and expected her father to burst in at any second, but he didn't.

Harun looked up at her, too confused to speak.

"I have awful news. Your mother is dead."

Harun blinked slowly. "When?"

"Yesterday. I am so sorry."

Alexandra buried her face in her hands.

"It is not your fault, Alexandra."

"But it is. I'm the one who caused her to come here."

"You are a very resourceful person, but death, no, even you are not that powerful."

Alexandra looked at him uncertainly. "Are you trying to be funny?"

"No. I am trying to let you know it will be all right." Harun took the watch from her. "For thirteen years I could not open this. Eventually I stopped trying. Why do you have the key?"

"I stole it from my father when I was six."

The sentence was unfathomable. There were no words. They studied one another, each uncomfortable under the other's gaze. This was not the mirror either would have chosen.

###

Did Aaron really think, just because he and Alexandra hadn't spoken in seventeen years, she would let him go to Egypt, where Sayeed was, with a coffin and not her?

On the train from Amman, Aaron muttered how the dead used to sail to the afterlife. Harun spoke about the sun god, Ra, sailing the sky in a boat. At Cairo they unloaded Farah's coffin and had it carried to the water. This would be her final voyage, her River Styx.

The felucca fit eight, but no tourists on the dock wanted their romantic memories tainted by a dead woman, so Aaron generously paid the Nubian captain to take the three of them. Farah's coffin was given pride of place at the bow, and the captain, who spoke no English, occasionally called out the sites from the tiller for Farah's benefit, addressing her as *malika altair,* which Harun roughly translated as "queen bird."

Aaron experienced the same dread he'd felt when he'd left Alexandria on the barge to Palestine and looked back to see nothing but a vague outline on the horizon. He had no final image of Farah waving goodbye, no photograph to cling to. Nothing but the vast empty sea. He sat in the felucca's bow to reread Farah's letters. He truly had loved and lost, and the rest of Tennyson's phrase was full of shit. He could feel Alexandra's and Harun's eyes on him as he turned page after page, each word sinking in further, barbed as a harpoon.

Alexandra brooded at the stern. She'd wanted to remain in Cairo to find Sayeed, but had no idea where he was, and felt uncomfortable abandoning her father so close to the journey's end. She intended to have Miranda do precisely that to Prospero in her and Sayeed's version of *The Tempest,* but away from pen and paper, she didn't have the courage to do it in real life.

As they'd left Syria, Harun told Aaron that, once they buried his mother, their reunion would be over. Alexandra understood the sentiment, but its coldness surprised her, as did her father's silent acceptance of Harun's rejection. It was his resigned acquiescence that compelled her to get onto the train and then this boat, despite her fury at herself for feeling sorry for him.

With nothing else to do, she unwrapped the gift he'd left on her vanity last night. On the frontispiece he'd written:

To my daughter,

This book brought me immense love and immense pain. It brought Farah and me together, and kept your mother and me apart. It is a great love story, and so belongs with someone still capable of great love.

Your father

A shadow fell across the page. Harun stood above her. "So that is the copy of the book my mother read out loud to him."

"Like a hakawati."

Harun smiled and turned to go, but Alexandra stopped him. "Do you know where in Cairo Sayeed is?"

"No."

"But you're sure he's there?"

Harun couldn't be certain of anything. Sayeed's fate ultimately rested with Leopold's weariness with petty intrigues. "Sayeed could be anywhere taking photographs at this point."

"Then I'll write to him at the museum, through Dr. Arman."

"That is a good idea." He gently squeezed her shoulder as he walked away. The gesture was spontaneous and foreign to him, but felt right. He sat on the edge of the boat and pulled out his pocket watch. Though Alexandra's key now dangled from a chain looped through the winding crown, Harun choose to fiddle with the closed cover.

A child's infectious laughter carried across the water. A larger felucca overtook them. Tourists called out to Harun in mangled Arabic and waved. He spotted a father and young son laughing as they tried to step on each other's shadow. It looked absurdly fun. The kind of game Harun had never fantasized playing with his dead British father.

He still had a mental image of him. One he'd concocted as a boy from pictures he'd found in library books about the war. The details were all there, though now there was a real face, a real father. Harun had trouble comprehending that this was the man who had inspired the charged atmosphere his mother had written about. He didn't know which father he preferred to discard: the dead British officer with knobby knees poking out beneath desert khakis, or this American. He'd lived so long with the other father that he wasn't inclined to give this new one a chance.

Alexandra set down the book and went in search of pen and paper. As she stepped around her father, he touched her leg.

"I left you behind, the way I left Farah. I'll never forgive myself for that."

"You didn't leave me behind. Mom and I left you."

"I could've tried to stop her. I could've tried to change."

A stream of excited words erupted from the captain.

"It's Alexandria," Harun explained. In the distance, the outskirts of the city rose out of the water. He stroked the closed pocket watch. "Another thirty minutes, I would say."

Aaron gestured to the watch. "Do you want to see how it works?"

Harun handed it and the key over.

"This is the balance wheel. It's like a pendulum, allowing the watch to keep constant time. And this handles auxiliary compensation. A fancy way of saying that it corrects for errors at extreme temperatures."

"If you are ever in Athens, go to the museum and see the Antikythera mechanism. It is an ancient watch that was buried in a shipwreck in 80 B.C. It has more gears and wheels than this one, and is inscribed with symbols for the sun, moon, Saturn, Mars, Jupiter, Venus, and Mercury."

Alexandra pulled out a sheet of blank paper from her canvas sack. She walked past the men as her father pointed out the escapement, center, and winding wheels.

Harun laughed. "So many wheels. We Egyptians somehow managed to build the pyramids a thousand years before we discovered the wheel."

Alexandra settled in at the far end of the boat and wrote:

Hello, Sayeed,

I'm on the Nile, just upriver from you. I've followed you to Egypt. When I'm through here, after I say goodbye to my father, I'll come look for you so we can finish what we started. I wish I could see your face after reading that sentence. Yes, after seventeen years, I'm with my father.

I've been thinking a lot about our *Tempest*. Maybe we were too harsh. Prospero deserves Miranda's ire, but also her understanding. Miranda lost a mother, but Prospero, a wife and lover. It must have been a blow, perhaps enough to drive him mad. I'd like to pose a question for us to answer. What if Prospero or Miranda tried to reshape their future through reimagining their past? What are the costs and advantages for father or daughter to retreat? Would the drama suffer, or might it unexpectedly blossom?

We're about to arrive in Alexandria. Now I know what I was named after. Actually, we're arriving just short of the city. Dad and Harun asked the captain to moor the felucca on the desert side so we could bury Harun's mother there. Turns out my dad and Farah Lakhosh were lovers during the war. Harun's my half-brother. I don't know what to think about any of it.

It's barely twilight. The stars and moon are already amazing. I know it sounds crazy, but it seems incredibly romantic to be buried in a desert, totally loved, and then lost forever.

I realize this letter has gotten off track. I can't explain what I feel for you. It doesn't make sense. But there it is. I may be making a fool of myself, but I don't really care. My way forward leads through you. I don't know how, or when, or where. I just know that it's true.

Can't wait to see you again.

Love,

Alexandra

The felucca moored near a small village. A donkey cart with three men soon trundled toward them. Harun climbed off the boat to talk to the driver.

The captain, Harun, and two of the men loaded the coffin onto the donkey cart. By then, the third man had returned with shovels and rope. Alexandra sat in front between the driver and Harun. Her father insisted on riding in back with Farah.

An hour from the village they lit kerosene lanterns and began to dig. It didn't take long before Farah's coffin was set into the grave. While the villagers filled the hole, Aaron gazed at the stars and Harun recited the Muslim prayer for the dead. Soon there was nothing but a small mound, no more than a drift, one among thousands.

Aaron sat beside the grave. "Alexandra . . . I have a favor to ask. Farah wrote about how I taught her hangman."

"She never found out your favorite word and I never knew you had one."

"Everyone has a favorite."

Aaron dragged his finger through the sand and drew a scaffold.

"Dad . . . no . . . You can't play hangman on a grave."

"It's Farah's marker, Alexandra. By tomorrow it'll be gone."

"I'll do it on one condition. If Harun doesn't mind, and he gets to play. Two against one."

"Seems fair."

Alexandra glanced up at Harun. He didn't seem perturbed, but curious. She patted the sand beside her and he sat. Aaron drew seven blank spaces beneath the empty gallows.

Alexandra drummed her fingers. "Hmm . . . seven-letter word. Harun, you go first."

"What do I do?"

"Most people start with vowels, but why don't you pick your favorite English letter."

"X."

Aaron smiled and drew an "X" in the first blank.

Alexandra turned to Harun in disbelief. "Wow! Good choice." Alexandra studied the rest of the blanks. "I'm inclined to say 'E,' but what do you think, Harun?"

"The word is probably Latin. Selecting 'E' would be a risk. What is your favorite consonant?"

"Right now it's 'S.'"

Aaron shook his head in dismay and filled in the last blank with an "S."

Alexandra rubbed her hands together with glee. "Oh, Harun, we are definitely going to beat him. Pick again."

Harun studied the blank spaces, then smiled. He filled in the five empty spaces with letters.

Aaron was speechless. Alexandra stared from the word to Harun. "What the hell is *xiphias*?"

"A swordfish. Now what?"

Aaron softly brushed away the game. "Now it's your turn."

Harun patted the sand. Beneath his hand his mother lay. He needed her to know he was capable of love. He drew a scaffold on the mound and eight blank spaces. Even if he won, and Alexandra and Aaron never guessed the right letters, he would share the word, his mother's favorite. He'd scratch it into the sand and let it linger between them. Only then would he decide what to do next.

THE WALL'S REQUIEM—OPUS 1

Klaus, Klaus, Klaus. You have had too much to drink. You are only eighteen and six months. Your new brown loafers were not made to run. The moon was full four days ago. Not to condescend, but that means it is still bright. If you carry the back of the ladder when the guards aim at your friend in front, you'll run into the bullets meant for Dieter and double your chances to die. The death strip was made for world-class sprinters. The guard towers for bully marksmen. As your nephew's generation will like to quip: This is not rocket science. You have siblings and parents. A "negative group of friends," according to Stasi informants. They will mourn your evaporation. Your sister will be interrogated. Your shoes will be given to her as a reminder of your treason. She will polish them once a year and give them to her teen-age son on his eighteenth birthday in a cloud of cigarette smoke and eardrum-busting Nick Cave. They will be lost before the night is over. You will be cremated so no one can prove how you died. You were born in Falkensee and mistake your birthplace for your abilities. You are not a falcon. You cannot fly.

THE WALL'S REQUIEM—OPUS 1

N 52° 30' 41"; E 13° 23' 24"—Thirty Meters North of Kronenstraße

Dig in, Fräulein. There is a divot you can't see, perfect for your small shoe. It's between your legs. That trembling delta. I will tell you some things while you catch your breath. Intimacy is hard work. Rabbits hunt dandelions. Do not shave your legs too soon. Go on, rest your wet cheek against my spalled face. I promise to give back your tears. So different from rain. You may not know this but rain exterminates memory. You can't imagine where my gravel has been. Where they scooped me from, what they bonded into me. My damp hope hardened around their gassy frost. I did not ask for this bed of nails in front of me. This rotten twisted wire carved into my crown. Rust streaks my spine, smears my belly, soiling the genitals the boy with the stutter and cabbage between his teeth spray-painted on my back. The woman who cradles a baby in the upstairs window on Friedrichstraße makes yellow marks on the glass. They come and go with her milk. Is she your mother . . . ? Is that your brother . . . ? Is she signaling you?

N 52° 30' 27"; E 13° 23' 24"—Checkpoint Charlie

Oy! Here they come. Five pale sewer faces. Another basement quintet emerges from their long pianissimo huddle. So many idealistic limbs. So slow. S o L a n g s a m. What a clumsy group. Ankles weak. Thighs paltry. Shoes too big. Ladder too short. They don't know it's deer season. Goose down duck blind time. Guards are different on Monday when they've killed on Sunday. The divine rush tough to give up. Give up! Hands, hooves in the air! Today is Monday, so you've chosen poorly, pale ones. I've got a vein of coal in here somewhere. The kind of honey pot you need to smudge sallow. Adorn flesh. Invisiblize mischief. Carbon under pressure when helium would be better. I'm sorry I don't know how to unleash my frozen smoke over Checkpoint Charlie. Some of me is—was—a Goethe scholar so I understand that *architecture is frozen music*. That I am *frozen* music. Which means I can't induce a chorale diversion either, much as I would like to help. Do you understand that *pain is short, and joy is eternal?* A Schiller scholar was sieved here too. They were father and son. Shot in the back with a hundred others. Pit your slow pale meat against my dispossessed bookworms and you will lose. The new moon can't protect you. You are snowdrifts against tar. Your pale foreheads could be lanterns at sea. Your fecklessness will pock and gouge me even more. I do not like brains. I do not like bone. I do not like blood. I do not like bullets to bore holes in me that only worms used to aerate.

N 52° 30' 33"; E 13° 25' 45"—Schilling Bridge

Where are my heart-shaped chocolates wrapped in pink paraphernalia, my "Be Mine," my "Ich liebe dich," my lusty dancing pigs with snouts up asses draped in candied ginger? There you are, Valentine moon. You socialist sickle with your sharp corners and winking eye. Having a bit of fun with a cloud? Such a perfect night. A curtain of mist on the Spree. The Schilling Bridge wrapped in lonesome guards. Everyone home fucking. Oh, St. Valentine, bastard son of Rome's Lupercalia, restorer of sight, aider to Christian lovers, secret bestower of illegal marriage vows, martyr of stones and clubs, where did they bury your severed head? So many fickle bodies fling themselves at me, want to wrap themselves over me, but I am not easy. Others, further along, have fewer boundaries, looser morals. I am painted pure white and not left filthy gray like them for a reason. Still, I am no longer a novelty. Not thought such a hunk any more. I am not easy, but I am kind. I always listen to their final cries after the hail of gunfire. "Ich liebe dich," I love you, "es tut mir leid," I'm sorry, "alles Gute zum Geburtstag, Happy birthday." Häää?! Get a load of that drunk monkey stumbling over the boiler company roof. Hey . . . you with the two left feet . . . What are you doing!? Oh Scheiße! Oh fuck! Oh St. Valentine, please talk some sense into this one. He is hopelessly unfit. Too soft in the middle. He'll never shimmy down that heating pipe. Well, I stand corrected. Whoa! Smart move, you! The guy landed in the dog run when the pack is being fed.

No no no no no, go the other way. Don't plaster yourself against me. I'm white, you're wearing black. What was that? Calm down . . . I can't understand you . . . You spent your last East marks on what . . . ?

N 52° 22' 35"; E 13° 25' 04"—Near Crossing Point at Drelinden/Drewitz

That first year, a song from the American sektor rocked my rebar. It never let up. The beat was new, squirmy, hot. It haunted me, taunted my makers, had what West Berliners called pelvis flypaper. My English wasn't too good yet, and then there was the syncopation, those background sirens, a seductively Latin flair, a bit too much of what I've learned may be reverberation meant to blur the senses, so it wasn't surprising what was sung and what I heard might not corroborate. Somewhere along the way the song gave up on rhyme, and with those sporadic bodies prostrate before me, cursing my not being a meter shorter, or a bit less slippery, or more penetrable, how (considering my position) could I have known "surrender" meant fucking and not capitulation, though of course the song was shamelessly begging for capitulation from one of the parties. Presumably the one with titties. Parts of me had studied the law. If this were 1938, I would be declared one-quarter impure and hard of hearing. Enough to be permanently jettisoned. So I confused "glory" with "gory," "magic" with "tragic," no one is perfect, except those who are. Over the years I heard the song less. Now on display in Kiev of all places, I've been subjected to irradiation and continuous dog piss. But when the occasional Elvis fan comes to gawk, a nostalgic swoon sweeps over me as I hear: *So, my darling, please surrender . . .*

N 52° 25' 34"; E 13° 07' 09"—Northeast of Potsdam

What a glorious spring! The Havel overfull from gluttonous upstream melt, the sky satin blue, no man's strip choked with weeds. Another week and their flowers will peak. Explosive color wild with nests, eggs sweet to burst. Ahhhh . . . The white wooden cross, planted for the two who drowned only meters from the bank almost invisible among the tangle. I watched one give out as four hands reached for him from the west while that searchlight in the watchtower over there lit his back. Stroke. Stroke. Stroke. That's how close he was. Sunk is the only word for what I witnessed. Sunk. The other one, superbly thin without his coat and sweater, fell through weak ice. I thought he was a young girl when he stepped off the bank. The water was still rippling under the surface. A skipping stone could've broken through. Why do so many choose to flee in winter? Is hypothermia one of those lost multisyllabic words no one is taught any more? Why have the weeds been left by the guards this year? It must be an augur of something. Halley's already shot by with its tail between its legs, very upsetting. I had expected something predictable yet wild, visible but unimaginable. Perhaps that was too much to hope for. It's hard to fathom I'll be here for another seventy-six years to see if it does better. And then there were those environmental and astronautic crises. Chernobyl. Challenger. Will the Havel's fish throw themselves on the bank in a mass suicide next? Will this become a lost world? With all that has gone on nothing seems impossible. I have seen many die. I used to keep count. The crosses helped. But then even those stopped. I'm beginning to suspect time has lost its synchronization.

N 52° 24' 03"; E 13° 31' 17"—North of Schönefeld Flughafen

Full moon, clear sky, Hallelujah! No one will come tonight. All points of the compass silent. Time to dream. Roam. Indulge the missing middle of this preposterous encirclement. Not to brag, but I am so much more than this monstrosity. Being forged under pressure has its upside, and while it's impossible to avoid the intermittent mayhem directed against me, because to quote Voltaire—*Those who can make you believe absurdities can make you commit atrocities*—there are peaceful full moon nights that remind one why they go on despite being persistently pelted with a fusillade of metal and derisive language, and defaced by a cultural cornucopia of drunks, anarchists, and faux revolutionaries. Being close enough to the Russian sektor to feel the psychotic effects of that dreadful language on its occupants, which may also account for their endless disrobing and flesh displays in front of uncurtained windows, I've concluded that, while I am not a monstrosity, I am a monumental folly. Why this distinction comforts me, I can't say, especially given that I am isolated in the outer ring of this quadrant, sans individuality and anything resembling a baguette, banger, or burger, exotic words I've heard on the wind from guards rotated here because they must have done something un-comrade-like. Words I'm convinced from their rapturously hushed intonation have to do with coital comfort. I've written a song about them. Would you like to hear it?

N 52° 32' 08"; E 13° 07' 30"—East of Falkensee, Near the English Sektor

As I was saying, Klaus, you are not a falcon. You cannot fly. Klaus, listen to me. You are still crouched in the overgrown vegetation assessing me. If I were to tell you there is a trip wire just past the signal fence, would it change your mind? You were never very good at sports, and, to be frank, you'll be doing Dieter a favor if you bop him on the head with a nearby rock or clod of earth. As bad as your situation turns out, his will be worse. Oh, he will make it over the last fence and leave you for dead, which in fact you will be, but his next five years will have the makings of a Puccini opera. Have some compassion, Klaus. Dieter is your best friend. If you don't care about your life, care about Dieter's. His end is worse than *Madama Butterfly*. Worse than *Turandot*. What he will endure. What his wife will endure. What their unborn child will endure. Have a conscience, Klaus. Bop him on the head. The two of you will wake in the field tomorrow with twin hangovers and have a good laugh.

N 50° 26' 46"; E 30° 30' 39"—Kiev, Ukraine:
Outside the German Embassy

All your love so warm and tender . . . Kiev, Jesus! Just my luck. Most people thought I was a bad idea, but now everyone wants a section of me outside their front door. Why is the German embassy memorializing me in Kiev? When did I become an accessory? So many of my comrades bask in the sun and tongues of Spain, Italy, South Africa. Twelve of my appendages—I do consider us all part of a whole and our dismemberment and scatterment as cruel as vivisection—ended up in Los Angeles. The way those two words roll off the tongue is so goddamn sexy. The only way to say Kiev is to bark. Some maladroit artist gave me a supposed facelift, a few pathetic pastel swirls and swipes, as if that alters anything. Concrete bleeds through pale pink and blue, dummkopf. Stumpy shrubs frame my base. Not very inspirational. Above me, tall buildings with narrow windows and narrower ledges provide perfect pigeon perches. No one fears me. No one curses me. No one touches me any more. It's horrible to have to go on like this. Pastel painted, poop pelted, and piss potted.

N 52° 30' 33"; E 13° 25' 45"—Schilling Bridge

A used guitar? Is that what you said? Don't cry. I've heard worse. One guy a few years back spent his last East marks on a trip to Moscow. Ironic, huh? Now . . . not that our visit hasn't been fun but . . . you're pressing your luck. Time to go home to your wife and do your Valentine's duty. Have some fun. Make whoopee. It's surprising the idioms I've acquired over the years. Since you're in no shape—in every sense of the word—to shimmy back up that pipe, my advice is duck under the bridge over there and Hey! Don't run off! Oh, Jesus . . . Not the river! Help! Help! Help!

THE WALL'S REQUIEM—OPUS 1

N 52° 24' 03"; E 13° 31' 17"—North of Schönefeld Flughafen

I lied. I have not written a song. I tried to write a song, but without intimate knowledge of what baguettes, bangers, and burgers are in a coital context, I am without direction. Are they positional preferences? Erotic instruments? Or are they poetic inducements to be shouted near coital climax? Who can I ask? The guards despise me. Sometimes they shoot at me out of boredom. Or more likely envy. If it weren't for me, their lives would be empty. And with this wide gap between us, my obviously superior status, and the way they can't stop gazing at me, it is almost as if I am their new God, as I believe their old one may have perished.

N 52° 30' 27"; E 13° 23' 24"—Checkpoint Charlie

Ahoy, lantern foreheads! Dangerous shoal! Road closed! Beware of dog! They never listen. The lone child among them, a girl, has those big fish eyes you see on certain dolls. The toy is familiar to me, one or two having been dropped at this address. Not quite the tasty bounty other totems receive, though I have had more than my share of sacrificial virgins. Fish Eyes, all of five or six, certainly classifies. Her corn-silk hair could be a flare, oh hell, a poem is seeping out. Goddamn Schiller scholars! Their willpower is inversely proportional to their egomania. Just treat the non sequitur *Now twilight dims* verse as a case *the water's flow* of hiccups. *And from the tower* this tends *the beacon's glow* to happen when *waves flickering o'er* a child is about to die. *Ah,* you can imagine *the dismal stream* how distressing *the lover's eye* and exhausting *sounds moan* these episodes *from heaven* are. *Huge wave on* Fuck *huge wave* there goes the *yawning gulf* searchlights! *Through an opening pall* oh no, Fish Eyes has frozen *grim earth.* Her body so small *poor maiden* the searchlight swallows her *bootless wail* completely. She is *lone victim* lost in *the stormy sea of* light. *The giant gulf is* I can't watch *grasping down.* No, even they wouldn't *still that heart,* would they?

THE WALL'S REQUIEM—OPUS 1

N 52° 25' 34"; E 13° 07' 09"—Northeast of Potsdam

And why not lose its synchronization? Time, not life, is the big mystery. If time has lost its sense of self, what is to stop Halley's from returning next year? Perhaps the cosmos is not unlike a bird's nest. An aerie of appetite and hunger, that when set trembling by planetary-sized paroxysms, falls prey to unknown desires. In such imbalance, strange, even preposterous things seem to happen. New religions are founded. Messiahs are born, or spontaneously generate among the masses. Why can't time become occasionally muddled, genuinely disoriented? Ahead. Behind. Now. Just words. Will you look at that! The electricity has gone out again.

N 50° 26' 46"; E 30° 30' 39"—Kiev, Ukraine:
Outside the German Embassy

You don't eat a dog, you don't eat a dog, you don't eat a dog, you don't! You don't eat a dog, you don't eat a dog, you don't eat a dog, you don't! Goddamn that song! It's everywhere. Haven't heard Elvis for years. Screams, bombs, bullets, every goddamn day. The building behind me is overrun with pro-Putin rebels. My shrubs are dying. I'm sure my comrades in sunny Spain and luscious Los Angeles aren't suffering from déjà fucking vu. Goddamn! There it is again. *You don't eat a dog, you don't eat a dog, you don't eat a dog, you don't!* Of course you don't, asshole, at least not in public. Some parts of me remember how hungry '45 was. I got three girls in here who sucked off soldiers for the protein. Anywho, tastes change, can't stop progress . . . or whatever this is. Still, I just learned how to say "I love you" in Ukrainian. Я тебе кохаю. It's not as easy as it looks, and the thought of having to go back to Russian repulses me. Hey, I didn't mean any criticism about those three girls. Lili, Hannah, and Emilie were great. It's not my place to judge because . . . uh . . . I have a confession. I am harboring a war criminal. Hitler's dreaded intelligence chief. I am 1/1,000,000,000th

Reinhard Heydrich, the "man with the iron heart." A part of his third rib was ground into my mortar. Even at 1/1,000,000,000th strength he is a supreme asshole. Like a homeopathic remedy whose dilution only makes the final solution more potent. That was an unfortunate choice of words.

N 52° 32' 08"; E 13° 07' 30"—East of Falkensee, Near the English Sektor

Klaus, I don't mean to be a jerk, but I told you so. Look at Dieter. Gets to the West, misses his mother, crosses back to East Berlin—for a hug or Gott knows what—gets arrested, spends a year in jail before West Germany pays for his release, a fantastisch use of taxpayer money NICHT, since Dieter crosses back over 240! times, falls in love, and gets engaged. Do you see where this is headed? Have you listened to your Puccini since we last spoke? Did I tell you that his fiancée already has an eight-year-old son? Each death is a bullet, Klaus. A bullet to someone's heart.

N 52° 30' 33"; E 13° 25' 45"—Schilling Bridge

Hey! Guards! Over there in the river! A drunk monkey is drowning! You can save him! It's Valentine's Day, guys! Have a heart! Be his! He just bought a guitar. Right now his wife is unwrapping the chocolate he left on her pillow in their under-heated apartment. Reading his wretched love poem by sooty kerosene light. Slipping into the red mittens her aunt in the West sent. Come on, guys . . . She's ovulating. Let him serenade her once. Take pity on the overweight slob. Tonight you are lovers, not butchers. Woodsmen with magic bullets that cannot kill a . . . Again, I stand corrected.

THE WALL'S REQUIEM—OPUS 1

I confess, Fräulein. The more time you spend on me, the more convinced I am you're making a mistake. You will likely die, and if you don't mind me saying, the way you set each foot just so against me, I think you have the makings of a gymnast. I'm not sure your attributes will be as appreciated on the other side. On this side, with state training and the right steroids, you'll be drowned in rose bouquets. I have this longing for you to live. You are lithe like my Veronika. She had the most tender way of spitting in my mouth. There was no part of her I didn't want to consume. From her I could make a stew. A cherry meringue. A pussy pelt. Forgive me, Fräulein. Your fluid body against my rigid face has spun me back. Can you hear my strangled sobs? The war's phosphorus still burns in my throat from that November night. You are too young to know about blockbuster bombs, but their name is apt. Veronika and I were near the zoo's aviary house when the RAF struck. The roof blew off. Hundreds of beautifully plumed birds instantly doused with incendiary bombs. Their clipped wings no escape. Frantic flaps whipped the flames across their earthbound bodies. Roasted monkeys tumbled from treetops. Snakes slithered away. Lions, leopards, and jaguars burst from their broken cages and stalked fashionable Berlin. That night they became Jews. Hunted and shot.

Once upon a time the electricity went out and time lost its synchronization. What was ahead? What was behind? Half of Berlin succumbed to the suspension of time and waited. The other half sped on. Waiting was the new cancer. The clock stopper of all tumors. Precursor to terminal meekness. A condition the ice nymph Leni Riefenstahl didn't know fuck about. How do I know? Because a part of me I'll call K knew Leni before she became LENI. K pointed her out when she showed up incognito in her designer sunglasses to gawk at us a few years back. Look at those lips! he'd said. For an aging infamous doyenne of Olym-

pic porn, not too shabby. But by then, having heard the story, I expected something mystically parasitic.

N 52° 30' 27"; E 13° 23' 24"—Checkpoint Charlie

Fish Eyes is on her back staring at me. She is the center of a poppy, her
parents and grandparents fallen petals around her. Fish Eyes' father
survived the Eastern Front, the wretched winter of '43. Her grandfather the disastrous Carpathian campaign of 1915. Fourteen toes and
thirteen fingers all that's left between them. Two hard-bitten soldiers
felled like fleas. What led them to this moment? Their fill of tyrants? A
sense of powerlessness? A newfound appreciation of individuality and
improvisation? Yes. Yes. And Yes. And what about the guards? What
led them to this moment? Their fill of tyrants? A sense of powerlessness? A newfound appreciation of individuality and improvisation?
Yes. Yes. And Yes. This is the outcome of humans interpreting the
same information differently. What can be called the unknown spaces
of our heartland. Yes, those do exist. You only need imagine "Flight of
the Bumblebee" executed by tuba instead of flute to comprehend the
disjunction. For those of you who find that too challenging, I recom-
mend reading a passage of Nietzsche while being tickled.

N 52° 24' 03"; E 13° 31' 17"—North of Schönefeld Flughafen

While I'm on the subject, I'm fairly certain gods are not supposed to
be treated with such disdain. I freely admit that I don't comprehend
my various geologies—nor as yet deciphered the baguette, banger,
burger mystery—but why that makes me the butt of others' hostility
is unsettling. It's true, I used to be more certain of things, and am
not entirely sure how I evolved into these multitudes within a singular
forgotten. Nevertheless, I share myself daily with my subjects, turn the
other cheek when attacked, and am the embodiment of charity. And
while I can come off as cold and enigmatic, I am generous in ways that

the best Gods are. And if I might momentarily digress and get back to songwriting and Voltaire, *Life is a shipwreck, but we must not forget to sing in the lifeboats.* Tra—la—laaa—la—laaa . . . Come on everyone, clap your hands and sing . . .

N 52° 25' 34"; E 13° 07' 09"—Northeast of Potsdam

So, as K tells it . . . Once upon a time his best friend W was desperate to kiss the ice nymph. W was Jewish, but that was before Der Fucker. W would do anything to be near L small e-n-i. Anything. Be her cross-dressed mannequin. Her slave doll forced to don her lingerie and dresses. Little Leni made W dance. Play pony. Wiggle his ass. Her too-tight panties against his piston popper was a special agony for him that endlessly amused her and her friends. Sometimes she rubbed his proboscis in things. Her Weimar lips were that powerful. Excuse me for a second. HEY! STOP FUCKING AROUND WITH THAT CIRCUIT BREAKER!

N 50° 26' 46"; E 30° 30' 39"—Kiev, Ukraine:
Outside the German Embassy

I have another confession. It's not just 1/1,000,000,000th Heydrich that I'm harboring. There seem to be some dudes—another great slang word I picked up in the '80s before being banished to this wretched hellhole—Nazi death-squad dudes, to be specific (or if you prefer their nom de guerre: Einsatzgruppen), remnants mixed in. The scum of the scum. I may look firm as hell on the outside, but things are more porous in here than is good for me. I'm sure it's on account of the Einsatzgruppen remnants that I ended up in Kiev. Scene of the crime and all. They killed almost 200,000 near here in two weeks back in . . . you know. That's 14,285.7 a day, 595.2 an hour, or 9.9 every minute. Isn't math great. It never grasps or gropes to prove its point. 9.9 every minute! It kinda gets me right here. OW! THAT REALLY HURT!

N 52° 25' 34"; E 13° 07' 09"—Northeast of Potsdam

Sorry about that. Where was I . . . ? Oh yeah, Little Leni's wondrous Weimar lips, which demanded something so appalling of W, he slit his wrists during dress-up. What did Little Leni do when confronted with so much blood? She stopped laughing long enough to ask her friends, *Jews bleed?* (She is not the only German to have wondered about that.) Whatever their answer, in that moment, Little Leni revealed her ability to compartmentalize whatever might interfere with her artistic process, exposing what triumphant LENI's will was made of. With a quick shove, she stashed W under her sofa so her father wouldn't find him in her camisole. Now you can see why I expected something more mystically parasitic from my first glimpse of the ice nymph.

N 52° 32' 08"; E 13° 07' 30"—East of Falkensee, Near the English Sektor

Okay, Klaus, let me walk you through this. Operas are so overwrought, all that gender swapping and poisoning can make a head spin. So, Act 2 ended with Dieter getting engaged to a nice East German girl. Act 3 opens on a beautiful summer day in August 1976. Blonde schoolgirls adorn the stage, pressing flowers into their diaries. The chorus sings *In the West toilet paper is two-ply, soft on the ass, decorated with flowers,* causing the schoolgirls to swoon. The air is sweet with the thought of West German chocolate. Dieter's betrothed enters stage right, gripping the hand of her eight-year-old son. He is pale, sickly, probably tubercular à la La Bohème, owing to Puccini's tendency to plagiarize himself and East Berlin's boycott on sun and oxygen. (Some chorus members drag oxygen tanks and wear breathing masks.) In a swoosh of pixie dust, Ms. Betrothed is transported to the dingy, contemptible office of the Pankow city district council to request permission to marry Dieter. The timpani urges . . . Dunnn dunnn . . . duuuunnn duun . . . duuunnnnnnnn dun dun dun dun . . . Spielberg's *Jaws* has entered der Zeitgeist.

THE WALL'S REQUIEM—OPUS 1

N 52° 30' 33"; E 13° 25' 45"—Schilling Bridge

The drunk monkey lies face down on the Spree's bank. Those who shot him smoke and joke over his body. They have desecrated St. Valentine. Farted on my socialist sickle moon. Made a mockery of love. I have always been a patriot but. I am taking a vow of silence until this madness ends.

N 50° 26' 46"; E 30° 30' 39"—Kiev, Ukraine: Outside the German Embassy

FUCK! I'VE BEEN HIT! It wasn't the 14, 2 8 5. 7 a   day, 5 9 5.   2 an hour,   9.9 a min ute   that   got to me. Goddamn rocket propelled   grenades.   Goddamn Putin-loving

      rebels.   I've seen   so   many   corpses   s o
much   chaos   never known   love   never had
so   much   as as   as   I   surreennderrrrr
    all   my   loooooveee   sooo
war m   an d d d   tennndeerrrr

N 52° 32' 08"; E 13° 07' 30"—East of Falkensee, Near the English Sektor

Just hang in a bit longer, Klaus. Almost there. The Pankow city district council not only denies Ms. Betrothed's request, but Dieter is slapped with a travel ban. (The slap is administered across his face by one of the blonde schoolgirls now outfitted in leather.) 5 1/2 months pass. Stage hands rip out newspaper pages in rhythmic counterpoint to evoke the passage of time. Our lovers grow desperate on separate sides of the stage. Ms. Betrothed's belly swells stage left to piccolo arpeggios. Dieter masturbates stage left to a lone bassoon. Enter lightbulb. Dieter, in a testosterone-fueled epiphany depicted in expressionistic *Cabinet of Dr. Caligari* shadows, applies for a visa to travel to Poland singing, *If Hitler could invade Poland from Germany, why can't I invade Germany from Poland?* as the chorus chants in canon (*He's a genius. He's a genius. He's a genius.*). The libretto leaves much to be desired.

N 52° 30' 41"; E 13° 23' 24"—Thirty Meters North of Kronenstraße

Hitlerjugend's honor, Fräulein. I shot the python. But I did not shoot the rattlesnake. I had no choice. Veronika was in the grass, cuddling a burnt baby monkey, and . . . excuse me, Fräulein . . . I just need a minute. Thirty years and it's still hard to bear. My beautiful Veronika and that tiny monkey, entwined by the python. It was a glimpse of Eden at the moment of our fall. I was too late. It had stolen all of Veronika's breath, consumed what I hadn't. Stay with me, Fräulein. Over there, where your mother leaves yellow marks on the window, is Sodom. You will do things in the West and wonder why. A canal of blood will leak from you so slowly you won't know you're dying. Do not cry, Fräulein. You have done your very best. Time to fall backward, my dear. Let your fingers and feet slip. Though do avoid my bed of nails.

N 52° 32' 08"; E 13° 07' 30"—East of Falkensee, Near the English Sektor

This is it, Klaus. The finale. Dieter leaps onto a moving train bound for Poland, but lacking all self-control—which should come as no surprise to you—leaps off one stop later in East Berlin. The chorus cries, *There was never one who loved so much!* Dieter finds his betrothed holed up in her grubby one-room apartment, an attic that bears a striking resemblance to the one in *La Bohème.* Her identification card has been confiscated. She no longer goes out. No longer eats. Her pale boy tortures cockroaches in the corner. Dieter hands him an East mark and tells him to go buy bread. The chorus cries, *No, mein Kind, don't go!* to no avail. Now that they are alone, Dieter caresses his betrothed's lips, hands, belly. They transfer their hopelessness to each other through her umbilical cord. The chorus links arms, sways as they croon, *Suicide is painless, it brings on many changes,* encouraging the audience to join in. The grubby one-room apartment swells with song. The February cold stings. One bop on the head, Klaus, and this tragedy could have been avoided.

N 52° 30' 27"; E 13° 23' 24"—Checkpoint Charlie

Fish Eyes . . . How many years has it been? You were the last to gaze at me with hope. I haven't received so much as a slash of paint in eons. My Schiller scholar stopped speaking after your body was removed. In solidarity, Goethe has gone mute too. Only rats visit now. I've begun to name the ones that overrun me after heavy rain for the women I had intercourse with. I know you don't know what that means, but trust me, it's vulgar to name rats after Gerta, Marie, Helena, Anna, Johanna, Emilia, Lea, Klara, Ida, Frieda, Marlene, Pauline, Franziska, Vanessa, I'm sorry, I'll stop. They are much thinner this year. The rats, not my lovers. Please don't think me crass. You forever altered me. Whereas I used to see those like you as entertainment—the blinding searchlights sweeping my bulwark was quite titillating—now my borders seep with fury and anguish. Though my music within is still frozen, once or twice since you were carried off, I've heard a soft rumble, perhaps a minor chord escaping. I don't think I'm imagining it, unless of course, I'm beginning to crack. I'd like to think it's a sign of my growing maturity—and not of my increasing instability—that I suddenly crave a bullet's caress.

N 52° 25' 34"; E 13° 07' 09"—Northeast of Potsdam

As I was saying before my Leni R. detour . . . If time has lost its synchronization, perhaps Chernobyl, Challenger, Halley's Comet, a former Nazi being elected president of Austria, the 6.5 million people who held hands across America to form a human chain from New York to California are fallout from disoriented time. Ahead. Behind. Now. Just words. Will you look at that! The electricity is back on.

TERMINATION SHOCK

Countdown

Fluorescents flood your crib day and night. You haven't moved in two years. There is the quiet of dying, and the noise of Detroit's inferno. There is the noise of your overripe smell, and the quiet of this call and response that couldn't have taken place, though I know all the parts. Dad's. Mine. Yours. Even the voice from the other side as it counts down.

10

It's time. Don't be difficult, Shirley. Don't force us to initiate something. Send lofty commands. Push clouds from their path. Not everyone requires a hearse to get from there to here.

9

You see a child's face, a girl, not pretty, a scarecrow, me. That scarecrow must be my daughter, you think, but what silly hair, what ugly shoes, what a glum face. She is the one who craved magenta. The liar with the sweet tooth. The one who calls me "You." She will make a good orphan.

8

Dad should put You somewhere out of sight. I'll pretend you're not this thing, but the surface of a lake where birds skim your body, gorging on gnats at twilight. This lake that is you is the one I've seen in a picture: Dad carrying you on his shoulders across the sand. If I ever find this lake with the birds skimming your body, I'll skip rocks across your face.

7

Our scarecrow calls you Dad, but calls me "You." Turn around and look at her, darling. I've barely breathed and she stands there in her jumper and baggy tights, impatient to get on with things, get me on my way, blame me for what will go wrong. She will make a good thief. Nothing is safe around her. Look at the way she looks at me. Even now she wants to steal the seconds I have left.

6

I found your diary with the honeymoon picture of You and Dad, balloon-headed puppets hanging by one hand from the Eiffel Tower. Even then you wanted to let go. I found your copy of *The Prophet*. You were not a strong bow for my arrow. I found my favorite book, *The Boxcar Children*. The one you read aloud every night. You think three is too young to remember, but I remember the orphans. That was your plan all along. And when you thought I was asleep, you hoped your other story could begin.

5

The scarecrow will do whatever you say, darling. Tell her to jump in the lake. Tell her to lie beneath the sycamore until the roots strangle her.

She doesn't know when to stop. Doesn't know how to smile. Doesn't know when to shut up. Doesn't know how to listen.

4

But I'm not asleep when your other story begins. In it, there isn't a girl. There is a boy instead. Not a real boy who has a name and can be punched, but a boy with octopus arms and brick feet. In the other story, you and the eight-armed boy live somewhere where none of this exists, where none of me exists. You and the eight-armed boy do things people here can't do: become seahorses, toasters, convertible tops.

3

Is that the tie we bought on our honeymoon? Are those my father's cufflinks? Yes, reach for me, darling. The sand is scorching my feet. I need you to

2

get out of the way, Shirley.

Another "to-do" to add to the list:
bury the scarecrow's hamster
defrost the lamb chops
teach him the foxtrot
get out of the way

This is not the time to wish you'd been a cat. Your top layer has already been blown to Lake Superior. Joined a storm that'll make landfall near Nova Scotia. You'll rip through summer cottages. Leave sailboats on roofs. Leave children huddled beneath potatoes in root cellars. Leave firewood for a decade. This is your path. Don't try to understand. Get out of the way. The telephone pole necks are broken. The deer fled. Cast everything off. Drop the knife in your mind. Let your legs jump over summer. If you don't get out of the way, you will never know release. Others' paths will be disrupted. Your second layer won't join the storm over the Pacific. You will not make landfall near Taipei. Will not drench uniforms or raise skirts. Will not know the feeling of a landslide beneath you. Will not cause love. Your third layer will miss its rendezvous near Corpus Christi. Your fourth, its mission in Vietnam. Get out of the way. You're running out of

1

Termination shock.

Voyager 2

When I was seventeen, after my boyfriend said he needed his space and I decided I was *done*—*done* and contemplating *it*—I imagined I'd do *it* in some unsloppy futuristic way that offered the option to embed my soul aboard Voyager 2.

The plan was to embed behind one of the thermoelectric generators, but possible side effects on my soul from the Pu-238 alarmed me, so I decided the Golden Record was a safer location. I researched every-thing about the Golden Record in advance so my soul wouldn't be surprised. My research filled two spiral-bound notebooks and took so long that, by the time it was done, I no longer felt *done* enough to do *it*.

I remember none of this until twenty-eight years later, after the guard-ian who raised me dies. Over a long weekend, I unearth this research in her rat-pack basement. I'm supposed to take only a quick peek into each box before heading straight to the dump, but rereading President Carter's message to the aliens makes me weep. "We cast this message into the cosmos . . . A present from a small distant world . . . We are attempting to survive our time so we may live into yours . . . This record represents our hope and determination . . ." I'm furious with myself. Why couldn't I ace calculus, survive centrifuge training, conquer my fear of heights and booster rockets to achieve liftoff?

Also buried beneath the dozens of schematic drawings and reams of data is: 1. a faded Polaroid of my slight and bare-chested father carrying my full-figured mother across the sand on his shoulders; 2. a pocket-sized captain's log titled: PERSONAL DIRECTIVES. Page 1 commands me in bold block letters, HAUNT EX TELEPATHICALLY FROM SPACE.

I am so impressed by my teenage focus and ingenuity that the man I live with—who grudgingly came to help me discard my past—finds me still sifting through this box in the morning. His expression is similar to one I saw years ago after I asked him if he was using me to avoid renting another apartment and he answered, "I don't know." We drove from Big Sur to LA, six hours, in silence. Upon arriving home, he packed his suitcases and left for Phoenix. I try to remember how we mended that rift as I show him the picture of my parents. He offers to go to Starbucks, but forgets my scone.

Whenever the man I live with gives me a nudge up the stairs, I chatter aimlessly to my ex, a silent intergalactic travelogue. *Uranus . . . What can I say? Seasons last twenty-one years. Dull, dull, dull . . . Neptune . . . Such an unearthly blue, cool methane wrapped in a cyclone, just what you'd expect from a big gas giant. How is your father? Still alive?*

Haunting my ex telepathically turns out to be the most relaxing part of the weekend. By the time we board the plane for home, I use a goofy signal to alert my ex of an incoming communiqué, and settle into easy chat about life aboard Voyager. Somewhere over Chicago, after taking twice the normal amount of Xanax to fly, I accidentally say, "Hello? Beep . . . Hello? Beep . . ." out loud.

The man I live with—already uneasy about my grief-mashed bumble-bee brain—has never taken a hit of pot in his life. He has no relationship to drugs. He doesn't drink. He is ultra-ultra-responsible. We're sitting in the exit row, and his worried look after my Hello? Beep . . . makes me fear he is about to have me reseated for everyone's safety. I do not want to be reseated. I've already ordered my free sparkling water. To ensure I'm not reseated, I tell him I'm working on a new novella where my soul embeds aboard Voyager 2, and that Hello? Beep . . . is the prelude to a communication with a Jet Propulsion Lab nerd who broke my heart.

He wants to believe me, but asks me to finish my transmission as a test.

"Hello? Beep . . . Hello? Beep . . . It's me. The one you left for the redheaded bitch. Where am I? You want that in miles or astronomical units?"

He criticizes it as too clichéd and goes back to taking notes in the margins of his Sherman tank modeling magazine. Beside an award-winning M4 model he jots: TOO MUCH RUST.

The man I live with prefers to travel without me. While I'd like to think this is because he prides himself on needing no one, it's probably because I suffer from engagement miscalculation: too engaging, or not engaging enough, as his restlessness requires. Chances are he shrugged off my transmission explanation, but to prove I'm capable of following emergency wing-door instructions, I flaunt my business savvy.

"You know . . . 'haunt ex telepathically' would make a great iPhone app. I could . . .

> a. pay some geek to develop it
> b. sell it to Apple for millions
> c. buy a horse
> d. get a dog
> e. teach the dog to ride the horse
> f. have the horse set up a foundation
> g. hand out grants to perpetually emerging artists
> h. stop teaching
> i. stop stopping
> j. do something useful"

The man I live with has this smile that reminds me of Canada: well-meaning, un-ironic, Peace Bridge. This is the smile my idea receives, along with his assessment of its business potential.

"The app already exists. It's called unlimited texting."

Over the Rockies we hit turbulence. He sweetly takes my hand and explains what's behind every creak and moan. The explanations require a B.S. in engineering to understand, but his voice is so calm and assured it has the effect of an Ikea instruction manual. I don't wake up until the plane is taxiing to the gate. This has not been a good trip for us. I must try harder . . . or something.

Trying harder is typing what I want to happen, or how I want the man I live with to behave, in tiny unreadable fonts that I print out, roll into spitballs, and put under his pillow, a new suggestion every night.

—Start cooking
—Smile more
—Croatia would be nice

A month goes by before he wakes up after me and makes the bed. He is irritatingly sexy in his 3.75x Walgreen's magnifiers that he uses to build model tanks with tracks the size of a preemie's pinky nail. He hands me an unrolled spitball and says, "What does this mean?"

The question seems favorably broad. "I think it means that Croatia is probably a nice place."

"What about this?" he asks.

This spitball's font is even smaller so he has to read it to me. "As we leave Neptune behind, I'm disturbed by Voyager's single-minded pursuit of the heliopause."

"It's one of my soul's complaints to my ex. Part of that novella I told you about."

"What are they doing under my pillow?"

"I've no idea."

He tilts back his magnifiers. His pale green eyes make me feel like I've swum too far out in Cass Lake. This is the moment I remember that, when I was four, my mother warned me I could drown in a teaspoon of water.

I snort a breath and ask, "What's a heliopause?"

Deflection is not my strong suit. I'm pretty sure he knows that the heliopause is between the heliosphere and the interstellar medium. Where our solar wind slows to form a shock wave. In diagrams it is often depicted as an oblong bubble trying to exit a giant, flame-nippled breast. But the man I live with doesn't answer the question. He pulls out a confounding Pema Chödrön line, or perhaps it's a Buddha quote: "There seems to be a discrepancy between the attitude of your conscious mind and your instincts."

For some reason, presumably nervous grief, I say, "Hurray!"

This doesn't stop the man I live with from taking me to Sun City to visit his elderly mother, though I suspect it's why he refuses to go for a walk the next morning. He warns me to take my cell phone and not to stray too far. This makes me feel like a cat, and I consider reminding him that I'm spayed. The retirement community must have been designed to thwart criminals, the streets laid out to replicate a mutant asphalt nautilus. The temperature climbs to ninety-five by 7 a.m. By 9 a.m. I'm still hopelessly lost. In those two hours I only encounter one couple, who, like Oz's scarecrow, point in opposite directions. I begin to panic.

The man I live with does not answer his cell phone, so I resort to calling a friend in Dallas. She asks me to find a street corner so she can Google me home. I drag myself another half-mile, drawn by a blinding silver cross. The directional totem tells my fortune. I am at the intersection of Desperado and Via Mañana. Really.

Yesterday, I dropped a three-pound weight on a pilates client's stomach. They went *UGH!* Just like in a cartoon. Instead of apologizing I said, *SPLAT.* It seemed funny at the time. Today, when they didn't show up for their appointment, I noticed they had never signed a liability waiver.

When I get home, the stairs to our apartment are littered in confetti, an incriminating trail of past suggestions and soul communiqués.

—Heartbreak sounds like a meerkat being chased down a hole by a king cobra

—Kiss me more when we have sex

—This morning was nightmarish. Voyager's high-gain antennae got stuck in an anamolic position and behaved so erratically I feared for my life

—I didn't know Voyager had the capacity to experience destabilizing effects—loss, confusion, insanity—but now I realize I can't blithely go on as before, letting Voyager do its thing and me mine

—Stop saying I don't know

—Don't bother visiting Greece. I got a glimpse of the Aegean arc while hurtling away from Earth, and the archipelago seemed utterly confused and devoid of geometric beauty

—Ask me to marry you so I can say no

I find the man I live with dabbing a paint called "European mud" on tank treads with a brush too small for Tom Thumb. He doesn't stop as I rail, "How dare you go through my wastebasket! That wastebasket is mine! I don't go through your wastebasket! I don't peek at your genealogy reports!" He looks up at me with his 3.5x magnification opti-visor over his 3.75x Walgreen's glasses. His green eyes bulge like a Philippine tarsier's. "If you're hungry, there's a salad for you in the fridge."

It was an impulsive ill-conceived attack, nearly as stupid as saying SPLAT. I clearly require recalibration, but instead of emailing my energy worker for an appointment, I channel my agitation into a soul complaint about the Golden Record's musical selection. *Do you know how nightmarish it is being consigned to listen to Peruvian panpipes for eternity?!*

The salad is delicious.

The man I live with suspects that the recent death of the woman who raised me, the rekindling of orphan memories, and the dark nature of my novella—not the one about my soul aboard Voyager, which doesn't exist, but my real novella about a fifteen-year-old orphan's agonizing but mystical twenty-one-day quarantine in the hut where her mother died of Ebola—may be contributing to my depression. He doesn't say this outright, but on my placemat at breakfast the current *New Yorker* lies open to an article about the filmmaker of *Noah*. This is highly suspicious as I'm always six weeks behind.

The article's writer identifies the filmmaker as someone who portrays mortals "called to self-annihilation." What is the man I live with trying to tell me? Is this a warning shot? I turn the page to a T. Coraghessan Boyle story, and read the first line, which isn't the complete sentence, but the sum of everything I feel: "Katie wanted to relive Katie at nine . . ."

"I want to go back," I blurt out.

The man I live with folds up his map of Peru and says, "I'm listening."

I close *The New Yorker* to avoid being distracted by what Katie wants. "I want to go back and relive being nine." He doesn't laugh or question me. He thoughtfully waits . . . a long time. Truth is, I do want to go back. Not to nine, but five. Before I knew the words "brain" and "tumor." I only chose nine because T. Boyle chose nine, and now it seems disingenuous to disrupt the spirit of the moment, especially since the man I live with is giving me his undivided, un-Peruvian attention. Why is he so patient? It's infuriating. I'm not prepared for this conversation. Not with a Zen Buddhist who wears relaxed-fit jeans and listens to Norah Jones. But it's important not to squander someone's goodwill, so with my well-honed bruised look I admit, "It's been a hard year."

It's been such a hard year the man I live with takes me hiking, but I trip over a root and land on my head. On the way back down the mountain, I'm haunted by our first date—when I accidentally flushed a baby possum down the toilet. Is this one more sign that we're doomed? The fact he felt it necessary to buy me a whistle for when we hike has never boded well. And the fact that I've remembered to put it on exactly once in seven years speaks volumes. Last year, after losing me on a trail a two-year old could follow, he resorted to purchasing walkie-talkies. Despite this being one of my pre-pubescent fantasy gifts, I'm 0 for 6 in remembering to put it into my backpack.

Today, I left it in the tent at the campground, which is now eerily deserted. Everyone else knows something we don't. Just after midnight we're let in on the secret. A freak fall storm. The temperature plummets fifty-five degrees. I put on every piece of clothing I brought and manage to wedge myself sideways in the mummy bag. After my earlier clumsiness, I vow not to wake the man I live with to unzip me, but contemplate my situation and trace it back to my dissembling over the *Noah* article. Only now does it hit me that the man I live with, a notorious article skimmer, probably never read the piece, and left it out not as a warning shot, but because he wanted to see the film.

Back at work, my boss requests a "tête-à-tête" in his office. He says "tête-à-tête" with a Midwestern accent that verges on sexual harassment. While his nasal whine ticks off my recent lapses in judgment, I "Hello? Beep . . ." my ex to distract myself. *It's pretty peaceful out here until our software commands take us closer to these noxious Roman Gods and we—ha ha, as if Voyager 2 and I are buddies, commander and XO, Kirk and Spock, Ziggy and Stardust—feel the deleterious effects of their gravitational pull. Who'd think a soul would be nostalgic for gravity? Oh, Christ, Voyager just spotted another moon. These things are like Chiclets out here.*

My boss asks me twice if I understand that I'm fired.

I practice my unemployment confession while negotiating the fire-scarred canyon in my Jetta. *I'm so done with teaching. I willed this to happen. My body can't take it any more. I'm supposed to be writing. My only accomplishment so far is to have outlived my parents. Thank God I'm not a clotheshorse. Thank God I can cook. Thank God I love rice cakes. I take full responsibility for the SPLAT, but this is fate. This is what happens if you go too long without doing something meaningful, without having any fun.*

How I got off on the "fun" tangent is unclear, but I'm fully absorbed in this new justification, and it upsets me to admit I can't recognize fun any more. When clients rambled on about their riotously "fun" weekends, the details filled me with rage. I'm grateful these people couldn't see my face as their exclamation-point descriptions assaulted me. In recompense for failing to see anything remotely fun in the time they'd wasted, for actively feeling pity for them, I routinely stayed late to twist their bodies, wringing out all the tension their "fun" weekends had caused them.

Once home, I don't confess anything. It's supermoon night, and the man I live with catches its last howl through the living-room window. He is uncharacteristically animated. From behind his back he produces a sleek white 1:72 scale X-29. He turns the plane in circles as if on a dais, does slow-motion barrel rolls. Whatever he has accomplished must be amazing. Too bad I can't see it. Though he prides himself on his eerie calm, in exasperation he shoves his opti-visor on my head. He has found a way to create and print decals in a font tinier than my spitball desires. On one side of the canopy is his name, on the other, mine. Holy shit! I'm his co-pilot.

I don't ask if there are two ejection seats in this aircraft because this is monumental, as good as having a song written about you. It is so wildly out of the norm that I throw my arms around his neck and do this twisty thing with my feet that is a life-long response to subconscious joy going conscious. And though I'm in the throes of spontaneous expansiveness, I inadvertently blunder into engagement miscalculation. "I heard somewhere that some people in love can't bear the agony that love requires. But I think the agony is worth it."

The word "agony" is regrettable, but his negative reaction to my heartfelt, though poorly vocalized, expression of love makes me suspicious of my hasty promotion in rank. I now suspect my inclusion on the canopy has less to do with his love for me, and more to do with jealousy about my relationship with Voyager. I confront him with this at dinner, and after one of his pensive three-minute pauses he asks, "What frightens you so much about sadness?"

Unlike me, the man I live with is a deflection specialist, a great ante-upper when he decides to speak. The only answer I can give is so pathetic that I gaze out the window through the Chinese elms at our neighbor cooking in his undershirt and boxers. His unfortunate resemblance to that over-televised twentieth-century archetype— paunch, grossly hairy—doesn't detract from his devotion in the kitchen. And I, desperate to out-pensive my partner, meditate on the dexterity required for such over-sized hands to delicately peel back the skins and de-seed so many blanched tomatoes. In fact, only while contemplating this lovingly homemade sauce do I fully grasp that the man I live with and I are in constant unacknowledged competition, and I will never win in the patience department.

Once, after a Valentine's Day snit, he enrolled in a nine-month silent meditation retreat and fled to Texas taking Alberto, my hanging stuffed squirrel monkey, with him. Two months after abandoning me, he breaks his silence to leave a lurid message on my rarely used flip phone to see how long it will take me to discover it. Every Sunday for the next seven months he calls to tell me he loves me and we repair the damage one week at a time. He never mentions the cell phone message. I don't discover it until a week before he returns. Years later I still play it, just to hear him describe all the things he'd love to do to me that he still hasn't done.

I "Hello? Beep . . ." my ex and telepathically admit that the idea of leaving the comfort and familiarity of the solar wind for termination shock terrifies me. The man I live with interrupts my silent communiqué to ask, "Where are you right now?"

"Nearing Pluto."

"What's it like?"

"Puttanesca."

Ignition

Dad stands next to your coffin until his legs cramp. His face has that possessed look he gets when he drives on Woodward Avenue in the snow. As if it will melt because his mind is on fire. I pirouette around him to unspool his thoughts. They're so unsettling they resist balance.

how will I pay off your grave the girl's school the funeral the camp the gun what to do with the girl the gun walk flee run toss the wigs rubber sheets where to send the girl should've left her at home goddamn house goddamn mortgage goddamn yard used to be a nursery Evergreen Woods destroyed one wood at a time is that rain haven't looked up in seven years or taken a breath not a real breath not really seven-years' war without peace you still died and the city hot fed up gone mad I get it I got a gun but I get it they want change want to set fires to oblivion they know when it's time to get carried off carried away riot I'll sell the house half the business get rid of everything not the girl never the girl why not nothing to remind me of you in her probably fell from Mars how dare you leave first how dare you lie there like something that can't be touched dark inside the day you think I can't follow you why not that's right I'll find you and then I never told you never told anyone there hasn't been a time no time not ever I've always been scared of thunder thank God a tornado please lightning please hail please don't spare us end this sick farce this farting fart farced FUCK can't hold a goddamn thought a ball in my head endless gray a riot counts for something are you looking can you see are you somewhere looking thinking what have I done if you can finish me off anytime is good now is good now or this minute this second or the space between them why can't I look at you

When Dad looks at you, it's as if he has been exposed to lightning. This is why people need dogs. Their paws act as a ground. When he looks away, I think I see you twitch, so I whisper, "Unh-uh . . . You had your chance." I don't know how heavy that lid is, but no one wants to shut it. Maybe they all feel sorry for you. Dad can't help himself. He looks at you again. Where did you get such power?

sorry I was a lousy dancer sorry I took away the car keys sorry I wouldn't let you drive the girl any more you didn't know how dangerous you were when the girl was little so little when you wanted to hold her I held my breath prayed you didn't drop her you were right to be afraid of having a child the girl scolds you in her sleep thinks this was your plan all along I might have to get her a dog direct her fierce love toward something beside me she gave up building model airplanes is obsessed with constructing miniature balsa wood ranch houses with intricate floor plans I could never afford I'm nearly bankrupt can't even pay for this I took the rings off your fingers   just in case.

I'm not sure why everyone thinks you're so pretty. Just because you have nice hair and nice clothes, "classy," they keep saying. Someone walked past a few minutes ago and picked a piece of lint off your dress. They stuck it in their pocket as if it were a Cracker Jack prize. Dad paces in front of you. Are you like Buckingham Palace? He showed me a picture of the soldiers in their silly furry hats once. Does someone need to tell him it's time to change the guard?

Heliopause

To explain the heliopause in the funnest possible terms, I walk to the CVS to buy a "heliosheath" as a joke. This is my first ever purchase of a condom, and when the self-serve cashier machine can't read the barcode after six attempts, the customer behind me comes to my aid. Call it kismet, but he is making the same purchase in much greater volume, and gifts me one with the warning, "This is the easy part."

While I'm gone, the man I live with volunteers to read the beginning of a new short story. I find him hunched over the coffee table, scrutinizing the pages the way he does an aeronautical chart before he flies a glider. In his closet is an FAA manual and a variety of straps he uses to affix things to other things, such as checklists to his thigh in case unexpected thermals force an emergency landing. I offer him the manual and a strap, and ask if my short story has sent his thermals wildly off course toward my heliopause. He doesn't laugh but gives me the "hand stop."

The man I live with has large hands and a short list of withering gestures that often precede his baroque silences. The "hand stop" is his most anti-Canadian. It halts every impulse in the person receiving it, and no matter what my state of mind or intention I am instantly reduced to a dog being given the finger.

"How did your parents meet? Did you ever see them kiss? Who made who laugh more?" he grills me.

This makes no sense. Where is this coming from? Is this a Buddhist misdirect? Such crazy talk calls for an absurd story problem to expose the glitch in his line of questioning. The man I live with loves algebra story problems. Loves them so much he volunteers as an algebra teacher to heavily inked ex-con ex-gang members studying for their GED. I don't know if he has ever tried the "hand stop" on them, but I do know he barrages them with what he calls "basic life skills" story problems, so he should have no trouble solving mine.

"Given a family where X equals me, Y my mom, and Z my dad: If X is 3 years old when Y's brain goes kaput, and Z dies 7 years later, only 8.5 weeks after Y—is there a greater than one, less than one, or a zero chance in hell X will know who was the bigger jokester, Y or Z?"

We do not to get to dramatize the heliopause with the "heliosheath" that night or the rest of the week. Apparently, my short story violates the second law of thermodynamics and my story problem violates his Cartesian space. The man I live with claims that the spontaneous production of order from disorder (the expected consequence of basic laws) does not hold when reading these pages.

June gloom descends. My VW's water pump breaks. There is a problem with the organic Fuji apple crop. I get a violent kink in my neck. Phantasms are dying at an alarming rate. Are these omens? Is it possible the man I live with, the man who had to ask me what Kafkaesque meant, is onto something and I need to try harder?

Liftoff

Y isn't ten minutes in the ground and already Z is considering leaving. Shoes still muddy. Fingernails gritty. Tossing clods of earth, such a primitive practice, like so much else on this planet. No reason to stay without her. It's the only reason he came.

Z, born to humble nobodies, uneducated connoisseurs of worry, two sisters before him, a featureless childhood; "limited horizons" is the well-trod phrase.

Y, conceived in a cloud of perpetual fermentation, tipplers all. Stout guts, wide feet for paddling and wading, three generations evolved from the sea. Y was the only sibling to negotiate gravity with grace.

Star-crossed lovers extraordinaire, mammal anarchists, such was their ability to plunge in and out of life without fear.

Z:

> (This is the version he whispers to the wallpaper, long after he goes to bed, a seismic plea. It begins on a day between seasons, the weather on everyone's tongue. The day the money runs out to finish medical school. Finding the words is almost impossible. At first, he only manages descriptive hiccups: Irish Catholic, peach skin, freckles, auburn hair, green eyes: small and big things that will be eclipsed.)

> To understand my inarticulateness, you have to understand the shock of seeing her again. If I tell you that one look exchanged can bridge lifetimes, you'll laugh, so I'll build a bridge from that look to that lifetime. The look itself, and the look received.

> Before she became Y, she flowed with the wild Hvítá. What became lips, legs, heart were flung headlong down the 105-foot crevice, broken open against jagged rocks in the Gullfoss's mist.

> Before I became Z, the earth sealed my golden roots in the tundra. Only a thousand-year flood could wrench me free. A flood

that swept me into the Hvítá, over the Gullfoss, past Brokey and Flately islands, a flood that ground the corn mill to dust, left codfish and lumpfish to pray in church pews, heaved sheep and cows into Eldfell's voracious volcano; stranded puffins, terns, whimbrels, and plovers with no perch, screeching in vain at the Cyclops lighthouse.

On Y's voice came, carried by the North Atlantic Gyre: "Look at me, darling, so it can begin."

Y: It was a nest of creation. Z looked first, how could he not? Looking back at Z, I felt—this is so hard to describe—a need to uncross my legs. But this was before I had legs. The sensation was utterly new. A bit dirty, I think. Yes, definitely dirty. An entirely new feeling that required a new set of words. Swift. Swallow. Dense. Hot. Succumb. Rocket. Succumb. Fuck. Succumb. I'm repeating myself.

Z: I spot her crossing 6 Mile. Auburn hair. Red lips. Beautiful lost things. Our unstoppable animal song so close. Turn your head, red lips. Show me what we remember. My heart has a dying valve, but I'm still a catch. A bit old, a few extra fault lines, but so tender it'll make up for being a bit old, a bit less than a doctor.

Y: What's wrong in my head? Why all this fog? Why does my nametag say cashier girl and not cashieress? "That'll be $12.78, miss. Yes, I was just outside, very strange, not summer, not fall. Thank you and come again." Dancing will stop the numbness. The floating. If a car hit me again, if a dog bit my leg, if a man curled his tongue inside my mouth, would I care?

Z: Our first fuck was an arabesque. My roots, her wave. We took chances. Strayed too far. I lost her. And now . . . She is helping a small boy at the candy counter. Bending over. The seam of her hose in pursuit of everything. Don't move. Don't move.

Y: The bell won't stop ringing. Some idiot is stalled in the doorway. If he had a sign hanging around his neck it would say, TAKE ME FREE. Ding ding ding ding ding . . . I want to shout, "Enter or leave!"

Z: She is in front of me, holding out her arms in that way that says, "Let's dance."

Y: His arms are velvet arrows. People come back, and then they don't.

Z: What to do with

Y: Everything.

Z: My heart has a valve that

Y: No one goes untouched.

Z: Don't break me into a million

Y: We'll consume time.

Z: Play it out until

Y: Until

Premonition Shock

Andre Dubus II is haunting me. I've never met him or read his work, but his soul is still haunting me. The only two facts I know about Dubus are he was a respected short-story writer and a Good Samaritan. His Good Samaritan-ness cost him both legs after he stopped to help two stranded motorists and was hit by another vehicle. In my mind, that vehicle has always been a large red bus.

For the past two nights I've jolted upright in bed to see a man's head floating dead center in my starry glow-in-the-dark Big Dipper. What Dubus looks like is a mystery to me. But being half-asleep I convince myself this is him, despite the head's uncanny resemblance to Hemingway. I refuse to check Google images, fearing he won't look like Hemingway, which could then mean Hemingway's soul, disguised as Dubus's soul, is haunting me.

The man I live with diagnoses my Dracula jolt as sleep apnea, but I suspect either Voyager is closing in on the termination shock and Dubus wants to warn me of something elusive, or the man I live with is about to perform one of his biannual disappearing acts.

Driving to work the next day, I hear NPR report on a man hit by a city bus. The story ends with a snippet of suitably melancholic music that NPR likes to play to close tragic stories. Only once in the past fifteen years have I heard them talk of war, death, or destruction and then grossly miscalculate their musical choice. Their selections for catastrophic economic news are absolute genius.

I don't tell the man I live with about Dubus's dipper-head, or the story on NPR, but the next morning, a quiet Sunday under a too-brilliant blue sky, we set out on a no-destination ramble. We don't linger over what happened on the tango floor last night—how his barridas set my adornos on fire—but aimlessly wander up and down hills in an afterglow of appreciation.

At what would be a busy weekday intersection, between a park and a high school, all is placid. Not a car in sight. Hearing a distant rumble, I lean forward to see a lone city bus coming from the west. My mind flashes to poor Andre Dubus II and the tragic NPR story, so I take five steps back from the curb. The man I live with does the same. A large red bus comes into view and roars past.

A voice inside me screams, "RUN NOW OR YOU'LL BE HIT!" I sprint across the seven empty lanes, though there isn't any traffic. I assume the man I live with is right behind me, but when I leap onto the curb and turn back, he is being his ultra-patient ultra-responsible self. Every cell inside me commands, Tell him to run, tell him to run, tell him to run, but I decide this is the moment I learn to control my anxiety and not foist my hypervigilant worry on someone else.

The orange flashing walk-man turns solid white, and the man I live with leisurely strolls across the empty intersection. He is six feet tall, with a seamless sway and legs drag queens dream about. I'm not often in this position, fifty feet away, able to casually admire how well designed he is. My anxiety and paranoia recede in a glow of gratitude, and I inexplicably find myself wondering about his sudden interest in exotic underwear.

He has recently gone on an underwear-buying spree, not just purchasing a rainbow of colors (including those more suited for neon signage), but styles the Chippendales might deploy. That his lingerie now outstrips mine should be unsettling, but instead I have this incredible urge to run into the street, pick him up, and twirl him around in circles; create our own post-war or post-apocalyptic or post-? moment. But he weighs twice as much as me, and prefers walking uninterrupted by chatter or mischief. And so I wait on the northeast corner, quiet and underwear-less, thoroughly enjoying my pilot's runway catwalk until the moment a super-silent Prius takes him out.

First-Stage Separation

Explosive bolts fire and the severed first stage falls into the ocean. Earth loses its grip on Y; Z's effect on earth diminishes. It is a smoky gray day, the sun everywhere and nowhere. The air made up of tiny mosaics if you squint just right. Air that doesn't stick or wrap around you, air that is barely air.

Z stands, paces, leans into the wall. Yesterday's calf cramps still jail his muscles. His body seems to be made of a new fabric, something humble yet inflexible, lacking durability.

At night, escape seizes hold of Z. During the day, calmer muscles prevail. The hours between 9 and 11 p.m., after the girl falls asleep, reserved for grief and worry—the chest tightening, the mounting debt, the leaky heart valve.

He had thought he and Y were singular. Defying parents, priests, rabbis. Believing—how silly it now seems at 10:15 p.m.—that love shapes life. He spends day after day trying to revise every moment of the past seven years to see which one will reset history.

Best friends fly in from New York to remind Z of life's purpose. All night they talk about the beauty and terror of the unexpected. They do not mince or sugarcoat. They are smarter than they look. And when they look at Z it is with telescopic eyes. They see the acceleration of his Big Bang. They gently guide the conversation, a Brooklyn chorus. Z's staccato whispers can't pierce their song.

CHORUS: We love the girl—
    Z: The war won't stop—

CHORUS: We'd be thrilled to be her guardians—
    Z: Day after day—

CHORUS: We've always wanted children—
    Z: The casualty list grows—

CHORUS: We'll teach her how to swim—
 Z: Sorrow grabs a gun—

CHORUS: We'll teach her Spanish—
 Z: Sorrow shoots off its mouth—

CHORUS: We'll celebrate her birthday—
 Z: Sorrow drains electricity—

CHORUS: Take her to museums—
 Z: Forgets where it buried the acorns—

CHORUS: Dance concerts—
 Z: Sorrow is a pile of rags—

CHORUS: Happenings—
 Z: When somebody loves you—

CHORUS: The Blue Angels—
 Z: Sorrow is a poached egg prepared not the way she made it—

CHORUS: Sorrow is being blind to the sorrow of others—

Radial Velocity

The man I live with is an unacknowledged aerial artist. In his encounter with the stealthy Prius, he uses the black beast's windshield
as a half-pipe. He shatters it to maximum dramatic effect to alert the
driver—whose view is now completely obscured—that this is the moment to brake, thus accelerating the centripetal force necessary for him
to finish his act by executing two spiraling aerial flips. The hybrid's
super silence accentuates every bone-crunching organ-squishing moment, especially the man I live with's breathtaking stick-it landing on
his back and head twenty feet away in the left-turn lane. It is a superb
demonstration of radial velocity, his body first speeding toward and
then away from another object along their axis. From my vantage point
on the northeast corner, he has died three separate times.

On his first death, my soul crosses the termination shock. The pressure of the interstellar medium pushes back against the solar wind.
No longer under the sun's influence I "Hello? Beep . . ." in a state of
traumatic confusion. *What about climbing Kilimanjaro? What about
the wildebeest migration? What about all that remains?*

On his second death, my soul suffers a series of bow shocks and I re-
experience the death of everyone I've ever loved in the order they left
me. A low scream hisses from the back of my throat, not unlike a lob-
ster's when dropped in boiling water.

On his third death, I know what it means to die and still be kept
breathing.

Escape Velocity

The time in the corner grocer when Y held out her arms to dance, Z thought: Now this will be funny, but not the funny it turned out to be. He tells his Brooklyn chorus about buying Y a soft gray muff, somewhere to hide her hands after her skin became too thin for the air. He has to stop himself from telling them: Happiness doesn't know how to use a gun.

Z locks the bathroom door to confront the mirror. The dark lines under his eyes descend halfway down his nose. So what's it going to be, he thinks, a tug-of-rope over quicksand? He turns on the shower and lets the mirror steam over. He is done pleading to Y in the dark. Instead of speech, he writes to Y on the glass WHAT SHOULD I DO, then retreats into the stall.

His hair has so receded that the top strands form a skinny peninsula. Before long it will evolve into an isolated island or iceberg, aligning perfectly with his internal state, which his best friends describe in the language of meteorologists and storm watchers. Not that Z is volatile or unpredictable. He hates mysteries, hates to pretend. Above all else, he is rational and judicious. And yet, when he exits the shower and returns thirty minutes later—after being distracted by the magenta one's refusal to put on her Brownie uniform—the only residue of Z's sentence visible on the mirror is the haunting unambiguous order: DO.

Before Z's best friends leave he tells them about his wounded heart valve. That he is past 50,000 miles and it must be replaced or else. At the airport, he stutters, "Should something happen . . ."

The Brooklyn chorus crosses the tarmac. At the plane they look back with their telescopic eyes and wonder if they should lie.

The magenta one waves goodbye from behind the big-as-her-head airport lollipop. When Z takes her hand she asks if she can buy a scrapbook. The thought of a photo album about Y lying on the coffee table is more than he can bear. But when they get home, he discovers the magenta one plans to use it to keep track of the Apollo missions. Her first question at dinner is about escape velocity. After redeeming a slew of Kellogg's box tops, her Beany-and-Cecil Beanycopter cap has finally arrived. She tells Z now she can fly to heaven.

Z tells her that to escape earth's gravity she must travel at seven miles per second. Each secretly believes they have the power to achieve this.

Terrestrial Bodies

The ambulance driver is doing thirty in a thirty-five zone. The siren takes me back to all the sirens of my youth, and I remember how I used to endlessly badger God: *Just once send the ambulance to someone else's house!* And then it happened, and I felt horrible about my neighbor's grandmother.

My unacknowledged aerial artist is strapped in an immobilization collar and body brace, and is behaving like a Canadian. He is not Canadian but I envy his spot-on impression of one.

Who else would stick such a landing, go sickeningly still, and then five seconds later come to and calmly announce, "I am alert"? Gore Vidal once declared "Joyce Carol Oates" the three most dispiriting words in the English language. Who knew the three most beautiful are "I am alert"?

Escape Tower Jettison

Nineteen miles above earth any astronaut knows the escape tower is useless and becomes dead weight. No turning back from there. *Jettison the escape tower* is Z's last thought before the anesthesia takes hold. He plans to spend time with Y while hovering between worlds at the moment the surgeon stops his heart. Y has only been gone 8.5 weeks. How far can she be?

Twenty miles above earth Y's soft blue curve is visible against blackness. Z sees her snuggling the Indian Ocean. Her legs are impossibly long. A cyclone stirs between her thighs.

Eighteen miles above earth Z sees Y make a fist and Peking goes dark.

Fifteen miles above earth structure and sequence evaporate. Z has no sense of what preceded or what follows.

Eleven miles above earth Z experiences a tapestry of turbulent speculation woven at the equator. Y's fraying curves drape Southeast Asia's uncontrolled burn.

Seven miles above earth something cold courses through Z's veins and he vomits a cloud.

Six miles above earth Y's fiery heat collides with the polar jet stream.

Two miles above earth Z watches Y's form disintegrate in a cloudburst.

Fifty feet above earth the atmosphere thickens. Hail pelts the granite epitaph: loving wife, mother.

Four feet above Z's anesthetized body, termination shock resets the rhythm of his wounded heart.

One millimeter above Z a surgical stapler punches stainless steel into his flesh.

TERMINATION SHOCK

Interstellar Medium

I'm taking bets. Now that the man I live with no longer needs a wheel-chair attendant and driver, he'll either abandon me again after his birthday in a few days, or when he returns from Peru. He is long over-due, but no one will take this bet.

For his birthday card I make an elaborate ink drawing and fold it into a gigantic cootie catcher with promised gifts hidden under each flap. I vow to get him whatever he chooses no matter the cost. When he flips back a flap it's the one thing he never wants, but that I can easily afford: a blowjob.

"Make it two out of three," I offer.

His next choice is "Redeem for one homemade item," meaning cook-ies, also within my price range. His third selection is "Redeem for one model," as in plane or tank. I tell him to go for broke and turn back every flap. Under the last flap he finds "Anything you want."

What he wants is a simple Italian dinner.

The thin-crust pizza's pocked surface resembles the moon. Olive cra-ters are strewn across the landscape. I feel nostalgic about that barren rock and all my other Voyager flybys, and don't want to eat it. I confess during dinner that I used to think I had the power to will people back to life. I do not confess that termination shock provokes an uncontrol-lable impulse to die.

A boy with a flashy widow's peak at a nearby table uses two deep-fried calamari rings as binoculars. He scans the room and fixates on the man I live with, who has a way with dogs and children. Their interchange fascinates me until the restaurant's walls and ceiling creep closer. Why is it suddenly so hot? What is happening?

The thought I'm having—the one that shrank the room and wrecked the thermostat—wrenches free. We are too old. It is too late. As the man I live with hollows out two eyeholes in a piece of bread and stares the kid down, I share my discovery at a frequency only a dog could hear.

"I never wanted children. The day I was spayed was amongst my happiest. I didn't know I would meet you. I'm sorry."

The man I live with excels at looking people in the eye. When he looks at you, you know you are being looked at. After he lowers the bread and asks how my soul novella is going, I deflect since it's unseemly to lie to him on his birthday when he has just begun to walk again.

"Did you know the Hiroshima blast could be seen on the moon?"

"By who?"

"By souls waiting to be let go."

He thinks this is a theme of my nonexistent novella and I don't correct him. I do tell him telepathic haunting is not new to me.

"I have spiritual guides, beings from where I'm originally from that I've talked to since I was a child. Spewing anger and confusion into the universe is my contribution to space junk."

He assumes I'm still talking about the novella and asks, "Do these beings ever respond?"

"Unfortunately, when I became human, I was recalibrated for sending, not receiving."

"Sounds like you need to build a different antenna."

"Or find an interstellar medium."

This time he laughs. "So what happens to the Jet Propulsion Lab nerd who dumped you?"

"He marries the engineer next door and has three kids."

"Happily ever after."

"Hell, no! The first kid suffers from ADHD. The second from OCD, and the third, the jewel of his solar system, embeds her soul aboard Cassini."

"Poetic justice."

"The best kind."

"Can I read it?"

"Someday."

The man I live with opens his last birthday gift just before midnight. I've repackaged the condom in a cigar-shaped box and written Voyager on its fuselage.

"Where are your soul and Voyager now," he wants to know.

"Past the termination shock and preparing for the bow shock."

"You don't sound excited."

"It's the point of no return. Nothing to bring us back. Only the stellar wind to pull us deeper into space."

He unwraps the condom and raises an eyebrow. "Voyager, huh?"

The Walgreens near us has a helium tank. I know this because the man I live with buys me a birthday balloon every year. When it loses gas during the month-long celebration, and begins to creep around our ankles like a decapitated ghoul, Walgreens gives it a helium boost. As a child, my birthday was overshadowed by my mother's illness, and the woman who raised me didn't believe in celebrations after age eight. In recompense, the man I live with gives me a full thirty days.

We gas up the condom and write a message along its equator: "Who Let the Dogs Out?" Then he gives me a back scratch as we watch it rise toward the Jewel of the Solar System.

Termination Shock

It hurts to breathe. The air is impossibly thin. Unreasonably thin. Z can't imagine how they expect him to live on this. It could be self-pity he is feeling, or the morphine. The nurse came in before the magenta one called to give him a morphine boost because of pain, but it seems equally possible that loss of air might be the penalty of diminished ambition.

Racecars whine around a course on the hospital's small black-and-white television. Z can't keep track of what's happening. Some cars are smears of gray; others appear upside down. When the doctor on call stops by, Z doesn't mention that the air in his brain might be too thin to hold images upright.

Z's thoughts stray to his magenta one. Earlier on the phone, she wouldn't stop talking about becoming an astronaut, but the sentences smudged in his ears as if there wasn't enough air pressure to carry sound waves. "Moon! Moon! Moon! babble babble babble . . . Einstein! babble . . . Relativity! babble . . . Saturn! squeal . . . ! Apollo! babble . . . Dark side of! shriek . . . ! Rocket! squeal . . . ! Alone! shriek . . . ! No radio! shriek . . . ! Tang! babble babble . . ."

At some point he stopped listening until his sister's voice came on the line to ask, "Do you want me to bring her by for a visit?"

"Don't bother. I'll be home tomorrow."

If there was a goodbye, he didn't hear it.

The receiver rests in his palm. An obsession laps his airless brain. Can he help the magenta one more from the other side? "The other side" is the exact formation of the irrational thought. It elevates Z's temperature and heart rate. Sets off the alarm on his heart monitor. Sends feet scurrying into his room.

The way arms jab above him he can imagine being a downed contender in a prizefight. If only one of those arms would open a passage for air, then he could beat the count and rise. But as things are, it is so much easier to stay down, eye level with the dinner tray—a horizon of Jell-O, mashed potatoes, peas, chicken, dinner roll, margarine pad.

Y beckons from just beyond the jiggling mound of lime-green cubes. "Keep looking at me, darling, so we can begin again."

Things We Can See from Earth

We can see what has already happened. The impact craters, the spent fuel, beginnings and endings, births and deaths, all the topographies of love and hate; celestial magnetism living high.

Is it possible that when the man I live with has his biannual mood supernova and does unspeakably cruel things, or doesn't speak at all and flees to the desert, where cafés sell antigravity sculptures in which clowns with *Creature from the Black Lagoon* faces spacewalk beside astronauts and scuba divers in jetpacks, he is fulfilling a cosmic cycle?

"Puttanesca!" I say. It is 12:01. His birthday over. The condom nearly out of sight.

"Cassini is getting ready for its Titan flyby," I divulge.

The man I live with pops out the screen of our living-room window and aligns the telescope with Saturn. It's a pleasure to watch him finesse the coordinates. He catcall-whistles at the sky. "Take a look at those rings."

They're so graceful it seems uncivilized to respond above a whisper. "No wonder Saturn is called the Jewel of the Solar System."

He wraps his arms around me as I gaze through the eyepiece. I silently "Hello? Beep . . ." my ex with advice, not a soul complaint. *Plant tomatoes. Point the telescope in the right direction. Concentrate on the heart. Ignore the impact craters. Small and big things will be eclipsed.*

JUNIPER
JUNIPER PRIZE FOR FICTION

This volume is the sixteenth recipient
of the Juniper Prize for Fiction,
established in 2004 by the
University of Massachusetts Press
in collaboration with the
UMass Amherst MFA Program
for Poets and Writers, to be
presented annually for an outstanding
work of literary fiction. Like its sister award,
the Juniper Prize for Poetry established
in 1976, the prize is named in honor
of Robert Francis (1901–1987),
who lived for many years at
Fort Juniper, Amherst, Massachusetts.